Praise for *Swallowing the Sun:*

Greenwich Council
Library & Information Service

IN HOUSE
QUALITY
SYSTEMS

Mobile and Home Service at Plumstead Library
Plumstead High Street, SE18 1JL
020 8319 5875

Please return by

20/08/07

-- JUL 2015

Morden

-- NOV 2017

Godfrey NOV 2019

Thank
You!

To renew, please contact any Greenwich library

Issue: 02   Issue Date: 06.06.00   Ref: RM.RBL.LIS

'This is a fantastic book: an original and thoughtful story,
told with s   *GREENWICH LIBRARIES*   *day Independent*

SWALLOWING
THE SUN

DAVID PARK

BLOOMSBURY

First published in Great Britain in 2004

This paperback edition published 2005

Copyright © 2004 by David Park

The moral right of the author has been asserted

Bloomsbury Publishing Plc, 38 Soho Square, London W1D 3HB

A CIP catalogue record for this book
is available from the British Library

ISBN 0 7475 7417 0

10 9 8 7 6 5 4 3 2 1

Typeset by Hewer Text Ltd, Edinburgh
Printed in Great Britain by Clays Ltd, St Ives plc

www.bloomsbury.com/davidpark

For Alberta, always.

THE THREE OF THEM are in the yard where the white-washed walls are grimed and rendered in shadow by the dropping dusk. His father's soiled vest has a puckered hole over his heart and the misshapen loops of his braces sag by his side like buckled wheels. The cigarette clenched in his mouth has almost disappeared into a dot of red. As his head bobs and angles and the words spew out, the red circle moves round the tight square of the yard like a firefly. Around the tight square of the ring. Then his father takes the cigarette out of his mouth and spits at their feet with a hawking scrape of his throat, and as if with the greater freedom it brings, his voice climbs higher and he's calling them 'little cunts' and 'bastards'.

His head is framed for a moment by the square of yellow light coming from the kitchen window but he's moving constantly, weaving in front of them, sometimes turning little circles of himself. Working himself up. And the two of them aren't worth a piss in the wind, an arseful of roasted snow. What sort of useless little cunts would let toerags like the Thompsons take their bike off them? It's fuckin' dresses they ought to be wearing. It's handbags they should be carrying. Bloody nancy boys the pair of them. While his father shakes his head to the sky he sneaks a glance at Rob but he's looking at his feet, trying to shrivel himself smaller, trying to make himself invisible. He looks again at the red dot of his father's cigarette. It's stopped moving. He's taking it slowly out of his mouth, drawing on the final dregs before flicking it with his thumb and first finger into the corner of the yard. It tumbles in a little flurry of spark into the seam of shadow at the base of the wall.

They know it's coming now. He can hear Rob make a kind of whimpering noise, feels him edge a little closer to his shoulder. He wants to push him away – it's not fair of him. What can he do? What can he ever do but let his father tire himself out on him, take the first flush of the anger.

'It was my fault, Da. I'm the oldest, I should have stopped him.' His voice flickers and breaks like the tumble of his father's cigarette butt. The open-handed slap shudders his whole body, flaming his cheek and all the parts of himself that can't be seen.

'Of course it was your fault! Of course it was your fault, Martin – I don't expect any better from him any more. But you're no better than he is – lettin' yourself be pissed on by shite like the Thompsons.'

'He had his brothers, Da!' Rob suddenly shouts.

'Shut your face! Don't you even speak to me. Don't you ever speak to me again, you useless piece of piss.'

They both know they've only made it worse. They hear it in the pitch and rhythm of his voice, see it in the tightening strut and jerk of his movements, know that something has to be expelled. Something got rid of that can't be kept in any longer, and they stiffen and brace themselves.

'Take off your shirts.' And when they look at him in confusion: 'Take off your shirts now!'

Their imaginations fuel their fear – they've never been here before. As his fingers tremble with the buttons he weighs up the chances of making it through the door into the entry. But he knows the bolt can sometimes stick and that if he didn't make it he'd be trapped between the shut door and his father. He looks around the yard desperate to see something that might be used as a weapon but sees only the skeletons of rusted bike frames hanging from hooks screwed into the walls, the concrete coal bunker, a dressing table stripped of its mirror and drawers. Maybe the bolt would slip smoothly and he'd be gone. It would mean leaving Rob but in this moment his fear is stronger than what he feels for his brother. The decision is made for him because he has thought about it too long, the chance has gone, and his father's impatient hands are pulling at their shirts, trailing them over their heads in a pop of buttons.

'Now take your stance like men – the way you've been shown.' He shows them again, hunching himself into a tight bristle, his raised fists masking his face so that only his eyes scream out over the top of his fingers. They stand in front of him, his mirror image and he can smell his father's sweat and the sweet scent of their own piss and fear as he comes closer. He punches each of them on the side of the head – a short stabbing blow that thuds dully against their temples like a piston. Rob stumbles backwards.

'Keep up your fuckin' guard!' his father shouts and hits them again, on the other side of their heads. 'Are you just goin' to stand there and let someone paste you?'

He half blocks his father's next blow with his forearms, but his bones feel like twigs that might snap. Rob doesn't manage to block his fist and catches it again on his temple. He's starting to cry, a kind of smothered sob

3

that never rises above a murmur. From next door comes the sound of a television set; there are people all around them living lives that are different to the one that is theirs.

'Stop that fuckin' snivellin',' his father demands, 'before I give you something to gurn about.' But as he says the words, his breathing is laboured and soon he stops and stands with his hands on his hips. There is a thick furze of black hair under his arms. Perhaps it's over. Perhaps it's over and they've made it. 'Square up to each other,' he says and then his voice changes for a moment and he rests his arms on their shoulders. 'The world's full of people like the Thompsons and they'll walk all over you if you don't know how to defend yourselves. It's for your own good. You have to be able to look after yourselves.' He skims the backs of their heads lightly with the back of his hand in a gesture of playfulness. Of affection.

'Rob, take a pop at him. Your best shot. Make him step back. Make his eyes water.' His brother looks into his eyes and he sees the red flare on the side of his head, the thin trickle of snot he tries to sniff away. He nods his head to tell him to do it, then nods again, watches as his brother screws his eyes shut and swings a blow at him that is aimed at his shoulder but flails mostly into air. There is the snort of his father's derision, the sound of music from their neighbours' television.

'Show him how, Martin, show him how or I'll do the showing. Make him step back. Make his eyes water. Don't let that bastard Thompson take anything belonging to you ever again.'

Rob is looking at him. He's nodding but his eyes are frightened. More frightened than he's ever seen them.

4

'Show him, Martin! Show him, son!'

He clenches his fist. Something catches his eye and for a second he glances up at the house, sees his mother's face hanging ghostly behind the glass.

A CONSTELLATION. THAT'S HOW he thinks of it. Ten beautiful stars, each one shining brightly in the night sky. They had always been told that she would do well, but no one at the parents' evenings had ever mentioned stars. He hadn't even known that such things existed, so when she had told him on the morning of the results he had been filled with apprehension, thinking that perhaps the stars indicated a reservation, a steward's enquiry that might soon strip her of the bit of paper she held in her hand and award it to someone else. When he asked about the stars Rachel had laughed as she explained and then everyone had laughed. Even Tom. Just for a moment, before he realised he was laughing, even Tom had laughed. Ten A-star grades. Top of the tree, top of the tallest mountain, it's a miracle. But whenever he thinks of it, he feels what everyone must feel in the presence of a miracle – that it's a trick, a sleight of hand that will leave him looking foolish and deceived as soon as he allows himself to trust it.

He knows it will be better when he sees the certificate which will be presented to her this afternoon; like the cheque in the hand after the lottery win: the indisputable confirmation that fantasy has been transmuted into reality; the tangible evidence of what the mind is frightened to believe. He looks at the stage and sees the table stacked with the glinting wink of silverware and knows that the certificate is there and part of him wants to hurry towards it and hold it. To kiss its undeniable truth.

The memory of another time when he held a certificate to his mouth and kissed it, suddenly imposes itself on his memory. It's in an echoing, tiled corridor that smells of polish, and comes just after closing the heavy, wood-panelled door of the office. Holds it to his lips tenderly and in a sudden release kisses his father's name, gives it to Rob to kiss, then slipping it into his jacket pocket, hurries with him towards the sharp-edged throw of light breaking from the street outside. But he wants no thought of that world to intrude into the perfection of the present and so he tries to push the memory away and stares again at the table of silver.

The prizegiving's about to start. The teachers process into the hall, the younger ones self-conscious and a little giddy in their academic gowns and hoods but he likes the gowns, thinks that they add weight to the occasion, the appropriate dignity. They file on to the stage and stand at their seats as the headmistress, school governors and dignitaries assume their places. He takes the opportunity to strain forward in his seat once again, in order to see if he can spot Rachel, but Alison calms him into restraint. The rows and rows of white-shirted prize-winners and parti-cipants conceal her and he feels a pulse of frustration. Two blonde-haired girls whisper together, their heads angled into each other like stooks of corn, while others discreetly point and smile at what their teachers consider the best their wardrobe can offer. She should be wearing the stars in her hair in a garland, a wreath of ten diamonds. She should be sitting on the stage, not with the others, and not because she's better than the other girls but because her journey has been longer, more difficult, and above all because it started with him.

And he can think of nothing that he gave to help her. No

part of his brain or being. She climbed this mountain on her own and when he thinks of the miserable school he went to and the pathetic little pyre of his own qualifications, it fills him with shame and confusion. He wishes he could put a match to it, burn it out of his memory for ever. They never had prize days – were told that for every one boy who got a prize there were hundreds who didn't. Maybe no one ever did anything that merited a prize, maybe they couldn't find chairs for the parents that weren't decorated with phalluses or sectarian graffiti. It comforts him a little to think that if perhaps, just perhaps, they had been given things to aim for, some encouragement to go beyond the narrow and fixed expectations, they might have achieved, if not stars, then something worthwhile.

But when he looks at the table with the silverware and the certificates it scares him, too, because if he can find no connection with these stars, then what connects him with his daughter? What makes him her father? He looks at Alison, his wife, who sits in her best suit and the make-up that she hasn't worn in a long time and he wonders if it was some hereditary misprint, some freak of genetics that produced such a child. He thinks of the items he stands watch over in the museum, the bones and fossils, the reproductions of the extinct; remembers the North's oldest footprint of a reptile found in sandstone on Scrabo Hill 230 million years ago, and he wonders if it is part of an evolutionary process – a step forward to something better, which throws off the husks of the past and discards all that is dead and worthless. But how can seventeen years, seventeen years, which to him feel like the blink of an eye, produce such a result? And there is even more fear edging his confusion because if she has travelled such a

9

distance in so short a time, then what is to stop her travelling on ever further, until, when she looks back, they are nothing more than a speck on a half-forgotten horizon? If her parents are no part of her achievement, what is to stop her discarding them as an unnecessary burden? He grips his programme, then flicks the pages as if the answer might spring out. There is a long list of university entrants. Already they have been talking to her about the possibility of Oxford or Cambridge. It sounds like a different continent, a different universe and for a second he feels frightened by the stars.

In the museum the lads called him 'The Star Man' when they heard. Before the variations started: Stars in his Eyes, Patrick Moore, Twinkle, Twinkle Little Star – he's heard them all and none of them made him feel anything other than proud and in the voices of those who used them, he could hear admiration, a desire to share some of the glory through their association with him.

The headmistress stands at the rostrum and welcomes everyone and then the choir is singing, their voices filling the hall and he's never heard of the composer or the title but it sounds like the music you might hear in a cathedral. The faces of the girls are earnest, malleable; moulding the softness of their features to the rise and fall of their voices. He looks at Alison and she smiles back at him and it feels as if they've just stepped inside a new world and that there is something sacred about it, something holy and he wonders should he bow his head. For a second he averts his eyes, looks at the floor and then in a sudden moment of panic he thinks that he doesn't belong here, with these people who have more money than he has, who live in big houses. People who know each other and have enough knowledge and confidence not to be sitting in their very best clothes.

Shuffling in his seat he stares at the door where the prefects stand with handfuls of programmes and wonders if there is some other way out of the hall. The collar of his new shirt is too tight and he tries to loosen it by pushing a finger down between it and his neck. His foot kicks the chair in front. It's too warm in the hall. He looks around at the closed windows. Why did no one think to open them? The collar constricts like a noose. He finds it harder to breathe. Perhaps he could slip out as the choir is finishing, leave unnoticed while they retake their seats. Maybe his being here spoils the moment, taints what is about to happen. The whiteness of the girls' shirts, the burnish and glint of the silver, the brightness of the stars – all begin to whisper to him that he doesn't belong in this place. He closes his eyes and for a second he feels as if he's in a newly painted room and his hands are black with soot and, as he struggles to find an exit, his grimed prints press their pattern on the walls.

The touch of a hand. Pressed over his. He looks down and it's Alison's and it pulls him back to the moment and she's looking at him and silently asking if he's all right. He nods and forces a smile and then it's too late because the choir is finished, only the echoing memory of the music trembling in the corners of the hall, and the headmistress is delivering her speech. He tries to calm himself as he always does by thinking of the objects he watches over every day, anchoring himself by focusing on their physical reality, the cases where their permanence is preserved and stored. So as she delivers her speech and talks of the results, the percentage passes, the appearance in the *Sunday Times* league table, he thinks of sixteen polished stone axes, their heads grey and smooth like fish; weaving looms from the linen mills; giant steam engines with pistons, valves and dials.

While she talks of the successes of the year, then the great sporting victories and the girls selected for Ulster in hockey and tennis, he repeats silently the factory slogans from the mills, 'Trade is the golden girdle of the globe', 'Man goeth forth unto his work and to his labour until the evening', thinks of display cases full of coins, flint-headed arrows, standing stones, the giant Irish elk with its antlers spread the length of a man's body.

Then she's introducing the guest speaker and he feels calmer. It's some former pupil who's running her own company and they start to give out the prizes and he claps each of them, starting with the youngest first-former and he keeps on clapping even when his hands are sore because he knows that each one who hurries across the stage brings the moment closer when he will receive the confirmation that he needs. The girls all nod their heads quickly like little pecking birds as they shake hands and as they walk across the stage stare at the floor as if watching out for a pitfall, some obstacle that will cause them to stumble. No one looks out at the audience and some let their hair fall and curtain their face. On the ground floor of the museum there is a pond with terrapin and goldfish. The bottom of it is spattered with coins. Why do people always throw coins into water? Is it the payment they think they need to pay for their wish? Is it the price that must be paid for warding off evil spirits?

And then the moment arrives, almost before he's re-alised, and as they read out the stars, there's a ripple of admiration from the audience but he doesn't clap more loudly or draw attention to himself; instead he sits perfectly still and watches as she gets a few seconds of conversation and a quick pat of commendation. They almost forget to hand her the cup for the best results and as she walks off, Alison is straining forward and clapping and this time he calms her with a restraining touch. And now he only wants to be invisible, to be nothing more than a particle of light reflected in the silver of the cup she carries. He rubs his hands as if to dry the sudden dampness that seeps into the palms and glances about him to gauge if anyone realises he's her father. All around him stretches a sea of white shirts, the sheen of silver, the noise of clapping, the fistle of programmes. But now it's real and no one can take it away from her. And to hell with them all because he knows he's her father but, as if to prove it to himself, he scoops up thick handfuls of memories, starting with the first time he held her, a blood-ied lightness after the long hours of Ali's struggle and the nurses had to prise her from him. Then he lets the mem-ories drip through his fingers like droplets of water until they settle and form into a silent pool below the surface of his being.

There is a new calmness now as he listens to the guest speaker's address and he even nods his head as she talks about the future, about opportunity, about the things that are important. He even smiles at her jokes – the little digs at men, the giving of the future to women – and does his best to concentrate. The splash of children dropping their pennies into the water, the press of their faces against the cases where the past is stored, safe and perfect. Where everything is explained. His mother's face flitting like a ghost behind the glass. It feels as if the future is being given to Rachel, given with the stars. She is a good girl. Why should she choose to forget them? He has a photograph of her on the inside of his locker at work. It's always been his favourite. She's about four years old and wearing a blue dress covered with white, yellow-centred flowers. She has no shoes on her feet and she's holding a small camera to her eye. But the camera is the wrong way round – she's looking through the lens and he likes to think of the light of the world flowing into that eye. All the light of the world. Light and the future, more than he's ever known. More than he could ever grasp for himself.

The choir are finishing the afternoon and they're singing 'Yesterday' by the Beatles. He doesn't understand why they've picked it, but at least it's something he knows and Alison smiles at him as she sings quietly along. The voices are soft and whispery like the wind through grass. He thinks that no one could ever believe in yesterday, no one could ever hold it to their heart like a bird throbbing between the hands. There is only the future now. Only the future, so why now does he think of Takabuti, her mummy's face black and wizened like a walnut as she sleeps in her coffin? Children hunch over the glass – it's the exhibit they always want to see, the one they want to touch, the one by which they want to be frightened. On the lid is a prayer asking good fortune from the Sun God, asking for good burial and on the breast of her coffin there is a goddess depicted as a beautiful young woman kneeling with outstretched wings. The goddess of the skies who wears the sun in her hair.

*

It isn't the inner circle of hell. Thankfully, at seventeen her birthday requires a greater degree of sophistication than McDonald's and so she has selected Pizza Hut. He's not unhappy with the choice and if he has to eat somewhere other than in his own home, then he thinks there are worse places and he almost feels relaxed in the booth they share. But while they are busy with their birthday chatter, he watches a woman at the salad bar as she pulls her baggy sweatshirt over the hump of her behind in a counter balance to the rising pyramid of food in her bowl. There is an expertise in her movements – the deft handling of the tongs as she builds the textured layers. The sides of this pyramid are a structure of red and green peppers, softened and held in place by a smear of cheese and coleslaw. Higher still. He decides it is the payment of money that precludes shame, thinks that everything in the salad bar should be free so people might be spared this humiliation. Alison is asking what he thinks of his pizza and he mumbles a vague reply. Rachel and Tom are squabbling over who has eaten more than their share of the savoury fries.

He can't take his eyes away. She has paused for a reassessment of possibilities, for a final perusal of the options. He remembers once seeing a woman putting salad in her ashtray, rather than pay for a bowl. But this one's going higher. He sees no limit to what she thinks is her need, her entitlement through payment, and then he feels embarrassment for her and looks about in the hope that some loved one might come and put his arm round her and shepherd her back to the privacy of their table.

'Are you going to have a sweet, Martin?' Alison asks.

'No, I don't think so.' The thought of eating more food that he doesn't need places his nose in the communal pig trough, makes him share the world's greed.

'Go on, have something, it'll not kill you,' she says. 'Spoil yourself.'

'Come on, Dad, you have to have something special – it's my birthday tea,' Rachel pleads, her eyes fluttering, her face contorted in her favourite parody of childhood. She often uses it now, mostly when she's asking for something – money, permission to go somewhere, to stay out late. The expression says that she is an adult but to please, to get what she wants, she will impersonate a child. But every time she does it, it only serves to remind him that she is no longer a child and when he says yes, it is because he wants her to stop the act. So he nods and picks some ice-cream extravaganza whose name it embarrasses him even to say.

Alison tries to catch the waitress's eye and instinctively starts to stack the plates as if she's clearing the kitchen table at home. The woman at the salad bar has finished now and turning away, carries the trembling edifice in front of her chest like a wobbling third breast. He looks at her face and it's devoid of any trace of shame. There is only the grim concentration of a competitor in a big race. He doesn't want Rachel to be seventeen and he doesn't understand but somehow it's this woman's fault for taking too much, for leaving nothing for anyone else. And it's the way time takes away something he wants to hold on to and the woman falters a little and maybe everything's going to spill all over the floor. He's praying to God it doesn't spill and his hand grips the end of the table. Then she's passed and he hates her a little.

Tom picks some morsel off the stacked plates and Rachel tells him off and the moment gets lost in the squabble. 'Spoil yourself', the words linger corrosively in his mind and he looks at Alison as she pacifies and clucks at her children and wonders how she doesn't know, and for one terrible moment he thinks of telling her as soon as they get home.

'Would you like to order dessert?' the waitress asks and he stares ahead as if she's not really there and waits for Alison to speak. But she starts to ask them if they enjoyed their meal, if everything was all right for them, and he has to nod slightly, wondering why they have to endure these little rituals, these impersonations of the personal. The girl is pretty, even his brief glance reveals that. Perhaps only a

16

couple of years older than Rachel. A student probably, trying to make a bit of money to help her pay her way. And she is too hot and so softly blows the stray strand of hair that has slipped on to her brow. The way a child might do. It lifts lightly, then falls back to its original place. He tries not to look at her as Alison gives the order.

Another two years and Rachel will be in university and that's going to cost a packet and Alison will be at him again about going for promotion, or getting a different job. The future fault-lines of argument and counter-argument splay out in predictable patterns. He's safe where he is – he's not giving that up. He'll do extra hours, grab whatever over-time comes his way and there's bound to be grants. But he's staying where he is. Staying for ever. She might even go to Oxbridge. He decides to look it up on the map, see exactly where it is, how you'd get there. And he thinks again of the stars, allows himself to suggest that despite what he felt at the start, whatever way they're looked at, a part, even some thin little sliver of them has to belong to him. And Alison. These things don't fall out of the air. Whether it's genes or even just encouragement, somewhere there has to be a part of him in it all.

The waitress returns with exotic ice creams and as she sets them on the table he wants to whisper to her about the stars. He lowers his head in embarrassment, ponders the best way to tackle the ice cream, then glances about to check if anyone is watching him.

'Martin, now might be a good time,' Alison says and for a second he's confused but then remembers the small package in his pocket.

'Wouldn't it be better in the car on the way home?' he asks.

'No Martin, now would be better,' she insists and so

with the back of his hand he wipes away any ice cream there might be on his mouth and shuffles the package across the table to his daughter. 'Martin!' Alison hisses at him, her eyes wide with exasperation.

'Happy birthday, Rachel,' he says softly. She scrunches off the paper without an attempt at sophistication and her pleasure at the mobile phone is all on the surface and unfiltered by any sense of teen cool. It's what she's wanted, it's what she's been asking for and for some reason they've made her wait. It's red and shiny and she waves it in the air as if that's how signals are picked up.

'Can I get one for my birthday?' Tom asks, and in the tone of his voice is the message that to be denied would constitute an inequality of treatment. It is a tone his parents increasingly recognise as the inevitable consequence of having a sister whose achievements so constantly eclipse his own.

'Who would you ring on a mobile phone, Tom?' he asks and Alison and Rachel smile, despite themselves. He thinks it is an unkind thing to ask but something makes him do it to his son who has no friends except the family computer, and the characters who run and jump across the screen, who fire their lasers at the touch of his fingers. It is his glasses he touches now with the tip of his finger, adding a whorled print to the existing smear.

'There's lots of people I could ring,' he asserts.

'Who, Tom?' he persists.

'Martin, leave him alone,' Alison says as Rachel puts her arm round her brother in a gushing display of mock sympathy. 'Rachel's older than you, Tom. She had to wait. But maybe if you get a better set of exam results at the end of third year, we might think of it.'

Tom blinks his eyes and shrugs off his sister's teasing

arm. 'That's not fair,' he says, and the words make him sound smaller and younger than the thirteen-year-old boy who's puddled into overweight. 'That's not fair,' he repeats, pointing the long spoon at them over the top of his glass. There is a little furrow of white on the top of his lip and he uses his nose to snuffle his glasses back on to the bridge of his nose.

'Hello, is that the loony bin?' Rachel asks into her phone. 'I've got a younger brother here who's taking a mad psycho. He's starting to foam at the mouth, can you come and take him away?'

'Ha, ha,' Tom says, wiping his mouth and digging the spoon into the bottom of the glass to spear the last remnants. 'Very funny – not.'

'I think Tom should get a phone,' Rachel says, starting to read the instruction leaflet. 'He could use it to phone Esther Rantzen on Childline, tell them all his problems. How badly everyone treats him.'

'That's enough,' Alison says. 'No one treats Tom badly. Don't be horrible to him, Rachel. Keep working hard and we'll see about a phone. But I'll tell you one thing – it's up to you both to pay for your calls. Your dad and I aren't made of money so you needn't expect us to subsidise your conversations.' She leans across the table and uses a napkin to wipe away some of what her son has missed on his lip.

'So am I going to get one?' Tom says, screwing his eyes closed at his mother's touch.

'We'll see, we'll see. I'm not saying any more than that.'

The answer appears to mollify him and smirking at his sister, he licks the spoon clean. Now they think they've finished. They're getting ready to go but the waitress is coming back towards them and she's carrying a little cake with sparkly candles. He knows nothing about this, Alison must have arranged it without telling him. 'Happy birthday,' the waitress says, carefully setting it on the table and passing each of them a side plate and fork. 'How embarrassing!' Rachel says, but he can see she's pleased. 'Blame your mother,' he says and then Alison gets her to blow out the candles and make a wish. He wonders what she wishes for at seventeen but knows that to disclose it would be to destroy the chances of it coming true. He thinks of all the other birthdays, the blowing out of the candles. All the wishes. What were they for? For a bicycle, a puppy, the latest fad? For a front tooth to replace the gappy smile? What does she wish for now at this moment, at seventeen? For the future? For Oxford and Cambridge? For more stars? For love? He watches the determination on her face as her breath sweeps round the candles, the same determination that has marked everything she's ever done. From first steps, to riding a bike, to learning to swim, to school, to everything. Her eyes are wide and blue. Or are they grey? He can't be sure. Everything is changing. She's growing older. She'll probably never do this ever again. It's probably her very last wish. Her hand brushes back her blonde hair from her face. They're blue, they must be blue.

'What did you wish for?' Tom asks.

'She can't say,' Alison says, 'or it won't come true.'

Rachel suddenly pulls her hair into pigtails and makes a pantomime, pretty girl face.

'Sugar and spice and puppy dog tails,' she lisps.

'Should have been for a better face,' Tom answers, smiling at his own joke.

'Sticks and stones,' she says and gives her brother a peck on the cheek.

'Yuck!' he says, scraping his cheek clean, then elaborately flicking the invisible contagion from his fingers.

There is a little thread of blue vein on her eyelid, so light you might not even notice that it's there. 'Be nice to your sister on her birthday,' he says.

'She's never nice to me.'

'He doesn't know how to be nice,' Rachel says, picking at a piece of icing with her fingers.

'You should be nice to her,' Alison tells him, 'in a couple of years she'll be going away to university and then it'll be too late.'

'Can I have her room when she's gone?' he asks.

'No you can't, weevil,' Rachel insists and for the first time he thinks she's serious. 'I'll still be coming home for holidays and things, so keep your mitts off. Stay in your own cave, your little hidey-hole, your Stygian gloom.' The light washes against the smear of his lens and bleaches out his eyes as he turns his head.

'Well, when you're away, who's to stop me?'

'Tell him, Dad, tell him he can't,' she says, appealing to his authority in a way she hasn't done in a long time.

'It's Rachel's room, she'll be coming back to it, so no one's moving anywhere,' he says, pleased to see Alison nodding her head in support. But he knows that Tom thinks he's found a weak spot in his otherwise infallible sister so he expects to hear the issue used again and as the waitress places what's left of the cake in a box for them to take home, he seems almost happy.

Afterwards in the car they feel like a family. Tom sits in the front with him and it feels like the old days when they used to do things together, go places. He takes the long way home. He doesn't want to get there. Alison is happy: he watches her in the mirror as she squeezes against Rachel and they gossip and giggle like girls in the same gang. How could he ever tell her? Tom slumps down in the seat so that it looks as if his spine is impossibly curved. He's opening the top button on his trousers – he's put on weight again. There is a faint cheesy smell from him and it seems to stir and seep from his trainers as he leans forward to put on the radio. As the sound of garage fills the car he shakes his head at his son and pushes in his own cassette. It's Billie Holiday. His children groan but he insists he's not listening to what he calls 'that rubbish' and ignores the rising wave of their complaint. Later on he will look in the dictionary he keeps in his locker at work, try to find out what a Stygian gloom is.

'You belong in a museum, Dad,' Rachel says and everyone, including Tom, smiles. It's the family's favourite joke.

*

He spends his life looking at people and things. Sometimes he walks about a little, sometimes he checks things – dials, temperatures, doors; things like that. He feels comfortable with the little rituals, the routines that have to be followed. They rotate the areas for which they are responsible – it's to prevent boredom, to keep them on their toes, but he's never bored, can't understand those who are. Although he has his favourites, his dislikes also, he's glad they do that. The whole of the museum is open to him and he feels as if he shares ownership of everything it contains. He loves the very building, its smells and surfaces, the way there is an inner catacomb of corridors and rooms that the public never get to see, the way the outer galleries fit perfectly over this inner body like a tailored suit. He knows the doors, the pathways that link the two worlds, moves effortlessly and quietly between the two.

He watches the visitors, too. They change – with the weather, the day of the week, the time of year. He watches them but they don't see him. It's as if he watches them from behind the protection of a glass and even when their eyes rest on him it's only for a second and then they move on. He likes to stand still, become part of the building. He likes to be invisible. And on those rare occasions he's called on to speak it's no more than to give a direction to the toilets or the café, or point out the nearest exit. He takes a detailed interest in everything he has to watch over, knows each exhibit with an intimacy that is prompted by respect and mostly with affection. But it's driven also by self-interest because now he understands the value of knowledge and so he stores it all away as an investment that will one day pay a dividend, and just maybe that dividend will be to know enough things to stay within the orbit of his daughter. Out on the rim perhaps, out on the very edge – it doesn't matter how far away, so long as he's there and not blown by the currents of time and space into another world that's coloured and shaped by shame or ignorance. So as he walks he reads the labels, the explanations, tries to commit them to his memory, repeating learned phrases like a catechism.

It irritates him to see those of his colleagues who parade their indifference, or even disdain, for what is all around them, and thinks they don't have the vocation. Because he considers it to be a vocation – preserving the best things of the past, keeping them safe for the future. Safe for people to look at. He believes, too, that looking is what a museum should be based on – looking and learning. There used to be a children's magazine called *Look and Learn* but it belonged in the distant world of encyclopaedias and train sets, of games like Monopoly and Scalextric. But there's still time to learn, to make up for what was missed in the past.

But looking isn't good enough any more. Participation, touch, full sensory experience – these are the fashion now, the words they use, as if they think that things can be understood like Braille with the tips of the fingers. His unvoiced opinion is that it's a gimmick, a cheap card trick that results only in disrespect and in the young a belief that everything must fall inside the entitlement of their reach, and so he is fearful of where it will end. Of what damage will ensue.

He hates the birthday present they gave to Rachel. Alison had insisted that it was what she wanted and even though he knew it was the truth, he could generate no enthusiasm for it because he hates mobile phones, thinks they only encourage people to make a show of themselves. To speak in public what should be spoken in private. His opinion is that they should be banned everywhere in the museum – apart from the café, perhaps, as a compromise. He winces when they go off in the galleries and would love to be able to confiscate them. His objection to them is held so strongly that he has committed it to paper, to management, suggesting that they should insist that all phones are checked into the cloakrooms, but in response received only a short note expressing sympathy and stating that the matter would be kept under review. None of his colleagues seem to care one way or the other.

There's something else that has started to get to him – working the Sunday afternoon shift. It's not the noise of the crowds or the shuffling vacuousness of their faces, it's not the street kids playing chasey, that affects him the most. It's the steady procession of separated fathers with their designated access hours to put in that upsets him in a way he has never known before. Pumped up on fast-food lunches and fizzy drinks, the kids scamper ahead, while their fathers struggle to keep up, their showy attempts at fatherhood being ignored. They feel the obligation to point out things to their sons and daughters, to compensate for their absence of instruction during the rest of the week. The children are always overexcited, pleased to be with them but still determined to show the edge of their unspoken resentment at what they see as a betrayal, their rejection by someone to whom they had given their trust. So he watches them exploit the fathers' sense of guilt and extract as much as they can from their pockets in the café or shop but withhold the forgiveness for which they're desperate.

He watches them and it frightens him. He can think of no worse place to stand with his children. It scares him so much that sometimes he feels physically sick. He tries to reassure himself that he has a skill for secrecy: it was how they grew up, it was the foundation on which everything else was built, the cement that held it all together. A family without links to the outside world, a house with windows that only looked out and a door permanently closed to uninvited callers. Sometimes boys from school who didn't know would call for them, ask if he or Rob was in, and his father would say they weren't and slam the door in their faces. Once he had called them both to him and put his arms on their shoulders, pulled them close and they had huddled behind the same closed door as he explained: 'This family doesn't need anyone. So long as we've got each other, we've got everything we need. Together we're strong but if we let outsiders in they'll destroy that strength. Turn each of us against the other.' He remembers it all so clearly because his father had used the word 'love'. 'I love this family, I won't let anyone out there destroy it,' and he said the word with an intensity that shocked and frightened them. When he'd asked them individually if they understood what he was saying they had nodded and he'd given them his blessing by tousling their hair and calling them 'Good boys, good boys.'

He knows all about secrecy. It's in his very blood. No one had to know. As a child, the thought of the world finding out about home had frightened him more than anything that had to be endured there. And so he had pretended to be like everyone else with a consummate cunning that covered up every sign, every potential clue that might have hinted at the truth. And he did it not out of fear, but out of an all-pervading sense of shame. He could take anything from his father, salve any bruise with the comforting compress of hatred but recoiled at the thought of the world's discovery. He hadn't even told Alison everything, just enough to let her think she understood and discourage her from further intrusion. How could anyone who wasn't part of it ever understand? How could he explain what it was like to live constantly on the edge of fear, to take each step as if you were walking on the thinnest of ice which might suddenly crack and plunge you into the darkness of the waters below? The wrong thing said, the wrong way you held a fork or spoon, the wrong time to be happy. But even that could have been coped with, but for the fact that the wrong thing was never the same, could not be predicted. Like throwing a handful of pebbles into the air – the splay and pattern of their fall were always different, could never be fully anticipated. And so to survive, to stop the plunge through the ice, required him to watch and listen, to sense. Answers were not to be found in seismic shifts, because by then it was too late, but in reading the slightest signs, straining for the faintest signals: the inflection and timbre of his voice, the edged lilt of his laughter, the tread of his feet on the stairs. Knowing when to be invisible, knowing when to be present.

So he has all the skills of secrecy, of giving nothing away, of holding it in. He could get a star in it. He could win a prize. It's to do with not wanting the lies of the past to stain the present that he's created, but even that desire is less powerful than the fear that has held him in its fist all his life, and which whispers to him that if the truth is discovered, he will stand naked and alone, exposed on the shore of the world's scorn. So why now does he feel the impulse to tell Alison, the unrelenting weight of his secret threatening to crush the life of him? So how could he, even for a moment, think of telling, of risking losing it all, of being swept in a matter of seconds out of their embrace for ever, of being one of those Sunday afternoon fathers, trying to catch up with his kids, struggling to find some way of making a connection, desperate to hang in there, to show he still cares? Asserting his entitlement to love.

In another month the exhibition will be over. Dismantled and taken away. He'll never see her or it again – he'll work it that he's on a different shift when she's taking it away. He tells himself he can do it. Knows he can. Child's play. And he'll make up for it – he's got the whole rest of his life to make up for it, to atone. He thinks of Alison, thinks of Rachel, thinks of Tom. So much already they don't know; this, too, can be buried deep in the pyre. And one day he tells himself that he'll find the match that lights the pyre, sends the consuming flames spurting skywards in great leaping tongues. But it is not the rush and crackle of the burning that he hears, it is Alison's voice and she's saying, 'It'll not kill you. Go on, spoil yourself.' And despite it all, despite everything, he still wants to tell her that it's too late, that he's already spoilt.

*

It was Tenko who appeared from behind a glass case, his eyes rolling, his head nodding in the confirmation of his own wisdom.

'It's pure shite!' he said. 'Pure unadulterated shite.'

'What is?' he asked.

'The new exhibition they're starting to set up on Four. Whoever brought that lot in needs their head seeing to.'

'What is it?' he asked again.

'A complete and utter bollocks!' Tenko answered, shaking his head slowly from side to side as if blown by the breeze of his incomprehension. 'Bunch of wankers out of art college. Supposed to be the cream. Wouldn't like to see the rest. The sculptures look like something you'd throw on the bonfire, put together from what you'd find on the skip. Paintings are all like somebody's thrown up on canvas and put frames round them. Has to be a piss-take, Marty. Has to be.'

'I'm up there later on. Something to look forward to then.'

'God help you – it'll be like being asked to look after the toilets, standing in front of thon mess. There should be a bonus to cover the humiliation.' Only the cackle of his radio stopped the flow of his invective. 'Pure shite,' he insisted, whispering as he walked off, his right hand waving in what was either a farewell or a final gesture of disdain.

As always, he thought Tenko talked too much and too loudly. (Tenko, because once at a union meeting to discuss new work rotas, he claimed that it would be like being in a concentration camp.) His voice seemed to set up waves of vibration that swelled and rebounded from the walls; even after he had vanished his presence left a print in the stillness of the almost empty gallery. He watched a young woman glancing disinterestedly at the displays, finding nothing to delay her more than a few seconds at each one. Sometimes without realising it she touched the glass with her fingers. He wished she wouldn't, but said nothing.

When it was time to go to Four he found the closed-off gallery busy with people setting up work, carrying materials and bits of their displays. A couple of museum curators were advising and helping. He wondered why it was necessary for him to be there. There was noise and movement everywhere and no matter where he stood or moved he seemed to end up in someone's way. At intervals mobile phones would go off and one of the artists nearest to him was wearing a personal stereo. He looked at his watch and wondered how he would put in his time, how long it would take before the gallery was able to reclaim its normal calm. He tried a few different positions, found some paths to skirt the chaos, before going to stand beside one of the phones, as if his proximity might cause it to ring with a request to go somewhere else. Most of the paintings going on the wall were abstracts, big panels of blocks of garish colour – pinks and purples. One had bits of newspaper headlines pressed into the surface and one was framed by what looked like passport-booth photographs. There were metal sculptures, combining thin shining planes and industrial piping beside more delicate, ceramic masks. The white masks portrayed some form of degeneration, beginning with a young woman's face and locks of hair, then moving through a sequence where a part of the face was blistered or broken, until the final twisted mask resembled less a young woman and more a gargoyle, its eyes hooded, the mouth contorted into a leer.

From the ceiling two young men were hanging a battered, black Raleigh bicycle, the heavy old-fashioned type that you saw sometimes outside a butcher's shop as decoration, and from it they were draping the paraphernalia of modern cycling. Entwined in the spokes or tied to the handlebars were flashes of fluorescence in the form of helmets, sunglasses, drinking bottles, Lycra shorts. The bike was suspended on chains and the balance of the student on top of the stepladder seemed increasingly precarious. He went over and put his hand to the ladder.

'No point dying for your art, son,' he said.

'Thanks boss,' the boy replied. 'On second thoughts though, it might boost the sale price.'

'Everything's for sale then?' he asked.

'Sure, and if you like, we'll do you a good deal.'

'Naw, you're all right thanks. Couldn't see the wife going on it. The most we hang from the ceiling is balloons at Christmas.'

'Well if you change your mind, give us a shout.'

'What's it called?' he asked.

'What's it called in the catalogue?' the boy said to his helper while he came down from the ladder.

'*Time Cycle 1*', he answered before slugging from a bottle of water. 'If you buy it you can always ride it home.'

'What's it cost?'

'Two thousand five hundred. But you get it installed for that,' the boy said, passing the bottle to his friend.

'Buy me a better car that would, but good luck to you, lads,' he said as he stepped back to look at it one last time. 'Get a sale and you'll be suppin' on the champagne.'

He wondered if Tenko was right but was reluctant to

admit the possibility. There had to be something in it all or the museum wouldn't have opened its doors to it. Looking about him at the industry of the students he told himself that not seeing it, or understanding it, was the product of his ignorance, the absence of education. If Rachel was here he knew she would be able to explain it to him. And there was something else that Tenko didn't grasp, something he had read in a book or heard on television. It was that when people dismissed things by saying that anyone could have done it, what they didn't realise was that the art was in the thinking – thinking up the idea in the first place. And not everyone could do that. Only artists could do that. So as he looked round the gallery, he told himself that these young people were artists because they could think up their art, have the ideas. If he was smarter and had been given a half-decent education he would be able to understand these ideas, be able to see the things the way they were supposed to be seen. Tenko would be wiser not to broadcast his stupidity, be like him and not rush to judgements that would only reveal how little he knew or understood. Look and learn – that was the rule.

'Could you help me?' she asked. She had appeared as if from nowhere. He looked about to see where she had come from, then realised it was from the black-draped, tent-shaped structure that had been built in the corner of the room. He hadn't realised anyone was in it and the flapping door had been closed so that he couldn't see inside.

'Do you think you could give me a few seconds?' she asked. A little older than the rest of the students but dressed in similar style and wearing a ring in her eyebrow and about six in one ear. She was smiling at him as if that inducement would increase her prospects of success. He hesitated, worried that she was going to ask him to do something that would expose his ignorance, his lack of skill.

'If I can,' he said. 'But you're probably asking the wrong guy.'

'No, I think you'll be just perfect,' she said studying him in a way that confused him. Her blonde hair was cut short, almost boyish in appearance, with only some longer strands that fell across her forehead softening the effect. He thought she was about thirty, maybe even a couple of years more. 'I need you to come inside,' she said, pointing over her shoulder. Then without any explanation she turned and held open the black cloth flap for him to enter.

Outside black, inside white. Everywhere white and, running and circling round the walls from some kind of projector, clouds and colours and images of sky and land and seascape. 'Stand just here,' she said, her hand guiding him backwards and then she looked him up and down again as if measuring him for a suit. 'I think that'll do just fine.' Sky ran across her face. 'And enough headroom, too.' Her body was the waves of the sea. 'I just need to check I've got the space right.' He was conscious of her scent, the closeness of her body in the confined space. He wondered what was on his own face and body but when he looked down all he could see were undulating ripples of light. It felt as if he was hanging over the prow of a boat looking at the skim of sunlight on water.

'I haven't got the sound installed yet,' she said, as her hand reached to the top of one of the sides, then moved down its length through the wavery quiver like a snake. 'Seems to be really secure and solid. Don't want anything falling on anyone.'

'Sound?' he asked.

'Yeah, there's a soundtrack to go with it. It's the best part. Took ages to make.'

'And what's on it?'

'It's a collage of different natural sounds – the wind, the rain, the sea. Whispering voices, birdsong, lots of breathing. That sort of thing. It's on a looped tape, goes on playing.'

It felt as if there was something he should say in response, some question he should ask but he was scared of saying the wrong thing and so at first he only nodded as if he understood, as if everything made sense. Her face was wind-driven clouds, streaming across the sky of her skin. He wondered what it was like to live inside the world of ideas, this world where Rachel, too, was going to live. He held his hand up to the light and watched the splay of pattern. He wanted to compliment her, to tell her how good it felt but didn't know what were the right words and for a second he turned to his children for help. Should he say it was 'cool', should he say it was 'wicked'? But he knew the words wouldn't come out of his mouth, so he hesitated and in that second she was thanking him for his help and holding open the flap for him to leave. He had to say something, to show her he understood.

'It's good, really good.'

'Thanks,' she said, 'but it'll be better when I get the soundtrack organised. You need both parts to get the full effect.'

He nodded his head. 'If you need any more help, give me a shout.'

'Thanks. What's your name? Mine's Lorrie.' She held out her hand and as he shook it, half expected it still to bear the brush of light rather than the dullness of metal, stone-less rings. 'Listen, I need to bring a couple of boxes up from the car, what's the quickest way to get there?'

He took her down the back stairs, let her use a private door. Helped carry one of the boxes. In it were threaded garlands of shells, latticed frames of leaves and pebbles, beaded and stitched symbols on squares of cloth and leather which she used to decorate the outside of the tent, pinning and stapling them to the black cloth. He found himself watching her, interested in the way her body moved so fluidly, so much energy pushing against its slender frame. And in her movements was a total concentration, an indifference to whatever position she pushed herself into, or how she might look to anyone else. Somehow he managed to drop a hint of his curiosity about what she had created and she explained that it was 'an installation', told him things he pretended he understood.

Afterwards she bought him a thank-you drink and they talked. She was doing a Master's, was thirty-one years old, had taught for a while in London and if she couldn't find anything better would probably drift back into it. As she talked about her work it sounded as if she wasn't really sure about anything herself and that made him feel less frightened of what he might say.

'Why did you come back to Belfast?' he asked her.

'Tired of being a Paddy. Tired of Hackney. Tired of my accent sounding strange in my own ears.'

'But is London not a more exciting place than here?'

'There's a real buzz over here now, everything's changed while I was away. I really like it – there's lots of things happening.'

'It's the peace dividend,' he said in a monotone, not knowing why he said it but knowing it sounded stupid. So stupid they both laughed and it felt good to laugh with someone else. Someone who understood about art and ideas.

'When I left, Belfast city centre was like a ghost town by seven o'clock. Do you remember that song by The Specials? Every time I heard it in London I used to think of Belfast.'

'So what song makes you think of Belfast now?'

'I don't know. "Copacabana", "I Will Survive", "Boogie Nights".'

They talked about music – she loved Billie Holiday – had another drink and then he had lingered to the point where going forward felt as easy as going back. Her flat was in the streets behind the University and he helped her carry the boxes of leftover material up the stairs and when they got there everything she said and everything she did made him less scared of what they already knew. And when she looked at him, it was always as if she liked him and that made him feel good and he wondered if being washed in enough people's like could be the thing that would make him clean. Like everyone else. The same as everyone else.

The bed was narrow and draped in different coloured fabrics. Bright colours – orange, green and yellow. The headboard was slatted wood and linking some of the slats were the same necklaces of shells and feathers he had seen in the museum. Her hand in his was small but strong, and when she led him towards it he felt like a child but somehow everything she did made him trust her and he wanted to believe that she knew enough things to help him, that she had some secret knowledge. As they lay on top of it he cradled her head with both his hands as she kissed him and could feel its whole shape, the springy spikiness of her hair at the back and sides, the softness where it fell across her brow. At first the warm moistness of her mouth seemed doomed to break against the closed tightness of his, but it was insistent and uncompromising and he could not avoid it or resist, until everything in his head gave way and he kissed her in the same way. Then she was opening his clothes, with sure deft movements of her hands but making no effort to remove hers until the very last moment and then it was only the lower part.

There was a large high window facing the bed, screened from the outside by a green voile curtain with scalloped leaves. The last strength of the evening sun streamed through it, casting trembling little shadows of leaves on the wall. A breeze disturbed it as he entered her, making him turn his head and for a second it felt like an eye watching him but as he hesitated she moved her hips and took him fully. And now he didn't care if it was an eye because in that moment part of him wanted to tell the world that there was someone else who would give him and take from him all that people could. And that had to count for something. She gasped and under him he could feel her body squirm and try to settle into an accommodation but already now he knew that it was not his love that he had to give her but his unrelenting need and so he pummelled and bruised himself in her, firing himself on as she pressed her palm against his hip in an attempt to lever him off a little.

'Easy boy,' she whispered, her arm tightening round his neck. 'Easy, easy.' Her breath was in his ear, her fingers splayed against the warp and strain of his back but he heard only uglier words, wanted to fuck them silent so there was no respite until he shuddered into a sudden cry of defeat.

'I'm sorry,' he said, shocked into profuse gestures of gentleness, touching her face with his fingers, stroking her hair. 'I'm sorry.'

'Where did that come from?' she asked. 'You felt like a man who's just got out of prison after about ten years.'

He rolled onto his back and put a hand across his face to hide his embarrassment, to shield his nakedness from her scrutiny. But she pulled it away and calmed his brow with her fingers, furrowing them across his skin and massaging his temples. His breath streamed from him in a loud rush.

'It's all right,' she said. 'It's all right. I can feel your heart still pounding.' He started to look for his clothes but she stopped him. 'Stay there, don't move.' He watched her move from the bed. The backs of her legs were lightly muscled and brown. They had a light stipple of freckles below her knees. She put music on her CD – it was an instrumental piece with guitar and flute, and then she returned with two small candles which she lit and placed at either side of the bed. In her hand was a small, red jar.

'Turn over on your front.' He mumbled something about having to go but she silenced him with a shush the way you would speak to a child and her hands started to work on his back, kneading and stretching, sometimes kneading inwards with the knuckles of her thumbs. 'You don't have a spine, you've an iron rod. There's great knots of tension.' He felt her hands smoothing and pressing, smelt the pungent tang of whatever she was working into his skin. Turning his head towards the window the light warmed the side of his cheek and in its cadences rippled the sense of light and space.

'You do this for all your men?' he asked.

'Never met anyone who needed it as much as you. And there aren't so many if you're asking.' Her thumbs dug deliberately deep, making him wince and squirm.

'Don't be such a baby. Lie still. And try to breathe slowly and regularly.'

He pressed his face into the burn of colour on the bed and smelt her scent. Tried to breathe and not to think, to block out all the thoughts beginning to clatter noisily round his head. Her hands felt as if they were doing him good, draining away things that he needed to get rid of. Maybe she was helping him, helping to make him better and not just for himself but for the people he loved. Making him better for Alison. It was the first time – the only time, he told himself. It was just like a medicine – that's how he told himself to think of it. And afterwards he would go back home and be better for her, better for all of them and he'd be cleaner and lighter with whatever lingered below his surface salved and mended. After a while she stopped moving her hands and rested her head on his back. His skin felt primed and alive, alert to the slightest sensation. For a long time she lay on his back like a coat, a protection from everything that might fall on him and her breath lisped against his shoulder. Her fingers traced the line of his hair on his neck then pushed lightly into his scalp, the tips of her nails gently scratching his skin. He felt sleepy, aware of the first waves softly breaking against him, urging him to give himself up to it and now only the music was inside his head and in the sleepy blink of his eyes he saw the wisp of smoke from the candles.

But she didn't let him sleep and as he started awake he felt her hand between his legs, stirring and easing him into life and then she turned him over and sat astride him.

'I have tiny breasts,' she said as she pulled her jumper over her head. 'Like a girl's. Sorry.'

'They're beautiful,' he said before seeing them. 'Just beautiful.' When he did, he touched them lightly and kissed them and then in his excitement he started to push and lift into her but she stopped him by pressing both her palms against his chest. 'My turn,' she insisted. 'Just relax,' He tried to do as he was told and watched as she rose lightly and fell on him, and the scalloped leaves flitted across her body in a wavering frieze of light. 'Isn't that better?' she asked. It felt as if they were back in the tent, sheltered and brushed by the travelling transfer of cloud and sky. He traced the wiry rhythm of her body, let his fingers linger on the ridge of her lower ribs as he let the ebb and fall of her breathing mingle in his senses with the music and the sweetness of the scents that seemed to suffuse the bed.

She leaned back and rested her hands on his legs. In the movement the tiny tremble of leaves across her skin looked like little notes of music on the score of her body. Her voice broke into its own faltering sounds to accompany her movements, her breasts pulled flat and tight to her chest so that they had almost disappeared but her rhythm had become quicker, more insistent and as she closed her eyes he told himself again that it was a medicine, something that might help to make him well. But as he did so, something broke inside his head and he's in the tent again but this time flitting and running across the walls are a sudden constellation, cold and sharp in the darkness of the sky, and a group of children huddled round a glass case and as he eases them aside it is the black and wizened face of Takabuti he sees and even in the hollow sockets of her eyes, a gaze he knows he cannot escape.

Afterwards as he drives home, everything, even the controls of the car, seems changed under his touch. He feels as if he's falling away from himself, his hands too heavy and clumsy to hold fast to what might steady him. He's in a kind of freefall and the churning in his stomach and the frenetic flurry of ideas running across his mind seem at odds with the slowing pace of the car. Before he gets home he has to sort it in his head or he knows he'll stagger through the door and spew it at her feet, and every mile that brings him closer sees him slip from whatever dream he was momentarily lost in nearer to the rim of the realities that gird his life.

He bursts into snatches of speech then back into broken breathing like a radio struggling to hold the signal, cursing himself, as if only he can inflict enough pain then it might start to pay the price because already he thinks there will be a price that has to be paid. He slows as he approaches a green light, hoping that it will turn to red and delay him a little longer but it only beckons him on, indifferent to whatever it is he wants. And what he wants now more than anything is to go back to where he was before he did this thing. It's started to rain and as the road ahead sheens and darkens, he can't escape the fall of his guilt, can't wipe it from the tightening consciousness of shame.

When he tries to piece the different parts together, he tells himself that he's been deceived. The colours, the moving frieze of images, the scents, the music – all of it conspired to drug him and detach him from the world in which he lives. He tries to give the blame to her, to make himself the victim, but the solace is only momentary and then for the first time he stops thinking of himself and thinks of Alison, of what he's done to her. Done to the only person who ever loved him. And the flail of swear words streams once more against the windscreen and splashes back against his face.

All of their shared memory shoots through him like a burst of electricity – every second of their courtship, every changing stage of feeling – it fires itself complete and alive, terrible now in its luminosity as it lights up every shadowy crevice where he tries to hide. But every particle of the memory feels altered in some way by what he's done, so as they reform and reshape themselves, he's afraid to let the images take hold, in case they too have been damaged beyond repair. At first everything seems the same. So, as always, it is her hair he thinks of when he remembers. The black flow of it, his desire to touch it as strong as the impulse to let your hand slip below the surface of moving water. To feel the strands between his fingers. It moves as she walks and sometimes he watches her and envies the hand that pushes it back from her face.

They work in a lemonade factory on the Castlereagh Road. He humps crates and loads delivery lorries, she works in the canteen. Sometimes if he manages the queue right he times it so that she serves him but he never speaks other than to give his order. All he looks at are her hands which wear no rings and if she ever smiles at him he never knows because this close he can't look her in the face. He worries she might look at him and somehow know that he's been watching her and be disgusted or frightened, so for six months the closest he comes is taking the plate or cup and saucer from her and looking at her hands. He could take an examination on them, knows every contour and colouring of the skin, the shade and shape of her nails.

'There you go,' is what she says to him as she serves him. It's what she says to everyone. There you go. It takes him six months to speak to her. It's when the first Workers' Strike paralyses the city and the factory is told to close. As they leave there are already hijacked vans and cars blocking the road. He doesn't notice her behind him at first but recognises her voice immediately.

'Do you think there'll still be buses running?' she asks.

'No, they'all be off,' he answers. 'Off or burning.'

'Nothing for it but to walk,' she says.

'Where do you live?' he asks, glancing at her and suddenly blushing as if he has asked too personal a question. When she tells him and he says it is not that far from him, she asks if they can go together. A week later they go to the cinema. Touches her hair for the first time, his hand trembling at the thought, and right from the start it feels right. Uncomplicated, right. Better than he could ever have hoped for. Until the moment she says, 'So when are you taking me home to meet your family?'

He'd already been to her house a score of times, met her parents. He knew it was coming but he's no better prepared for it, despite all his planning, for all his practised responses and so he starts to lie to her, to make excuses that sound half-believable. But then he stops and for the first time in his life he thinks that the truth might be less shameful than the lies. So he tries to tell her, not everything, but just enough to make her understand and all the time he's scared of losing her because of the shame he feels at being different, of being stained. But she doesn't understand and for the first time he realises that it's not possible to understand because the world she lives in is a different country and it's nowhere near the borders of his. So she thinks his father has a bit of a temper, that sometimes things aren't good between them and because she doesn't understand she still wants to meet them. Keeps on until he has no other option but to say yes.

He's told Rob to clear off so at first it's only the two of them and his mother. And maybe this will be enough for her. They drink tea out of the best cups and try to make conversation and all the time he's waiting for his father and thinking that just maybe he won't come. But before enough time has decently elapsed for him to suggest to Alison that they should move on, he hears the back door open and his father's feet in the kitchen. He glances at his mother but she looks away and stares at the cup she's holding in her hand as if she's suddenly noticed something in the dregs of tea.

He's a little flushed but he's not drunk and he apologises for being late as he drops into one of the chairs. He even shakes her hand and then he sits and looks at her, smiling all the time as he opens the laces of his shoes.

'Any tea left in the pot?' he asks.

'I'll make some fresh,' his mother says, standing up, then pausing turns to Alison, 'Come into the kitchen and give me a hand.'

But as Alison rises, his father lifts his hand and says, 'She's a guest, we don't ask guests to make tea.'

'I don't mind,' Alison says.

'Rest yourself, sure I've hardly got a look at you yet.' He leans back in his chair and smiles at her. 'Well, aren't you a right bobby-dazzler! How our Martin managed to get a look in with a picture like you beats me.'

'I'm only after all his money,' she says.

'And spirit too,' he says, slipping his feet out of his shoes. 'Beats me how you've managed it, but you've done well for yourself, Martin.' Then he asks her some questions about where she lives and her family, even tells her a funny story and makes her take another cup of tea.

Later when they're walking back she tells him his father wasn't so bad as he'd made out and in relief and gratitude he nods his head as if she's right. When she pulls him into the doorway of a closed shop and holds him tight, he buries his face in the thick splay of her hair and even when she's searching for his mouth he holds his head fixed and hidden.

A year later they're married. There's no one from his family there. His father has fallen out with them over the arrangements for the wedding, feels his place isn't being acknowledged properly in some way no one understands. He doesn't tell Rob where the wedding is in case his father takes it out on him. Afterwards the silent and then the abusive phone calls start, sometimes in the middle of the night. It's beginning to frighten Alison – he doesn't know what to do and then he goes and talks to someone and they tell him that they'll look after it for him. So one night, just after he has come home from work, his father gets a knock on his door and when he answers it there is a man standing on his doorstep who asks him his name, then tells him that he is to stay clear of his son and his new wife. As he's about to reply, to clench his fists, the stranger opens his coat just wide enough to reveal the revolver stuffed into the waist-band of his trousers. Now there are no words, only the slow shutting of a front door and a stranger walking away and seeming to button his coat against the cold.

*

She's in the kitchen making the next day's packed lunches. Three lunch boxes sit in a row on the kitchen worktop. Each one will be a slight variation of the other according to taste, according to need – in Tom's, raw carrot and grapes alongside the tiny triangular sandwiches with their crusts cut off, and a little chocolate bar that describes itself as 'fun-sized'. Although he denies it, they think he supplements his lunch with purchases from the tuck shop.

She doesn't turn to look at him when he enters the kitchen and he's glad because he thinks it must be written across his face, every blink of his eyes signalling the blatant truth like semaphore. He thinks the very smell of it must seep from his pores and so he doesn't touch her or go closer but slumps at the kitchen table.

44

'You're late,' she says, turning to glance briefly at him. Her voice has no condemnation, only concern.

'They're setting up a new exhibition. Ran over time.'

'Cheese or ham tomorrow?'

'Either,' he says. 'And thanks.'

'What for?' she asks.

'For making my lunch.'

'All part of the service. Do you want some tea?'

'I got something on the way home,' he lies, because he cannot bear the thought of her doing more for him; in her kindness his deceit is magnified and edged with guilt. He tries again to tell himself that he did it for her. That it wasn't an entirely selfish act but if he can no longer convince himself then what hope has he of convincing anyone else?

'How was your day?' she asks and as he answers, he listens to his voice and thinks it sounds different – weightless, fluttering round the kitchen like a trapped moth. She's tidying and cleaning the chopping board, scraping the crumbs of bread and cheese with the edge of her knife and each little scratch of the blade feels like a cut inside his head. Tell her now, tell her right now while it still feels like a confused mistake, raw and uncovered, before it has the chance to fester and harden into reality. He was lost, climbing those stairs – that was all – momentarily stumbling into the wrong place. And now more than anything, as much as he's ever wanted anything, he wants to come back to his home. Go to her now, steady the busyness of her body by resting his hands on her shoulders. Only once in twenty years, only the once and never again, he can tell her and maybe that will mean just enough for her to forgive him. And if there's punishment, and he thinks that there should be, then he will accept it gladly and openly.

'Alison.' He calls so gently, it's almost a whisper. She doesn't turn but presses the lids closed on the lunch boxes. 'Ali.' She turns and looks at him as she places the boxes in the fridge. 'Do you think we can find the money for Rachel to go to Oxford?' There is one punishment he can't stop thinking of – the one thing that he knows he could not endure and the fear of losing all of them warps and silences the words he wanted to say.

'She hasn't got in yet, so let's not count our chickens before they're hatched,' she says while she dries cutlery and lets it tumble noisily into the drawer. 'There's bound to be grants. And I've been thinking that maybe when the canteen is closed during school holidays I could find a part-time job. Safeways are looking for checkout people. Maybe there's a late afternoon shift would suit.'

He feels a new shame that she should have to think of adding more work to what she does already, determines to take on more overtime, even, as much as he dislikes the idea, considers the possibility he has long resisted, of applying for the next promotion that comes up. He goes to tell her but thinks the words he must use will feel like a lie in his throat and so he asks her what the children are doing.

'Same as always,' she says, looking at him more carefully. 'Rachel's in her room working, Tom's using his time slot on the computer.' He nods and wonders if he looks different to her as he slips away.

He goes to Tom first in the front room, feels a sudden burst of affection for him that he hasn't felt in a long time. It's as if he's come so close to losing everything that only now does he know the value of what he has. Tom doesn't take his eyes from the computer or acknowledge his presence in any way. Only his hands are alive with movement, the short chubby fingers stabbing and fretting over the keyboard. There is dirt under his fingernails. He stands behind him and watches the running woman jump and somersault, make her way down stone corridors. 'Are you winning?' he asks, but the only response is a nod while a finger pushes his glasses back to the bridge of his nose. He pats him on the shoulders and leaves, tells himself that he'll spend more time with him, maybe try to find some sport or physical activity that they could do together. He pauses at the door and looks back. Tom's head is pecking like a bird at the screen, urging on the girl. Where did the weight come from? It seemed to creep up on him, and now it's getting worse all the time with every diet they try to keep him on collapsing in a matter of days because he doesn't seem to care, because he wants to eat the things he shouldn't. He thinks of Tom's lunch box in the fridge and goes back and wordlessly places a pound on the top of the computer and watches a hand silently pocket it.

On the stairs he can hear the music from Rachel's room. She always plays music when she works. Sometimes her mother asks her how she can concentrate with 'that racket', worries that she won't be able to perform in the silence of the examination hall. Her door is half open but she doesn't hear him because of the music and because as she sits at her desk her back is to him. Her head is bowed into the light from the reading lamp, she has nothing on her feet, books are sprawled in all directions to her page, with more dumped on the bed. He doesn't go in or speak – he never goes in when she's there or when she's working. He stands and watches her work, absorbs the way she sometimes flicks the hair from her eyes, the angle at which she holds her pen, and the way when she's thinking hard she holds it level with her cheek like a spear she's going to throw. What

47

would she think of him if she knew? Would she pierce his heart with her hatred? He can never tell them – he knows that now. Never, never tell and so he'll bury it deeper and deeper with all the rest until some time far in the future; it might just rot away to the nothing that it was.

He goes to the bathroom and showers, slops great splashes of water against his face again and again, feels his face and searches his skin for traces but sees nothing. He has started to hate her, to blame her for making it so easy and although he doesn't want to, he thinks again of his father huddling with them behind the locked front door. She tried to destroy what he has, to destroy his family and he has to hate her for that. But then as the water sluices against him he remembers the moving leaves on her body, the flutter and press of her hands on his skin, the tautening of her breasts and for a second he feels himself stirring until he stops the water and presses his body against the cold-ness of the tiles.

*

It's not the shape of Lara's body which he loves best. He leaves it to the other kids to talk and joke about her breasts. He never joins in because sooner or later someone will talk about his and then he'll have to laugh and pretend it's funny. What he loves best about the way she looks is her eyes. Almond-shaped tiger eyes, jet black in the pupils and they don't blink or smile. Eyes that see in the dark. Eyes that are never scared. These are the eyes he would like for himself. Not his half-blind, watery blur of blue under puffy lids.

It is his favourite of all the games, nothing else comes close. It seems more real than anything in his life, it's where he would stay and live if only he could. He has started to think that if he can master it, follow the right path, over-come all the obstacles, then he will find the answers that he needs. And in the playing, only in the playing, his body is subsumed by the movements of hers and so as he journeys deeper into the labyrinth, his whole being is alive and fluid, moving through the elements with consummate ease. Here he is light and unhindered by any constraint and so he can run without the shudder and shake of flesh, without the burning stitch and the shuffling protest of his breath. There is only the firm press of feet, the kick and effortless glide through water. He loves to watch her climb and jump – gets it wrong sometimes so he can make her do it again and again. Jump and jump, propelled into the air as if on wings. And with it the soft little moan, a simple bruise of the air.

Who can stop her progress? What sniggers, passed round the class like a parcel in a game that he never wins, what jokes and daily inventory of names – a list that's always added to and replenished when it's grown a little stale – what slap of hands can, even for a second, stop him hurtling forward to the very heart of the temple? Let the scorpions and snarling dogs leap from the shadows and be blown away by the unfettered fury of his anger, the banishing flash of light and bang of her guns from which there is no escape. For Ross, Chapman, Rollo, Leechy and all the others, there is pay-back time. The blowing-away. His dampening fingers stab the keys with all the weight of his body, eyes blinking with pleasure at the pulses of his desire. Let them try to tip his possessions into the toilet or out of the classroom window, let them try to take his money and sweets; let all of them try. Because now he is as light as air, running, running, and none of them can touch him or resist the angry retribution of his fingertips. Run-ning and climbing, bursting into the square of blue light above, before striking out in new directions. Running and running and no one can get close, not even the words they shout after him, and when he turns and stares, it is with tiger eyes, and now the only fear is theirs and it squirms and spirals in their throats, coiling tighter and tighter until it starts to choke the bastard life out of them and as they gasp for air he bends close to their faces and whispers 'Suffer!' And the one he bends closest to with his tiger eyes, and whispers to with most pleasure, is always Chapman. But suddenly it's not his own voice he hears, but his mother calling to him, telling him that his time is up and he must shut down the computer. Then, as the screen darkens in front of him, he fingers the coin in his pocket and wonders if it will be enough.

*

She is working on her essay. This is her room. About eleven feet by nine. Not very big. A single bed with a white quilted headboard – she doesn't like the headboard, thinks it looks tacky. She's seen a gothic-style wrought iron one in a magazine that she'd like. Wants a new duvet cover as well. This green one with its yellow flowers is too childish now. She's seen a white one in the Argos catalogue that has black Japanese writing on it. She wonders what the writing says, jokes to herself that it's probably a trick on foreign devils and says something like 'A whore sleeps in this bed'. More and more things in the room have started to irritate her recently with their slightly embarrassing echoes of childhood, or earlier phases of her taste. She wonders how she ever thought some of the stuff was cool – stuff like the yellow, floral wallpaper with the matching curtains from Dunne's. The prissy little tie-backs, the colour co-ordinated border. Even the light shade. How terribly fashionable she had thought everything was, how sophisticated that everything matched. Getting the wallpaper up right had nearly broken her father's heart but he had kept at it until he'd done a good job. There was only one place where it didn't join properly and you wouldn't really notice it, unless someone told you. Now there's not much to be seen of it anyway. Where it isn't hidden by the pretend-pine MFI wardrobe and dressing table it is mostly covered with her pictures and posters. There's a big poster of Kurt Cobain, one of Liam Gallagher with a cigarette drooping from his lips and his hand raised in a two-fingered salute to the camera. There's a poster of Ash, a black and white magazine photograph of Marilyn Monroe, and a film poster of *Billy Elliot* that the girl in X-tra Vision kept for her. Above her bed there's a postcard of Mount Fuji, one of Mount Etna erupting, and one of Everest. She likes mountains. In school, Lisa says it's an unconscious wish fulfilment thing for bigger breasts. But what she likes about them is not the fact that they tower above everything else, not the way they dwarf everything, but how they have a sense of aloofness, of detachment. Like they don't care about anything else, what anyone else thinks. And they're cool, snow-capped, not driven by mood swings and crazy, stupid passions that burn out quicker than new fashions.

There is more snow beside her bed on the desk at which she works. It's a little glass dome and when she shakes it, snow falls on an alpine village. Lorna gave it to her at Christmas – it's the type of cute / naff little present that everyone exchanges with each other and is given with extravagant hugs and pretend kisses. But the reason it's beside her bed is that she really likes it, not pretend like, but really likes. She shakes it every night before she goes to sleep and watches the snow swirl and settle on the sleeping village. It reminds her of her favourite poem, 'Stopping by Woods on a Snowy Evening' by Robert Frost. She likes things that make her feel cold. 'The woods are lovely, dark and deep.' She repeats it to herself like a mantra. At the start of every exam. When she's scared. 'The woods are lovely, dark and deep.' It helps her to think that just maybe the things that are meant to scare you are the very things that will take you in their arms, hold you tighter than anyone ever can.

Beside the snow-shaker and in front of the book-rack are her other favourite objects, her talismans. A pink pebble picked off the beach whose smoothness calms and pleases her hand; a little piece of grey stone pressed with the outline of a fish that she bought in a fossil shop; a ball of plasticine that she never uses except to roll and mould in her hand; a carved and spangled wooden box that in its sweet-smelling inside contains a tiny alabaster elephant, some rings and earrings; her personal stereo; her mobile phone; a hand-held black lacquered mirror; a picture of herself as a child on the beach in a frame decorated with shells. Only her favourite books are kept in the rack, all the others are piled on top of each other in the space between the wardrobe and the dressing table, so it holds Alex Garland's *The Beach*, *Oranges are Not the Only Fruit*, *A Room with a View*, *Sophie's World*, *Generation X*, *A Dictionary of Mythology*, Toni Morrison's *Beloved*, *Heidi*, *The Collected Poems of Robert Frost*, *The Great Gatsby*, *The Old Man and the Sea*, *The Woman who Walked into Doors*, *My First Atlas*, *Miss Smilla's Feeling for Snow*, *Snow Falling on Cedars*, and *The Silence of the Lambs*. Between pages forty-six and forty-seven of *Heidi* there is a condom, given to her by the girls in school. For the first time. She wonders when she should use it but doesn't know the answer. Worries that she'll use it for the wrong guy. Give it away to the wrong person.

Also on the desk is a tray with computer discs, CDs and videos. Playing now, as she works, is Radiohead. On the top of the dressing table are combs and cosmetics, saucers with cheap jewellery and knick-knacks and on top of the wardrobe a tennis racquet, some box files full of school stuff, rolled-up discarded posters, unused bags and two empty shoe boxes that she thinks will come in useful for something. In the bottom of the wardrobe is a swimming float, a hockey stick and shin pads, and a small case that contains a pair of shoes from each significant stage of her life, starting with the very first pair and moving through the years. It was her father who started the collection and when she discovered it, she kept it going. Everyone collects something but she has never told anyone she collects her own shoes.

She sits at her desk and works on her essay, which she wants to get done even though it's not due for another week. It's about Polonius and his relationship with Ophelia and Laertes. She finds it hard not to show how much she hates this family and her only uncertainty is which of the three she hates the most. Perhaps her conclusion should be that they deserve each other, deserve the misery life brings them. What is it with Polonius? What makes this pompous, bumbling old man always want to snoop and spy? His whole fawning, ingratiating life is about gathering information, about being useful to those above him but even when he sees things with his own eyes he sees them wrongly, his understanding inevitably flawed and distorted. She thinks he is a voyeur, that there must be some sexual thrill for him in all this hiding and watching. She hates, too, the way he speaks to Ophelia, the way he calls her 'a green girl', tells her to think herself 'a baby', the way he treats everything she says with undisguised scorn and disgust. Ophelia should stand up for herself, tell him where to go but all she says is 'I shall obey, my lord' and if it isn't enough getting all that interference from her father, she has to listen to it from her brother as well. On and on they both rattle, never listening or thinking even for a second about what she might want.

Laertes is the guy she never wants to give it to. Not if he's the last guy in the world, not if the condom's hurtling past its sell-by date because he's like most of the guys she meets every day, where everything is on the surface and they're loud and shouting about what they've done or what they're going to do. About their honour in one shape or another. Always needing someone on their shoulder to restrain them, to hold them back from desperate deeds. The stupid way they drive their cars, the stupid way they drink, their phoney pretence of camaraderie. Of being in a gang. She hates gangs, in-crowds, so why then is it so important for her to be on the inside like everyone else? Sometimes, in the past, she's pretended to be less smart than she is, because too smart is bad – a swot, freaky, different from the rest. A bit sad, a loner. 'Get a life' – that's what they probably say. Get a life. After the stars, there isn't any point pretending so she has to compensate in other ways to show she's just like everyone else. Be a little sloppy and rebellious in the way she knots her tie, listen to the right music, be a little wacky sometimes. No one says much to her face, no one calls her Einstein or Brainbox: the most anyone says as they wait for results or hand in their projects is, 'It's all right for you.' It's not much, but she hates it as much as the worst insult she can imagine. Do they really think it's all right for her? If they do, they've no idea about the worry, the unrelenting sense of failure that lurks just below the surface, the way that everything she does never feels good enough. That at any moment her world could come collapsing round her.

Why can't she be like a mountain? For a second she closes her file and looks at the postcard she's stuck on its front. It's *Fuji above the Lightning* by Hokusai where the white-tipped peak holds itself above the forks, as if disdaining even to look at the stir of the storm below. Some of the girls have used their condom, bragged about it; soon someone will ask her if she's used hers.

She goes back to her work and reads Polonius's advice to Laertes before he goes off to France. She's reluctant to admit it but is forced to concede that much of it is good. But how can someone who is so stupid give good advice? And the more she reads it, the more it's obvious that every precept with which he lumbers his son is the very opposite of what he practises in his own life. 'To thine own self be true,' would perhaps mean more if it didn't come from the mouth of a man who will contort himself into any shape that advancement requires. And what good would it be if your own self was inadequate or unformed? What good then to be true to something that was less than what you wanted to be? Even to know what your self really is, when sometimes it feels vague and fleeting like a ghost glimpsed in a mirror.

She knows he's standing in the doorway watching her – she can always tell without looking. It doesn't make her uncomfortable. He won't stay long – a few seconds and then he'll be gone. Why does he never come in? Why does he never come in and sit on the bed and talk to her? Does he think that what she does is so important she can't be disturbed, that she has no time to fritter away talking to her father? She know he's intimidated by what's in the books, even a little frightened of them. She sees it in the way he opens them surreptitiously when he thinks she's not looking, the way he lifts them and holds them, traces their titles with his fingers. Maybe she should tell him that they're full of things that don't mean very much in the real world. That they don't tell you how to be happy. Maybe he knows better, more important things than can be found between their covers. So why doesn't he come in now, sit on her bed and give her some advice? Tell her the things he knows. About how you find someone to love. When you give yourself. She swivels on her chair to signal him in, but there is no one there and when she turns the music down, she hears only the sound of running water. She lifts the little glass dome, shakes it softly and watches the snow fall.

*

Her feet are sore from standing all day. She sits on the edge of the bed and rubs them with a cooling foot gel she bought in Boots. As she does so, she reads the label which says 'With mint, arnica and witch hazel'. She's not sure it does much good but she likes the sound of the words, the scent of it, the feel of it on her skin. These few moments at the day's end feel like they give her back her body, salvage it from the hours of heat and cooking in the canteen, the rawness of pans and ovens, the slop and leftover mess, the unrelenting noise of children. She examines the back of her leg for the spreading blue web of veins. Sometimes she feels as if she's falling apart before her very eyes. She stands and starts to brush her hair. Tonight it feels as if it's soaked in all the grease and food smells of the day. She can't wash it every single day and into her movement seeps a frustration at not being able to brush the smells away. What's the point anyway of cooking different meals when all they want are burgers and chips? And some days there's more thrown about than eaten and it all ends up on the floor. She pushes her face closer to the glass and pulls and stretches the skin on her cheeks into a leaner, tighter shape, then runs one hand slowly down her neck as if to smooth it. Sometimes she feels as if she never wants to see or touch food again.

'Martin, what are we going to do about Tom?' she asks. 'He's put on more weight this week. I found a store of chocolate and sweets hidden in his room. If he puts on any more weight, more of his clothes aren't going to fit him.'

'I don't know, I just don't know,' he says. 'He's got to want to do it for himself. And I think he's starting to smell.'

She holds the ends of her hair and sniffs them. 'Maybe we should take him back to the doctor.'

'It didn't do much good last time. They just give you some diet sheets which he sticks to for about a day. He's got no will-power.'

She angles her head to the glass so that she can see him in the bed. 'Martin, do you think you could talk to him? I've tried, maybe it would be better coming from you.' She watches as he rubs his forehead with the palm of his hand as if he's trying to ease away some pain. Her eye catches a thread of grey in her hair and she holds it to the mirror, separating it from the other strands with her fingers.

'I don't know what to say to him, Ali. I think you're better at it – he'll listen to you. I don't know what goes on inside his head.'

'You're his father,' she says as she pulls at the hair and suddenly she feels angry at everything – at her job, at the mess on the canteen floor, at the grey hair. 'Why don't you try to spend some time with him, go somewhere, do something with him?'

'You know I've tried, but he's not interested in sport or anything else I can see except stickin' his head in that computer. If Rachel didn't need it, I'd get rid of it.'

'What do other fathers do?' she asks. 'And maybe we've given too much attention to Rachel. I think he should get that mobile phone. Tell him if he even loses a couple of pounds we'll get it for him. What do you think?'

'I'll try anything you think might work. I'll talk to him, think of something for us to do together.'

She takes her final look in the mirror – the right side of her face, the left side, her neck, fingers some little blemish she's suddenly noticed on her forehead and then licks the tip of her finger to try to brush it away.

'What's it all about?' she asks herself out loud. 'Why does everything have to be such a struggle?' Then before she finally replaces the lid on the foot gel, she takes one last sniff, inhales the scent of mint, arnica and witch hazel and tries to let it journey deep inside her.

*

He wants her to come to bed. He wants her to come now, so he doesn't want to talk about Tom, doctors or anything else. He wants her to hurry so much that he almost goes to her and pulls her away from the mirror. Her hair looks shiny and alive – he watches the way it sways with the movement of her head. She should let it grow longer again, the way it was when she was younger. Before the children came. He likes the way she holds her head as she brushes her hair, the sound as it moves through the strands but now he is impatient to hold her in his arms, to pour out the love that rises up inside him and begs for release. All their past life courses through his being, all the things shared and hidden to the world. She was the first to love him, the very first to show that he was worth loving and he owes her for that. With her, he's safer than anywhere else he's been in his life and he lacerates himself with curses when he thinks how close he's come to losing that, to throwing it all away. And what for – a transfer of light that runs through his hands and can't be grasped? Let her come to bed, let her come now and he'll hold her once more in his arms and be safe again and he'll give his love more tenderly, more fully than he's ever given it. Tenderness, gentleness, all the time she deserves, and although it's hard for him he will tell her that he loves her. He will say the words she used to tease him about his reluctance to use. And he'll mean them more than he's ever meant anything in his whole life.

Now she's coming, coming at last. There is a slowness in her movements, a weariness that is unfamiliar to him. He flaps back the duvet on her side but not enough to show that he is ready to love her. She sinks into the bed but as he stretches out his arm she moves to her side and reaches for her book. 'Are you going to read?' he asks, trying to suppress his disappointment.

'Just for a few minutes,' she says. 'Just to get the day out of my head.'

He feels only the stirring of his doubt now, a loss of confidence, wonders if she will be able to read in his body the drive of his desperation, the depth of his need. She knows more about him than anyone else, so just maybe if he comes to her now she will know what he has done. It's a risk that he will take because he cannot let the day end without trying to take himself back to the place he belongs, that place where he wants to be more than anywhere else.

He moves close, strokes the back of her hair, runs the tip of one finger down the nape of her neck and then across her shoulder. 'My hair needs washed,' she says, still reading her book. He traces the outline of her shoulder.

'Martin,' she says, snuggling back into him.

'What?' he asks.

'Buy a lottery ticket tomorrow. It's a rollover. Do a lucky dip.' She reaches a hand over her shoulder for him to hold. It still carries the sweet scent. His other hand moves slowly under her arm and across her side until it cups her breast.

'I'm lucky already,' he says. 'The luckiest man alive.'

She stops reading and sets the book on the bedside table. Turning to face him she asks, 'Are you all right?' She scans his face and there is curiosity in her eyes. 'Is there something wrong?'

He knows he has already said too much, the kind of words she doesn't hear him say. 'I'm fine,' he says, not looking at her, even when she places her hand on his cheek. 'I'm tired too.'

Now she thinks she's doing what they do for each other – being strong when it's the other's turn to be weak. So she puts her arm around him and tells him everything will be all right, that everything will work out fine, but the more she does it the more he feels a fraud. That he's extracted her care under false pretences, that it's unearned. He will pay her back from now on, starting even in this very moment when he will love her with all the tenderness that he can muster, give her every gentle demonstration of his love. Use words if he has to. He'll take that risk. So he pulls her close and strokes the back of her hair, kisses her lightly on her eyelids, watches as a smile starts to cross her face. Watches as it collapses into quiet swearing as the phone in the hall rings.

'Maybe it's for Rachel,' he says.

'They don't ring this late. Go and answer it before it wakens everyone.' She turns back on her side, facing out of the bed, one arm pushed under her pillow, the other hugging herself. They both know what the call is but don't say it, as if saying the words increases the prospect of it being real. There is no worse sound for them now, each ring deadening and frightening, cutting them off from each other. 'Hurry, Martin,' she says, pushing her head into the pillow.

When he answers it's not his mother's voice telling him that she's hearing voices, that there are people trying to break in or that she can hear some child crying in the street. It's not her saying that people are stealing things from her, or that in the middle of the night she needs to go to the shops or visit some long-dead relation.

'Martin, it's Pat – she's gone walkabout again. I've had a look round but I don't see her. Do you want me to phone the police?'

'No, I'll be over in ten minutes. Thanks for calling. You go to bed. I'm sorry about this.'

'She was a bit agitated today, talking to herself a lot. Don't really know what it was all about. George just noticed the lights on and the front door open when he was lockin' up. I'll keep an eye out in case she turns up.'

He thanks Pat again, apologises for the trouble and is silently grateful she is a home-help who seems to care for more than the pittance she gets paid. When he goes back to the bedroom Alison asks, 'Your mother?' He nods as he scrambles into his clothes, then searches the dressing table for the car keys.

'She's gone walkabout. Have you seen the car keys?' She gets out of bed and finds them for him.

'We can't go on like this, Martin. Something's going to have to be done for her. It's not fair to her or anyone else. You're going to have to speak to Rob about it, make him do his bit as well.'

'I know. I have to go. Don't wait up. It'll probably take a while to get her settled. We'll talk tomorrow.' He goes to kiss her but hesitates and then the moment is gone and he's hurrying down the stairs and into the car and the cold night air.

Something has wakened him. It's someone stirring, moving. He can't see clearly so he rubs his eyes to try to push the darkness out of them. It's Rob, standing up, moving about his bed, 'Rob,' he whispers. There is no answer. 'Rob,' he whispers more loudly. The light comes in brittle and gritty shafts that spear the thinness of the curtains. From outside there is the yellow seep of a street lamp and as he squints, it looks like the sun is rising and about to burst into daylight but it remains fixed, like a promise that is never delivered. He sits up in the bed. 'Rob, what the frig are you doing?'

'Shut up before you wake him!' Rob whispers, and his voice is frayed and thin, but edged with determination.

He can see now that he's putting things into his school bag and he's tipped the contents on the bed, that the bed is stuffed with something that makes it look as if he's still sleeping in it.

'What the frig are you doing?' he asks again.

'I'm leaving,' Rob says. 'Gettin' out of here.'

Part of him wants to laugh, part of him wants to giggle but he knows that if he doesn't get this right then there will be no laughter in its consequences. He wants to tell him to wise up, that thirteen-year-old boys who've never been to the end of the Newtownards Road on their own don't run away. Kids who are scared of their own shadow. To get back into bed and dream something nice until the morning but instead he says, 'Right, running away. When did you think this up?'

'I've been planning it for ages.'

'And what about me, Rob? You weren't going to tell me? Just go?'

'Had to be a secret.' There is a thin seam of pride in his achievement, the secrecy of his planning.

'You think I'd tell anyone? You think I'd tell him?' He flecks his voice with hurt. And now his younger brother is caught on the barbs of disloyalty and ingratitude.

'I know you wouldn't tell him, Martin. I know that.'

'We always look out for each other, Rob. You and me – we always take care of each other.' His voice is wounded.

'I was going to write to you,' he says. 'Honest, I was.'

Now he has him, now he can reel him in. And he knows, too, by the shape in the bed that this has sprung from a film he's been watching, some fantasy that he's seen and shaped as his own.

'So where are you going?' he asks and he lets the question echo with his admiration.

'London, probably, or maybe Australia.'

'Right. Fuckin' hell, that's a great idea. You've really thought this out. Just imagine his face if he gets a postcard from Australia!' They both snigger a little. Now it's time to bring him back. 'And you have plenty of money?'

'A couple of quid.'

'So how were you planning to get to London or Australia?' he asks, as if he's keen to share his brother's expertise.

Rob hesitates, searches desperately for an answer. 'Maybe go down the docks, hide on a boat. Or get a job on one.'

'Right, right. Good idea,' he says, as if he's really impressed. 'But listen Rob, I know this is your idea and you've really planned it out, but I was wondering if you would let me come too?'

'You want to come? Maybe it would be best if we both went because he'd probably take it out on the one left behind. Wouldn't he?'

'Too right he would. We could look out for each other, the way we always do.'

'Yeah,' Rob says.

'But listen, if there's two of us we're going to need more money. We're only going to be able to do it if we have some money. We need to start saving, gathering it up. Listen, I know a great place we could hide it, somewhere that no one will ever find. What do you say?'

'We'll save the money and then we'll both be able to go,' Rob says.

'And listen Rob, can you imagine his face when he gets a postcard from Australia?'

Rob sniggers but then there is a pulse of panic. 'Do you think he could find us in Australia?'

'It's too big, Australia's too big, Rob. He'd never find us. Get back into bed now.' He watches his brother do as he asks. 'And hide that bag.' Rob kicks the bag under the bed and retrieves the rolled-up coats from under the blankets.

'What'll we say on the postcard?' he asks.

'Fuck you, kangaroo!' he answers and Rob starts to giggle and snigger so loudly he has to tell him to be quiet, but he's so excited, so pumped up, he has to invoke his fear of their father hearing to silence him.

*

Happy families. She tries to curl into the heat he left in the bed but already it's draining away as she listens while the car's engine kicks into life. Moving back to her side she slips her hand under her cheek and smells the scent still lingering on her fingers. Happy families. Knock, knock. Is Mrs Bun the baker at home? Mrs Bun the baker is not at home. Is Master Pill the chemist's son at home? The rain thunders against the caravan roof and it sounds as if someone is throwing great handfuls of gravel and stones against the windows. As they hold the cards in front of their faces like fans, they glance from time to time at the ceiling and once, when the whole caravan gives a little shudder, the children look over the tops of their cards with widened eyes that speak of pleasure and a pretence of fear.

They huddle round the little table and they've never felt as close as this. It's their first family holiday. A caravan in Groomsport caravan park. The caravan is called Bluebird and Rachel says it's like Dr Who's Tardis – bigger on the inside than the outside – and she's right because every-where there are beds that fold down and things that open up, so when the rain volleys against it, they still feel snug and safe, shut inside their own world. The children are in their slippers and dressing gowns. Happy families. Knock, knock. Is Mrs Chop the butcher's wife at home? Then as the fury of the rain momentarily fades, there is only the waxy fistle of the cards and the breathing of the children as they strain to make their families complete.

She wonders if it was the last time that everything seemed to fit. The last time that she felt in control. And

65

suddenly Martin asks how you win the game and as she reads the rules out loud she laughs at him, telling him, 'That play continues until the happy families are complete. When a player holds no more cards they are out of the game.'

There is a pain in her leg and she stretches a little and tries to stir a little heat in the bed. She wonders how long he'll be, tells herself that she should wait up for him to hear him say, as he always does, 'Give me some of your heat,' but knows already that she is slipping towards sleep. And now if anyone were to ask her, she would say that's all that marriage is about – a sharing of heat, trying to protect each other from the cold outside. She moves again towards his space – he'll be cold when he gets back. It's important that he's got her warmth to bring him home and when he comes he'll snuggle into her back and girdle her with his arm. She thinks about that moment and tells herself that when it happens, in that soft limbo world between sleep and consciousness, then just for a second it will make them both feel that everything is complete.

*

The drive down to and along the Newtownards Road only takes a short while. The other cars on the roads are mostly taxis but even this late, the streets are not empty. As he turns off the main road and enters the knotted tangle of streets where he grew up, a group of youths stands on a street corner and passes round a cider bottle. One of them looks no older than Tom. They look at the car as he passes but he doesn't look back. He knows the language, the way to be and look, the names to know in these streets he grew up in, but he's been away a long time and with younger ones there is still the danger of being thought a stranger.

Using his elbow he softly locks the doors as he watches them in his rear-view mirror, thinks they're probably the kids of the guys he used to run with and is glad he made it out, gave his own kids the chance of something better.

He's never seen so many flags, not even in the heart of the Troubles. They're on every pole and post, turf-markers in the new wars. Dogs pissing out their territory. But everywhere he looks, despite the redeveloped houses and the walkways, there is only deterioration and decay and part of him wants to tell every flag-waver that they're fighting the wrong bloody war, that they should be making something better for their kids. Kids like these two who wheel a shopping trolley loaded with bits of metal. They pass in front of the car and he stops for them and winds down the window.

'Hey lads, see an old woman walkin' about anywhere?' he asks.

'An old woman? Hey mister, are you a perv?' one of the boys says, coming closer to the car and staring in.

'It's my fuckin' ma, son,' he says, staring the kid in the eye, leaning towards him. 'She's losing the plot, wanders off.' He never takes his eyes off the kid, lets him see he's clocking him, weighing him up. That if he has to, he'll know him again.

'There was a woman down near the factory, maybe that's her,' the other boy says. 'Do you want us to help you find her?'

'Naw, you're all right. I'll go down and look.'

'If you pay us we'll help you,' the first one says. His eyes are narrow with suspicion but wide for the possibility of opportunity.

'You're all right, son, but I appreciate the offer.' Then, pointing to the trolley, he says, 'You should get that lot stored before anyone realises it's missing.'

'It's only scrap no one wants,' the boy answers. His voice is defiant, almost eager for an argument.

'That's right. Good luck to you.' As he drives off, he sees the boy throw back his head and spit on the back glass of the car. He turns down the next street, slows as he passes his mother's house with its lights on and then heads round to the old factory. She's standing there in her coat with a shopping bag as if she's waiting for a bus to come and take her somewhere. The air is cold against his face as he gets out of the car. He's too tired for a big effort, for some elaborate pretence.

'Let's go, Mum,' he says, taking her bag from her and leading her towards the car. 'Let's get you home and into your bed.' She looks at him and he doesn't know if she recognises him or not, but she suddenly asks, 'What time is it, Martin?' When he tells her, it doesn't seem to register but after a few moments she starts to rummage in her bag until she finds her purse. She hands him a five-pound note.

'I forgot it was your birthday. Buy yourself something.' He doesn't tell her that it's not his birthday but thanks her and takes the money. 'I've never forgotten before. I must be gettin' old,' she says, carefully shutting the purse and dropping it back into her bag.

When they reach her house she makes no effort to get out of the car. Pat is there now and opens the door and helps her out. Together they get her in and he waits downstairs as she gets his mother into bed, sitting in the living room and listening as Pat gently scolds and encourages her, calming and reassuring her. Talking to her like a mother. When she comes down he thanks her and gives her ten pounds. She won't take it but he insists until she reluctantly accepts.

'That's the third time this month she's done this,' she

says. 'I think you're going to have to speak to the doctor again, see if there's anything he can give to settle her at night. If she keeps doing this she'll get run over or something.'

'I'll get Alison to ring him in the morning. We can't go on like this. I'll stay a while until I'm sure she's over.' He lets Pat out, watches as she walks across the road to her house, then slumps back into the chair. He doesn't want to sit there, to be inside the house at all, but tells himself he has to, that maybe it won't be for much longer. If his mother doesn't leave, then the redeveloper's demolition ball will flatten it soon. Good fucking riddance, he thinks, the sooner the better, and part of him curses Rob who's never set foot in the house since the day he left it, who pulled the shutter down and never so much as lifts the phone to speak to her. But another part envies him, wishes he had done the same so that he wouldn't be sitting here in this place he doesn't want to be, where every piece of furniture, every smell and shadow, force memories on him he doesn't want to own. He reminds himself that he owes her nothing, not even a phone call but he knows it's not as simple as that and tries to cool his resentment by telling himself that she must have been a victim too. That she probably had as much fear as them. That she wasn't strong enough. But there are other voices in his head and they say that she should have done something, told someone, stuffed their possessions in cases and run off with them if that was the only way.

A car stutters past outside. The whole house seems to creak and shiver a little before it settles again. The pavement is just outside the window – any passer-by can look through the window – there are houses on either side of their walls. Across the entry another house looks into theirs. How can no one know? How can it be a secret? Maybe no one gives a shit about anyone else, everyone minding their own business and trying to think the best because it's always easier. And his father is a popular man with the world, always full of jokes, always good for a laugh, and it's important to him that he's liked, that he's a good father, so there are lots of staged performances and public parading of family. Everyone well turned-out and happy. How he would have worshipped Rachel's stars, how he would have used them to lift himself up and be the talk of the road.

He pushes his back against the chair, listens to the sudden heaviness of his breath, which sounds as if he's just run a race, and tries to calm himself with the knowledge that he never got his hands on them, never so much as saw his grandchildren before he died. It is the only justice that he can find, the only spark of comfort he can ignite from the welter of sensations that stream about him. He knows he has to go, has to get out of the house and climbing the stairs he stands at the doorway of his mother's bedroom but doesn't go in. For a few moments he stands motionless, listens to the fluted rise and fall of her broken breathing, then goes back down the stairs, trying not to touch anything with his hands. As he opens the front door he remembers the five-pound note and goes back just long enough to set it on the mantlepiece under the foot of the clock.

IT'S ALL BEEN ARRANGED by Alison. He's taking Tom to the Odyssey arena to see the Belfast Giants play ice hockey. She's got the tickets, and it's to be his big chance to talk to Tom, to try to get through to him. She's going to sit with his mother and they'll pick her up on the way back. Even Rachel's going out. Out with girls from school to celebrate someone's birthday. When he tells Tom about the ice hockey he isn't negative, for a few moments seems mildly interested.

After dropping Alison off, he wonders if it's the time to start the talk but he's not sure of the best way to begin and so he decides to leave it until just before the game – when they're sitting with nothing else to do and the start of the game can bring a natural end to the conversation because as yet he doesn't know what his conclusion will be. They drive over the Queen's Bridge and suddenly the city he thinks he knows feels dizzy, pumped up on its own adrenaline, straining and breaking away from what anchors it in his memory. Everywhere he looks there is new building, a new skyline of hotels and offices and here, by the river which his childhood associates with piles of rusting scrap metal and the army of shipyard workers, are new apartments tracing the dark snake of the water. In between the buildings, the city is decked in bright necklaces of neon. He can't take his eyes from its strangeness and is glad when the increasing flow of traffic forces him to slow almost to a crawl.

He opens the window of the car to let the faint odour of

Tom escape and the night air that rushes in feels sparked and stretched, ready to ignite into something that is new to him and about which he is uncertain. Crowds of people stream past, some of them wear ice-hockey shirts. Everyone looks at ease, there is no current of menace and he tells himself to relax. Soon they get funnelled into a giant car park and then into the arena itself and everywhere are families and groups of people who look as if they know what they're doing, as if it's normal to be going to ice hockey in Belfast on a Saturday night. He tries to blend in, to appear as if he too is knowledgeable and is part of what's happening. Before they find their seats, Tom leaves his side and comes back with two large Cokes and two large packets of M&M's. As he hands him one of each, it's clear that this is the bribe for allowing him to consume what he wants. It's not a good start but then here everything is bigger than he imagined it – the stadium, the crowds, the merchandising, the whole scale of it.

'What do you think, Tom?' he asks.

'It's all right,' Tom says before he covers the lower half of his face with the carton.

'Are you going to drink that all now or save some for later?' he asks.

'Don't know,' he answers. 'Don't want to let it go flat.'

How to start? What to say? A machine rollers the ice, following the pattern of a man cutting grass. 'It's not like going down to see the Glens, is it?' Tom shakes his head and opens the packet of sweets. 'Tom, I don't think you should eat those.'

'Why not?' he asks, looking at the packet as if there might be something wrong with it.

'Because your mum and me are worried about you, about the weight you're putting on. It's not good for your health.'

'I'm hungry,' he says, holding up one of the sweets between his finger and thumb as if it's a precious stone he's studying. He throws it to the back of his throat, his head jerking suddenly upwards like a seal swallowing a fish.

'You only think you're hungry,' he tells his son, unsure of whether he's talking sense or not. 'And we need to get some exercise going, burn off some of that stuff.' He gently pokes his son in the side with his elbow but feels him squirm away with resentment and regrets having done it. 'Does anyone ever say anything to you about it in the school?' There is no answer. 'Maybe we could do something together – what about swimming? Or I could fix up your old bike, find one myself and we could go for some rides at the weekend.' No answer. He knows he'll have to try a different angle.

'Sometimes my father narked on at me when I was your age. I used to hate it, so I don't want to do that, Tom. I hope you understand, son, that I'm only talking to you because we care about you and want you to be happy and healthy?' While he's talking someone walks to the middle of the ice, his leg movements heavy as if he's walking through water. He's the MC and he starts to wind up the crowd and pop music rumbles through the arena, galvanising and stirring the atmosphere. He goes on trying to talk to Tom but he's struggling for the right things to say, to find any point of connection, even some precarious little handhold which will allow him to cling to the face of his son's indifference.

'So PlayStation Two is supposed to be good? Costs a fortune though, doesn't it?' Tom's answer gets lost in the roar of the crowd and then they have to do Mexican waves. To be like everybody else they have to do it and all around them are people waving their arms like an act of fervent supplication. It's one of the most embarrassing things he's ever done in public but they can't break the wave, can't have everyone else looking at them. Even Tom lets his arms rise and fall limply. 'Look, maybe if we make a plan – nothing too drastic – then we could think of getting you a Playstation next Christmas. You'd have to stick to it this time, though.' They both have to throw their arms up again as the wave reverses direction. 'Just cutting down on things that are really bad for you. And Tom, there's one thing that I've never really said before.' Tom looks at him for the first time. His eyes are suspicious behind his finger-printed lenses. It looks as if he's finally going to say something but now they're playing YMCA and everyone is doing the actions and singing; so whatever was going to be said slips away as the packed arena shapes letters with their hands and arms and the swelling chorus of voices drowns out his own faltering words. From the tiers of seats across the rink it looks as if people are signalling to them, a kind of semaphore and diffidently and slowly, and a few seconds out of sync, Tom tries to copy the way they form the letters, before finally he gives up, slumps back into his seat and waits for the game to start.

*

He cradles the carton to his mouth, feels the bubbles break against his closed lips. Does anyone ever say anything to him at school? Not really, just every single day and every single period and every moment between periods. And on the bus before school and at lunchtime and in his head first thing in the morning as he wakes up, even before he's got his eyes open. Because even when they don't say anything he hears the echoes of what they've said before and the echoes feel trapped inside some cave from which they can

74

never escape. He opens his lips and rolls some of the Coke round his mouth like a boxer between rounds, before he swallows and licks the remaining flavour off his lips. Do they ever say anything in school? This is what they say. These are some of his names: Fat Boy, Fats, Blubber, Tits, Piggy, Flubber, Porky Pie, Monster Mash, The Incredible Bulk, Bouncy Castle, Tommy Tucker, Fatboy Slim, Roly Poly, Cheesy, Little Mo. Sometimes when the teacher calls the roll he is surprised to hear his real name used, almost as if he has forgotten what his real name is.

And his names stretch to eternity because every day there is a new one added to the list, usually by a kid who wants to please, so they think up something funny and clever and present it to Chapman and the others like a little gift, a ticket of admission. And if they're lucky and it makes Chapman, Rollo and Leechy laugh, then they might get brought into the club. Sometimes he laughs at the names himself because it's better that he's part of the joke and his laughter helps bring him a little closer to the circle; the worst thing you can be is someone who can't take a joke. And there is another reason: because to show a weakness, a particular point of pain, is only to invite more of the same, like a hammer beating down again and again on a nail until its head is buried deeply in the wood.

He doesn't like sport but this one holds his interest. It stops and starts so he hasn't time to get bored and everyone who plays the game is bulked up, twice their normal size but they skate over the ice like they're inflated only with the lightness of air and they can turn and twist as if they're carried on the currents of their own desire. Maybe he could play this game and he imagines slamming Chapman against the boards, trapping him between them and the great unstoppable rush of his weight. Sees him squashed and flattened with the air whistling out of him. His tiger eyes staring down at his crumpled heap. Suffer! Suffer! Pounding his head with the stick, the blade slicing through his helmet like a cleaver. Suffer! Suffer! Shit your pants, Chapman! Your ma's a whore, Chapman! Out on the ice two players start to fight, sticks thrown away, arms flailing, then locking like stags to push and shove. It's the biggest cheer of the evening and then it's over and they're sent to the sin bin. A few rows in front he can see someone with a hot dog, smell the onions. If you're the goalkeeper you have to be big – the bigger the better – because that means there's less goal visible and the goalkeeper doesn't even have to move much. He could be the goalkeeper, bulk himself out to fill all the available space. Catch the puck in the folds of his stomach.

*

In the car she asks them how it was, tries to gauge from their posture, the angle of their heads how things went. 'It's the end of the Troubles,' Martin says. 'They've finally cracked it because there's no Catholics or Protestants any more. Everyone's American. It's the end of sectarianism.' She doesn't understand so she asks Tom if he enjoyed himself but he says only that it was OK. The collar of his shirt is starting to fray. And she's going to have to throw out his trainers, replace them with something else. They're already gone far past Odor-Eaters and she thinks that if she is to put them in the washing machine again, they'll probably fall apart like papier mâché. Maybe at the weekend she'll take him down to Dunne's and get a cheap pair and if he starts to turn his nose up and talk of brand names she'll just have to tell him that they're not made of money, that you can only have what you've worked for.

While they squabble again over Tom's choice of radio station she thinks that just once in life it would be nice to have something good happen to you that you hadn't had to work for. Something that just fell into your lap. Something like luck. She remembers the lottery ticket behind the clock and wonders if it's her turn to be chosen. Tom points out a new yellow Volkswagen Beetle and says 'Yuk', describes it as the colour of puke. She's so pleased to hear him talk that she doesn't tell him off. 'Hard to live with,' she says and kneads her calf muscle with the tight grip of her fingers. There is the electric scribble of green neon and a flashing diamond flush of fast-food outlets. 'Can we get a McDonald's?' Tom asks. 'No', they say simultaneously. Only their tone is different – Martin's more insistent and tinged with his frustration. 'Just to take out, not to sit in,' Tom pleads as if the location of eating has serious significance.

'Listen, son, from now on when you think of Happy Meals think of something that's not goin' to put on the pounds. Think of fruit or . . .' He struggles to continue his list. 'Think of things that are good for you.'

Tom stares out the side window of the car. She leans forward, rubs the back of his hair but he moves his head away as if she's hurt him. Three young woman parade along the pavement, dressed for going out. She watches them as they giggle and laugh, their linked-arm, precarious, high-heeled strut, their bare legs, make her think of children walking into the sea to paddle. Soon it will ripple and foam about their feet. Soon they will shriek with pleasure or pain at the cold. She thinks of her own feet, and they suddenly feel hot and sticky and the prickly heat begins to spread through the rest of her body, as if carried in the currents that course through her veins. She wants to walk into the sea, to let its salty brine cool and ebb it away. She wants to link arms with these three girls, to have the strength of the chain, the lightness of having nothing to do but flow with whatever tides of laughter and release the night will bring.

She opens her window a little and thinks of Rachel, envies her that even at this moment, she is on someone's arm, her voice woven through others like thread that joins to make a pattern, a picture that can be coloured and shaded into anything that you want it to be. Envies her that everything is open and on the edge of becoming. The wind whistles and frets too loudly into the car and she closes it again. There is a pang of resentment now because she begins to think that Rachel will never know what it is to be as tired as this, that her feet will never carry such an ache. That she will never know what it is to brush food from a canteen floor, food that has been dropped or thrown, food that has been trampled and pressed into the vinyl tiles. She wants her to know – just for a few minutes – and then she will know what it means to have what has been given to her. Not ever to need to wait for luck to bring you something but to be able to work it with your own hands like clay, to shape it into whatever will be good for you. But she starts to feel guilty at wishing her daughter something bad, for however short a time, and tells herself that if it's true that you can only have in life what you've worked for, then Rachel has earned everything that has come to her. She worked for the stars; night after night sitting in her room, getting all that stuff out of books and into her head. How did Rachel remember it all when sometimes she has trouble remembering the simplest of things? She thinks of all the times she has brought supper to her – a round of toast or a couple of biscuits and a piece of fruit. Pictures her daughter sitting at her desk, head bowed over the books, the light from the desk lamp bleaching the colour out of her hair where she bisects its arc. Herself pausing for a few seconds before setting the plate on the edge of the desk, just inside the shadow and wanting to touch her hair, gather it in both her hands like she did when Rachel was a child, and pull it behind her head for the brush to burnish the strands. But instead saying something like, 'How's it going?' or 'Would you like anything else?' before she leaves again. As she goes down the stairs, she always touches her own hair, then tries to remember what her daughter's once felt like.

*

Heidi climbs the mountains. Heidi helps the poor little rich girl to walk. How surprised her father will be, when he learns the mountains have the power to heal. She lifts the condom from the pages of the book and looks at it for a second. Will this be the night? Will this be one more test for which she must find the answer? She slips it into her bag along with her money, her make-up, her mobile phone, then looks at herself in the mirror and almost feels like a woman. Perhaps this is the last step that must be taken before she can finally become one. She smoothes, then tousles her hair, pulls a bra strap more securely on to her shoulder, before giving the stiff pout of her lips a final dab with lipstick. Sometimes she thinks she looks good, but mostly she catches her image as if by stealth, when it's in the corner of her eye or the edge of her consciousness. Now, when she stands full-face to the mirror and the focus is unclouded, she sees more reasons for criticism and so she tries to spirit them away by narrowing her eyes. She wonders, too, if what she's wearing will win approval, blend in with the other girls, and the more she thinks about the coming evening, the more she feels nervous about getting everything right, of passing the test.

There is the sound of a car horn; Clare's arrived to pick her up. She quickly gathers the present for Kerry's birthday and hurries down the stairs. In the car the other girls tell her she looks great, that her make-up really suits her, that she should wear her hair that way more often.

'Got your dancing shoes on, girl?' Andrea says, in the tone she always uses with her, which is on the edge of patronising, as if she thinks that someone with so many brains can't live fully in the real world. She's smoking and is wearing a pink T-shirt printed with the words 'Beware: this bitch bites.'

'Definitely,' she answers and then thinks that her answer sounds wet. She glances at Andrea's face through the thin drift of smoke and wonders if the top is a piss-take or if she really thinks it looks good. 'Do you know the definition of indefinitely?' she suddenly asks the girls, avoiding their eyes as they look at her, perhaps thinking of calling her Professor or Mastermind. But there is only a second of puzzled silence. 'When his hair touches your hair,' she says quietly. Then the car is raucous and squealing with laughter and as they give their contorted faces to her, she looks out of the window and allows herself to smile.

In the bar of the club they join up with about a dozen other girls from school and a few others she doesn't know. Everyone is excited, complimenting each other, pecking each other's cheeks, handing over their birthday presents with gestures of mock flamboyance. They start to order drinks and she asks for a white wine, doesn't even recognise what some of the girls have asked for. The girls tease the waiter, compete in flirting with him but he just smiles and takes the order.

'Rachel,' Andrea calls, 'tell him your joke about indefinitely.'

'I don't think so,' she answers. 'He's not old enough.' Then as the waiter walks away, says, 'Nice bum, though.'

'You're a bit of a dark horse, Rachel,' Jennifer says. It's a compliment and she's pleased by it, accepts it silently by making her eyes wide and innocent. The way she sometimes does with her father.

'Can you see my nipples through this?' Andrea asks as she pushes her breasts up and forward with the squeeze of her arms, then feigns disappointment when they shake their heads. 'Everyone has to pull tonight,' she demands, 'but here's the plan. Get them interested, get them horned up, let them have a bit of a snog and then when they're gagging for it, tell them to piss off. It's girl power tonight. All the girlies together.'

The drinks arrive and a toast is drunk to girl power. The laughter and jagged shards of their voices attract the attention of guys standing at the bar. She sees they hold their bottles of beer in a way that signals both their maleness and their insecurity. One raises his bottle to his mouth and drinks from it as if kissing its mouth. The youngest-looking of them leans back with an elbow on the bar and smiles at her but she turns her eyes away and doesn't answer it. The light from the bar sheens the close shave of his hair into a shiver of blue and glints the row of earrings that fasten his ear lobe. She watches as he turns away again, drapes his arm over the boy standing next to him, then whispers in his ear something that scrunches their shoulders into laughter. She thinks again of Laertes and smiles. Young men desperate to protect the honour of their sisters, desperate to make whores of everyone else's. But she can't take her eyes off them, knows that they give off something that both scares and attracts her.

'See anything that you like?' Jennifer asks.

'Not yet,' she says, sipping at the wine that she thinks is the vilest thing she's ever tasted. She hopes that Andrea doesn't do what she's done before and introduce her as the girl with ten A-stars. If she does, she might as well say that she has a baby at home, or an infectious disease, because she knows already that boys don't want anyone they consider smarter than themselves and the ones who do see it as a challenge to light the fire of someone they think knows nothing other than books. And so they'll come with their charm, their sex, and rescue her from her sad nun's life, show her things that she's never known before. Thank God she doesn't wear glasses or else they'd act out those cringing embarrassments of scenes in films where men remove the glasses from bookish women before they kiss them and bestow the instant blossoming of unfettered passion and beauty. Maybe she should get a top like Andrea's or one that says 'Babe' or 'Hustler' in glitter across her chest.

Andrea's talking to two of the guys. She goes into one of the corner booths with them and out of sight.

'So do you think you'll go to Oxford then?' Joni asks. She has four peanuts in her palm which she eats slowly and mechanically, one at a time, with exactly the same rhythm and time interval. The dark stain of her lips is speckled with the light shimmer of salt.

'I'm not sure,' she answers, trying not to grimace at the bitterness of the wine on her tongue. She doesn't want to talk about it but knows it's the standard topic people feel is appropriate. The one they touch upon because they can't think of any other.

'I'd go if I got the chance,' Joni says, turning a gold bracelet on her wrist. Her bare arms are thin, the bracelet looks like the ring on the leg of a bird. 'You could get set up for life. Loads of rich hunks, loads of princes and sons of famous people.'

She wonders if Joni has used her condom yet. Every time she sees her, her body looks thinner. As if sex would hurt it, snap it in two. She wonders how much the first time will hurt, if she will bleed. All the more reason to find someone who isn't Laertes, who won't think of it as his sword or lance. Someone who won't spear her with his greed and selfishness.

Andrea returns and summons their group to follow her to the toilets. Six of them troop after her like her gang. She feels a little stupid, remembers how much she hates gangs, but pleased she's been included. It feels like a girlie thing, like they're going to talk about boys and who's just been dumped, or share make-up. Maybe it'll be Andrea's final team-talk, the plan of campaign, maybe she's about to share her knowledge about boys, about how to 'horn them up'. But as they stand in the empty toilet Andrea says nothing at first, only stares at their faces as if one of them is a traitor she's about to unmask. And then she smiles and pulls them close as if it's a sports huddle in which they're all going to make a pyramid of their hands. But when she looks at Andrea's hand extending into the circle, it is tightly clenched and it hangs there until she slowly opens it, finger by finger, like a magician revealing a card trick.

Some of the girls squeal, others shush them. She doesn't understand. The tiny sachet is closed again inside the hand. She thinks it must be condoms, for a second almost goes to say that she's already got one, but something stops her. Instead her eyes flick to the mirror that runs the length of the wall and she sees the thin bangled arm of Joni resting on the shoulder of Jennifer who in turn links to Lorna and Lisa. The hand opens again and now she knows it's not condoms.

'One for each of us,' Andrea says, taking the first one herself and funnelling the others carefully into her palm. 'Put on your dancing shoes,' she tells them and her voice is a parody of a little girl's. Hands pick the tabs – she's not sure whose, doesn't want to stare at faces. In the mirrors there is the sudden jerk of arms as if two sets of people are present. Then there's one left and it's offered to her and this time she does look and in Andrea's face she sees the challenge, the test she's setting. The tablet is white, imprinted with a dove. 'Pretty, isn't it?' Lisa says and she nods her head as she takes it in her hand. She's never failed a test in her life, never, never. Someone hands her the bottle of water and it's suddenly cold against her skin. In the mirror she sees the circle is still tight and linked and is she going to be the one to break it? For a second she wants to push them aside and see herself clearly in the glass, to talk to herself, to know the right answer before she lifts her pen and writes.

'It'll be cool, Rachel,' a voice says.

'We'll look after you,' Jennifer says.

'Nothing is this good,' another says.

They feel nearer, she can't see herself in the mirror, only the closing faces of these girls who are her friends. Friends who know better than her what is cool, who will take care of her and hold her tight. Someone strokes the back of her hair.

'No pressure,' Lorna says. 'Don't do anything you don't want to.'

'No pressure,' Andrea repeats. 'Don't do anything that

might hurt that brain of yours. Someone else can have it. No worries.' She holds out her hand for its return.

Mount Fuji above the lightning. She thinks of the great splintering forks that tear open the sky, feels them flash and rage about her now. How can she survive the storm, raise her head high above the tumult, the constant tumble of uncertainties? She's never found the answer in books and suddenly all their contents feel like dust-filled husks, like so much dust she wants to shake from her soul. No worries. No more pressure. And maybe it's time for her to step outside the covers of her books and live in herself. To be the same as everyone else. So without taking her eyes from Andrea's, she puts the tab in her mouth and swallows. Swallows the little dove. Someone says 'Indefinitely' and hands are patting her on the back and laughing, stroking her cheek and the back of her neck. Now they're all together and it feels good as the excited chorus of voices pipes louder and seems to merge seamlessly into its own indivisible harmony. But as they file out of the toilets, their hands touching the shoulders of the person in front, like a team making its way down the tunnel towards the arena, she lingers until she is the only one left. Then she walks back to the mirror and stands with her face close to the glass. She wants to reach out to herself, to reassure herself, but doesn't know how and instead stretches her hand to touch its reflection moving towards it. The fingertips meet in a little whorled cloud on the glass.

'The woods are lovely, dark and deep,' she says to herself, thinks that just maybe she was right when she thought the things that are meant to scare you, are the very things that will take you in their arms, hold you more tightly than anyone can. And now she tells herself that the time to be sad is gone and she must find her friends and begin to dance. Dance more fully than she has ever done before.

Before long there is a rush inside her, a surge that carries her on the stream of its flow. There is a stone inside her chest and it's tumbling down the slope in a free fall, quickening in speed and other stones are joining it and it's an avalanche rolling into the freedom below. She kisses Joni on the cheek and is kissed on the lips in reply. As she dances she watches Joni's gold bangle fall down the thinness of her raised arm, almost to the elbow. All the girls are around her and she knows now that she finally belongs and the knowledge seeps through her in a course that calms and soothes her but also leaves her untrammelled, unburdened, finally free to give herself to the music. So she closes her eyes and her swaying arms caress and shape the air and the music comes from within, running through the nerve ends and sense organs, curling like a garland of pretty flowers round her head.

When she opens her eyes she thinks the lights are beautiful. The blues and greens bleed into each other, spread through the other colours like liquid. She feels more open than she's ever felt and if she's a book, it's a book with its pages turning for everyone to see and every page is coloured by the love she feels. She thinks of one of her books lying on the ground, the wind fanning the pages, of the little books they made in school with a slight variation of a drawing on each page and when the pages are flicked the picture comes to life, animated, by the spin of the holder's fingers. So long to make, but so alive. Running, moving with the flick of the music's fingers. That's the way she is in this moment and it doesn't matter any more who sees each page because there's nothing to hide in her life and only the quickening rush she feels has any meaning.

Lisa comes to speak to her, she's shouting in her ear but she struggles to make out what's being said, so she nods in agreement and holds her hand for a second before releasing it again. Everything is falling away. She's stronger than she's ever been, so strong that it is the pulse of her own being that drives the music and her body is seamless, not made up of different limbs but an undulating oneness that encompasses the space around her, and subsumes the people all about her. She sees the group of boys hanging on the edges of the dance floor and feels sorry for them, sorry that they're trapped in their maleness. Sorry that their honour is pricked, that the world slights them in ways that must be defended. Her arms contour her shape in the air, her self portrait that she colours with beautiful tints, the parts of herself that no one's been allowed to see before. Sorry that their honour is in their pricks, that the tip of their swords must be 'envenomed'. She laughs, then shouts in a burst of air from her lungs. They, too, can be loved, know how good it is, if only they will throw away this stupid, paralysing sense of honour, screw their doddering, bumbling father's advice. Let their sister look out for herself.

She wants to go over to them, pick one out and lead him into the dance, until he, too, is carried naked and clean in the flow. But it is the girls – her friends – who are all around her now and they brush and touch each other with the sway and movement of their bodies. They are a flock of white doves which fountains into the clear canopy of sky. And for the first time there is space inside her head, as if she's brushed it clean, and when she goes home she's going to clear everything out of her room – all the things that restrict and constrict who she is. Everything will be clean and open, and like the bangle that dances on Joni's arm, nothing will tighten or pin her down and in the books she'll colour the pictures, add her own drawings. So much space just waiting to be claimed. She feels like the child her father took to the museum one Sunday morning when it was closed to the public and she had the whole place to herself. So much space, so many things to see and the freedom to run everywhere and see everything. Everything exists just for her, is open to her touch – it's as if she owns it all, owns all these beautiful objects – and there is so much space in the empty galleries and corridors that the skipping clack of her heeled Sunday shoes claims everywhere for herself, leaves the indelible print of her true self on everything.

She is running now through that space. Past the glass cases full of jewellery and coins, the butterflies and insects, the sea shells. Past the crystals and quartz, the gleam of the gem stones. Past the stone axes and the paintings. Past the giant deer and the beautiful glass and ceramics. Past Takabuti. And it's the first time that there are no other children draped across the glass so she can stop and look as long as she wants. But it's too scary when you're on your own so she doesn't look at her withered face, the dried-up blackness of her shrunken head. Her own mouth and throat are dry. She's been talking too much. What time is it? She's too warm. There is a pain somewhere, a tightness that she suddenly realises has been there for some time. She wants a drink and she looks about to ask someone, but the music is too loud and when she speaks something happens to her words and she's not sure if they have any sound beyond what she hears in her head. She's too warm and the heat is somewhere inside her body seeping out through the pores. She thinks of the mountains, of the coolness of the snow. She wants to be inside that little glass dome, for someone to take it in their hand and shake it. For the snow to fall and cover her. It's what she wants now more than anything. She needs to tell the girls, but no one's listening, no one's listening, and her arms which try to reach out to them are only the falter and flail of her dance.

*

He's already started to think of his unfaithfulness as a crime. A shameful and inexplicable crime; one that will escape detection but not punishment, because he has the capacity to inflict that on himself on a daily basis and in new and ever more bitter ways. So when he drives into his street and sees the police car parked outside their door, his first thought is that he's been discovered, called to account and every detail that he's tried to bury deep inside himself will be summoned to the surface and paraded for all to see.

'We've had a break-in,' Alison says.

'A break-in?' he asks, and for a second almost feels glad. Tom's hand squeaks the glass as he rubs it to get a better view. A policeman and policewoman get out of their car to meet them. They both have their caps in their hands and as they step forward, putting them on, the policewoman smoothes her hair with a movement that looks like a salute, then uses both hands to fix the cap securely in place.

'Mr Martin Waring?' she asks. Her voice is businesslike, neutral in its tone. It's clear that they've decided that she's the officer who will do the talking.

'That's right. Have we had a break-in?' he asks, already uncomfortable with the way she's staring at him, her unbroken gaze focused on his eyes. It makes him feel as if she's watching, waiting for him to tell her a lie. Behind her, her colleague hovers, as if he's not quite part of what's happening, his eyes directed at the side of their car.

'You're the father of Rachel Waring?' Her voice is suddenly soft, personal, and he mistrusts it even more than her other voice.

'We're her parents,' Alison says, brushing past his shoulder. 'What's wrong? Has something happened?' He hears the panic in her voice, wants to say something that will calm her, tell her that everything's all right, that there can't be anything to worry about with Rachel.

'I'm sorry to have to tell you that she's been involved in an accident. She's in the Ulster Hospital and if you get in the car we'll take you over now.'

'An accident? What sort of accident? Is she all right?' Alison's voice is high and quick. He goes to say something but nothing comes out and it feels as if something is blocking and constricting his throat.

'She took ill at the club she was at. She's in the hospital now and it would be best if the doctors tell you the details.' Alison fires out more questions but doesn't get any answers and as they get in the back of the car the policeman holds his hand over the top of their heads. In the car Alison sits on the edge of the seat and tries to get more information but it's as if the two officers are closed off, separated by the barrier of their seats, and their heads stay facing grimly forward. Sometimes they speak to each other but he can't hear what they're saying and only the cackle of the radio and sudden, frantic bursts of static break the silence. Alison pushes her elbow in his side and when he looks at her, the expression on her face nods him on.

'What sort of accident?' he asks again. His voice isn't his but someone else's, someone he doesn't even know. The policewoman half turns her face to them, her cheek brushed by a green light. She looks at her colleague but he is locked in the mechanics of his driving and doesn't return her glance.

'I'm not really able to tell you more because I don't know all the facts and it would be best if you heard first-hand from the doctors.'

'We're almost there,' the driver says. They're the first words he's spoken and in a few minutes when they look out of the windows they see the lights of the hospital. It's starting to rain and as the first drops stipple the wind-screen, the wipers are turned on and they scrape and scud across the glass. The car stops at the front door and the policewoman gets out and opens their door, then goes through the same routine with her hat as before. People coming out of the entrance look at them and as the car drives off, she leads them through the doors and it's clear she knows where she's going and they follow in silence, only Tom's trainers slithering occasionally over the tiles as if his feet were polishing them.

Long corridors, empty mostly but for the occasional nurse or orderly. They pass an old man in a dressing gown, sliding his slippered feet behind a zimmer frame in a whispery wake. He greets the policewoman who nods in reply. Taken ill at a club. He runs the words through his head again and again until he's constructed a range of possibilities: too much to drink – the other girls have taken advantage of her inexperience and plied her with booze; someone's spiked her drink – there was a programme on television about it recently; maybe just got sick and fainted or something. And everything will be all right when they get her home again because they know how to look after her, how to take good care of her. And she'll have a bit of a hangover, or a sticking plaster over a bump, and in a couple of days Alison will have a talk with her, but in a couple more days they'll have a laugh about it. Maybe Alison will ask him to give her a bit of a father's talk, just the way she did with Tom. He glances round for Tom and sees that he's started to lag behind a bit, so he signals him to keep up, watches as he shuffles more quickly towards them, notices the flounce and roll of his body as he starts to hurry. And there's another thing, this accident that has happened will be an opportunity to really be her father again, to hold her hand at the bedside, to drive her home, carry her things for her. She'll realise that she still needs them, that despite the stars she's still their child and that they're both there for her when she needs them.

He goes to tell Alison that she mustn't worry, that everything will be all right, but says nothing as he can see now that they're arriving at their destination. He's confused because it's not a ward but an empty waiting area and the lighting is dimmed, apart from the brightness coming from an office. There is another policewoman standing in the arc of light and at the sound of their footsteps she straightens and knocks the already open door. His feet kick an empty plastic cup from the shadows and sends it skiting under the seats. A vending machine glows red and black in the corner of the waiting area. Some of the chairs have magazines strewn across them. A young woman in a white coat has come out of the office with a man in a suit behind her, his hand straightening his tie. On his lapel is a plastic name-tag.

'Mr and Mrs Waring,' their policewoman announces, then stands aside in a gesture that suggests her job is over, that they have been safely delivered.

'Please come in,' the doctor says. 'It might be best if your son waits out here and you can speak to him yourself in a few moments.' At her words Tom slumps into a seat, out of breath and his eyes full of suspicion as if he thinks they're going to be talking about him.

In the office the man shuts the door behind them as soon as they are seated, then goes behind the desk but doesn't sit. 'Mr and Mrs Waring, you are the parents of Rachel Waring?' She reads their address to them and asks them to confirm it and Rachel's date of birth. Alison goes to interrupt, but he stays her voice by touching her on the arm and already he knows, but tries to tell himself that the doctor's voice is not going to confirm, but deny, what's started the crazy shake of fear that's seeding itself in his mind, the spores scattering and beginning to spread to every part of his being.

'This is a very painful moment and it is with the deepest regret that I have to tell you that your daughter Rachel died this evening at fifteen minutes past ten.' Her words vanish into the wail of Alison and then her screams of 'No! No!' Her movements beside him collapse into a sobbing thresh on the chair but he can't touch her, can't look at her, can't take his eyes from the face of this young woman telling him that Rachel is dead because he's desperate to see something that will tell him she's a liar, that with her youth and her inexperience she doesn't know what she's talking about. And so it's her arm that comes forward now to comfort his wife and the man comes from behind the desk and he's saying, 'We're very sorry, very sorry,' over and over as if the words will calm him, ease the pain. But there is no pain, no pain at all because now everything in the room – the doctor's voice, the tightened knot of this man's tie, the greyness of the filing cabinet and the wilt of the plant that sits on it, the cries of his wife – conspires to create an unreality that anaesthetises every nerve end and detaches him from where he is and what's happening to him. So it can all be ended with the flick of a switch, the changing of the channel, the wakening first gleam of the morning – some assertive act of his consciousness. Alison's questions, the doctor's answers, only filter slowly through the thick mesh of what his mind has created and if he is to stand up now, he will shake off everything they say like a dog that shakes itself free of so much water.

'She died from heart failure. Very quickly. She was dead on admittance to hospital. There was nothing we could do. The ambulance crew tried their very best. I'm very sorry, very sorry.'

In the photograph she wears a blue dress with white and yellow flowers. No shoes on her feet. She holds the camera to her eye. Eyes that he can't remember whether they're blue or grey. All the light of a future world flowing into her eye.

'Does Rachel have any known heart condition? Is there any history of heart disease in your family?' He stares at the doctor, tries to understand what's she's saying. She's said 'does', she's said, 'have'. It's all been a mistake – Rachel doesn't have a bad heart, she's never had anything more than a cold, hasn't missed a day of school in the last five years. Five years. Why do people throw coins into water? Because they think it will bring them luck? The next chance he has, he will throw all the coins he can find into water. What did she wish for that night in the restaurant? What did she wish for all those birthdays?

'I want to see her.' He stands up. 'There's been some mistake.'

'We'll take you to her now,' she says. 'I'm so sorry.

You'll have to tell your son. We thought it best if he heard from you.' She hands more tissues to Alison and he looks at her, at the twisted blur of her face, at the fistful of shredded paper, hears the gasping sobs that break like waves on the broken shore of her being and he still can't touch her or speak to her because he can't give himself to this grief, this grief he won't accept or believe is needed.

'We can't be sure until we've done an autopsy, what were the exact causes of death but we have reason to believe that Rachel took something at the club – possibly the drug Ecstasy. It's possible that this precipitated heart failure. I know this is very painful but have you any knowledge of Rachel ever taking any illicit substances?'

He almost smiles. He knows for sure now that it's the wrong girl. He thinks of telling the doctor about the stars, about who Rachel is, but instead says. 'Let me see this girl. It isn't Rachel.'

'I know this is very difficult,' the man says, 'and I wish you were right but Rachel's been identified by her friends. One of them came in the ambulance with her. Someone she's at school with. We'll take you now but is there a minister or family member you'd like us to contact for you? We could wait for them to arrive. It would give you time to speak to your son.'

'I want to see her now,' he says and then for the first time touches Alison, lightly and quickly on the sleeve of her coat. The man lifts the phone and tells someone they're coming. When they leave the office the policewoman comes with them but the doctor stays behind with Alison – she's offering her a sedative, asking who her local GP is. In the waiting area Tom is working at the vending machine, lifting its flaps, pressing buttons, looking for change. He goes to follow them but he tells him to stay. A few minutes later they are down in the casualty area. There is the muted sound of television, the echoing, discordant voices of people waiting and then in another corridor they push through plastic double doors and come to a closed door where two nurses whisper to each other, then fall silent at their approach. No one moves to open the door.

He has seen Rachel dead twice. Once when she was a baby and for the first time slept through the night. When he woke, looked at his sleeping wife, looked at the bedside clock and heard only the cold silence thicken and expand inside his head, he knew she was dead. Down the hall, his bare feet fired by the rising panic, the words 'cot death' slowly tightening round his throat: he flings the door open so hard it bounces against the radiator and clatters in the sleeping quiet of the house and his ears are honed and desperate for his daughter's breathing but all he hears is the beat of his heart. She's in the cot, part of the blanket covering the side of her face, and he pulls it back and for a moment she's still as stone, then suddenly her mouth puckers, before a wrinkle spreads across her face. And he's on his knees, hands holding the bars of the cot, face pressed against them, his eyes level with hers. He holds the bars a long time, then goes back to bed and hugs himself, careful not to waken Alison and in the morning says nothing.

The second time was only six months ago. He can't sleep, doesn't know why. Something in his head feels unsettled, unfinished, like a window or door that hasn't been locked against the world's intruders. Alison's breath comes in a steady stream, sometimes her shoulder shrugs the duvet tighter. He gets up and makes his way downstairs. In the hall there is the fray of flickering light – someone is watching television with the sound down. He thinks it must be Tom. Perhaps even sneaking more time on the computer. But when he goes in, it is Rachel on the settee, an outdoor coat draped over her. It is her back he sees because she is curled into the settee, her head pressed against its folds, buried in the shadows, and the light of the television is frantic, making her stillness more resolute, more permanent. He stands close, picks the open book from the floor and wants to speak to her, to shake her awake so that he can banish the stupid fears that scurry about his head. Instead he only stands close until she stirs and stretches a little before he returns the book to where he found it and goes to turn off the television, but then hesitates, reluctant to plunge the room into darkness. So he leaves it on and as it blinks like an eye he quietly leaves the room, glancing back over his shoulder when he reaches the door.

The sheet is slowly removed. Her eyes are closed. She is asleep. Soon she will stir and stretch, soon her mouth will pucker and the muscles in her face will wrinkle. Soon she will stretch her limbs into life. Her skin is washed in blue as if she's cold – the whole room is cold – why does no one turn on the heat? Maybe if he held her, he could cradle heat into her veins, smooth the blueness from her lips. His hand moves to touch her but doesn't. He can't bear for his fingers to touch this cold, a coldness he knows will burn his skin. Her eyes are closed, he can't see what colour they are.

There is a voice asking him if it's Rachel but he knows if he is to speak, his own voice will crack and splinter like glass. So he nods and the voice is saying other things but they're lost in the rush of what feels like a molten flow that threatens to carry everything before it. He tries to save himself, to dam the flood and so thinks of sixteen polished stone axes, of giant metal wheels and cogs of polished machinery, of money thrown into water but these things he knows and stores are powerless and breached by the relentless tide. But he cannot cry, can find no release as his fingers tighten on the sheet and the only voice he hears now is telling him that he's a little bastard, a useless little cunt for letting them take what was his.

He's circling him, moving constantly, weaving his words and movement into one curse and his hawking laughter is expelled from his throat like a spit. Laughing because he was stupid enough to think he'd escaped. There is the slap of his palm on his cheek which flames and quivers with the pain. He tries to think of the stars, to pull them out of the night sky and hold them like a shield in front of his eyes but they're brittle and snapped by the smash of his father's fist. He looks for help but there is only Rob cowering in the shadows, his mother's face behind the glass.

'Fuck off!' he hisses and there is the sound of the man leaving, the door closing behind him. 'Fuck off!' he whispers again. Leave him alone, leave her alone – together they'll be all right. He's going to choke on what's erupting inside him, what sears his throat, the lining of his stomach. He has to get it out or it'll burn him up and his hand drops the sheet and he walks to the corner of the room, to crouch with his back pushed into the walls. Then he streams it out on a wordless shout that falls and rises, over and over, bangs his head hard back against the wall as the cry finally collapses into a slowly fading echo of itself until it is replaced by the slow and broken rhythm of his breathing.

In the photograph she's wearing a blue dress patterned with white and yellow flowers. She holds a camera to her eye. She's got it the wrong way round. He looks at her closed eyes again. He never understood until now. There is no future – there is only past – and what flows into her eye isn't light but the darkness of the world. He watches as his father's flicked cigarette butt sparks and tumbles through the dusk and for a second ignites the seam of shadows lining the yard. On the lid of Takabuti's coffin there is a prayer requesting offerings and good fortune from the sun god. Asking for good burial. And the goddess is beautiful, depicted as a young woman kneeling with outstretched wings. The goddess of the skies. The goddess of the stars. She wears the sun in her hair, swallows the sun whole every night.

THEY HAVE TO WAIT for the post-mortem but he doesn't care because it delays the reality of the funeral a little longer. And now there is no time or will, only a slow sinking below the surface of his life where at first there is no volition beyond finding the next breath and sometimes even that, too, seems selfish and without purpose. Unable to sit for more than a few minutes, he forces himself to walk jittery circuits of the house, in and out of rooms, looking out of windows, touching the once familiar things that are now imbued with a separate strangeness, then pulling his hand away as if burnt by the sudden flame of their foreignness.

He needs to get out of the house if he is to survive. He thinks of Rob. Where is he? He searches for the Christmas card they got last year but when he finds it there is no address. The phone book doesn't reveal one either. He'll have to be told. He'll have to go up to the estate and find him. Why couldn't he keep in touch with them better than this? But as soon as he asks himself the question, he already knows the answer. They don't see each other because they can't look at each other without getting an in-their-faces reminder of what doesn't want to be remembered, and so it feels better to live their own lives, to separate out the strands of their shared past and hope that they will weaken and fray until they're not strong enough to hold them.

'I'll have to tell Rob,' he says and Alison looks at him as if she doesn't understand what he's just said before she nods. Maybe it's the tranquillisers she's been given that cause the delays in her responses, maybe it's because she's run away and is hiding somewhere deep inside herself. 'He'll have to know,' he says before he wonders why Rob has to know, why anything at all matters now. She says nothing but starts again to read again the newspaper that carries the report, as if reading it over and over will somehow help her to understand what has happened. He suddenly wants to tear it from her hands, rip it into the tiniest pieces, in the vain hope that that might destroy its reality. Maybe Rob has read it in the paper or heard it on the news but if he has, then why hasn't he come? He'll have to go, try to find him. Suddenly finding him takes on an importance that he doesn't really understand but he grasps it tightly because it gives him something on which to focus, something he can pursue.

In the front room Tom sits at the computer. The only light comes from the screen. He stands at the doorway and tries to calm his growing anger. From the speakers fires the sound of running, pounding feet. He sits there as if nothing has happened, as if everything is just as it always is, the only movement the press and squirm of his fingers. How can he do it? How can he sit there and not give a shit? His anger at his son is rising, gnawing at the edges of his being. 'Do you have to do that right now?' he asks, stepping into the room. 'Is there nothing else you could spend your time on at a time like this?' His voice is slipping out of control, there are things he wants to shout but there are no answers to his questions, no movement of his son's head in front of the screen's flicker. Being ignored stirs his fury and he walks towards him, intent on turning off the computer, his hands desperate now to push and pummel some response but as he reaches his son's shoulder, the side of his light-brushed face turns slowly towards him as if he's aware for the first time of his father's presence. His fingers never leave the keys, as on the screen her guns blow away the red-eyed dogs, but when he looks up at him, the lenses of his glasses are fogged and from behind their frame slides a single, globular tear that trembles for a second like mercury before it slithers down the flickering frieze of his cheek.

He'll have to go and tell Rob. It's a chance to get out of the house – the house which he now feels is suffocating him, slowly squeezing out his last gasps of air. He thinks it must be what it's like to be trapped by an avalanche, buried under deep folds of snow and when you want to raise your head to shout in pain, to shout for help, there is only the answering tightness of its press, crushing the last breaths from the lungs and filling your eyes and mouth with the choking coldness of snow. As he closes the front door quietly behind him he has to spit, try to spit it out of his mouth, but when he does there is only the sour rush of sickness in his throat and a dizziness in his head.

His hands grip the wheel and then he winds his window right down to let the night air stream about him. He starts the engine quickly as if frightened that someone will suddenly burst from the house and call him back. He wants to drive, would drive all night if he could, because in the mechanical responses, the changing of gears and ad-justments of speed, he finds a solace, a solitariness that calms him and creates a momentary clearing in his head where the charged wires and currents that spark and sear are stilled a little. It starts to rain – a thin but insistent drizzle, that smears and bleeds the neon of passing shops and street lights across the windscreen. He listens to the steadying swish of the wipers, like a regular heartbeat, and in the rhythm is able to think a little and wish that life could be steered as surely and cleanly as this, where the slightest touch of his hand, even his fingers, can take him where he wants to go, avoid the obstacles that might appear out of the darkness. For no reason other than to prolong his journey he drives past his mother's house, slowing as he goes by and sees that only a bedroom light is on. They have decided that they will not bring her to the funeral, that it would be too much of a strain on her, too much of a strain on them. He needs to have his hands clear, unencumbered, if he is to get through it. As he comes to the end of the street he thinks that it is her they should be burying, that she, too, has cheated him. Like all the others, she has cheated him of the future that Rachel was to give him and he feels a new pulse of hatred for her and as he stares at the coloured droplets of rain on the windscreen it is her face he sees again behind the glass. Featureless, blanched by the light. Never real, always flitting like a ghost through the different parts of the house but never leaving a print or any echo of her steps.

His mother's moans are low, tight-lipped, little expulsions of air that she thinks go no further than their shut door. He is louder, the bed is louder. 'He's hurting her, Martin, he's hurting her,' whispers Rob, his insistent hand shaking him out of the first waves of sleep. 'We'll have to do something. He's going to kill her.' He wakes himself and listens, gradually understands what it is he hears. Rob's hand continues to shake him until he's forced to push it away. He doesn't know what to say, so he tells Rob to get in bed beside him and talks to him about nothing until the noise rises and is finally over and the only sounds are what drift in from the outside world – a car's complaining engine, a name being called, the half-hearted bark of a dog. 'Is she dead?' Rob asks but he tells him that everything is all right, that it's over, that everything will be all right and he makes the words like a lullaby, repeating them over and over, until his brother finally closes his eyes and slips into sleep.

Everything will be all right. Everything will be all right in the morning. Now he tells himself the words, repeats them over and over to the slow rhythm of the wipers and wonders what difference there is between love and hate, if for his father they weren't the same thing, and for a moment as he threads his way back on to the Newtownards Road, he searches in his head for something into which he can pour all that he feels. He thinks of Lorrie and it ignites the slow burn of hatred. He hears a voice tell him that was where it started, that was the moment which sent things spinning into new orbits. That it was her fault, that she deceived and trapped him with her wavering nets of light, that what she gave him was like a drug that took away the consciousness of what he was doing. He remembers the sky running across the screen of her face, the trembling transfer of leaves on the movement of her body like little notes on a music score and suddenly he fires a stream of curses against the windscreen, little spots of his spit looking for a second as if they have mixed with the slew of the rain. Maybe after all there is a sense of order in the world, a sense of what is right, and when you transgress it then there is a price that has to be paid. He remembers the boy who spat on his car and the increasing flurry of the rain which beats against the glass becomes the spit of the world because it knows that it was no one's fault but his, and he is the one who is to blame.

He rubs the back of his hand across his mouth and suddenly his life is cold and exposed, pinned out on a table under the bright operating lights where there is nothing secret, or which can be hidden from the relentless probe of the knife. And he's passing an entry where twenty-five years earlier, as a member of a Tartan gang, he gave a kicking to a Taig who'd ventured to shops that were outside his own territory and in his head he hears the screams and whimpers of the boy, the clack and clog dance of their boots on the ridged concrete as they swarm about him in a competitive flurry of arms and legs, eager to be able to claim later that they were the warriors who inflicted the most damage. And they're almost done now, as for greater balance they stand with linked arms like a chorus line, their legs still swinging at a head and body that break and burst like a piece of rotten fruit. And he calls to Rob – Rob who's keeping watch – and invites his kid brother to be as big a man as they are and leave his print, but Rob's frightened and says there's people coming and so they run the length of the entry, their feet a tattoo on the beating drums of their hearts.

He wonders what happened to their victim, where he is. Hopes he got out, got away to London or Boston or New York. If he could find him now he'd tell him that his attacker's got his punishment. All these years later he's got what he deserves. As he drives he sees faces he recognises, even one of those whose arm linked with his and who still lives in the same street he grew up in, and he laughs with bitterness at himself for having thought that he was better than these faces because he had escaped the road. They'll have seen his name in the paper, heard about it on the television or radio and they'll think it's the price he paid for getting above himself, for turning his back on where he came from. For trying to forget. And he can't bear the thought of her name on their lips, the way they will dismiss the stars as worthless trinkets. If this is the price, then it's too high. He bangs his fist against the glass and tells himself again that it's too high. He was the one who had to pay, not her, not Rachel. Rachel never did anything to anyone, never in her whole life did she do anything to anyone and then the road is blurred and he makes the wipers work more quickly before he realises it is his tears he needs to clear.

*

Red-eyed dogs, spiders, All of them stand in his way. He doesn't know if he can make it. He's confused. Even though he's been running through this world for months, it suddenly feels foreign and he can't anticipate where they're lying in wait for him. He's tired, his eyes are sore but he's got to go on. Got to stay awake and alert or they'll get him too. Get him just like they got Rachel. And he's started to think that this is where he's running – running to the heart of the mystery where he'll find her and bring her back. He wants her back, more than he could have ever guessed, misses her calling him by his name – his real name. Misses seeing her sitting at her desk in the circle of light. Misses so many things that the memories peck at him like little birds and he doesn't want to do anything that will startle them and make them fly away. So he's always quiet now and tries to sit as still as he can. Even when he's playing the game. And he's got one more thing to be frightened of and it's that if these memories are to leave him, then they'll never come back and where Rachel used to be will be nothing but an empty space.

*

Every wall, every gable, every kerbstone and lamppost in the estate declares its affiliations, its loyalties and alle-giances. And all of the murals and the exhortations are fresh like some memory that's just been revived in case there is a risk of it being forgotten. So driving through the estate feels like the beginning of something and not something that's about to end or be put to sleep. There is a chip van parked on a square of grass but no customers make their way to it out of the gloom. He drives round hoping for some clue or chance sighting, passes a darkened row of shops, their windows hidden behind a web of wire mesh. Only the end one is open, a block of yellow light framed by the open doorway. It's a taxi firm and breeze blocks fill what once were windows. A couple of men stand smoking behind a black four-wheel drive which has personalised plates, their cigarettes writing patterns in the dusk. He slowly parks opposite it, allowing them plenty of time to see him, then gets out of the car and walks towards them, stopping halfway across the road to ask for Rob. Their cigarettes dropped slightly behind their backs, they stare like schoolboys who've been caught smoking, and at first they give him blankness and slow shakes of the head, as if he's speaking some language they don't quite understand.

'He's my brother,' he says, but their only response is a shrug and the slow return of the cigarettes to their lips. He's about to turn away when a voice calls out from inside the shop.

'Of course he is, Marty! Long time no see.' A man in a leather jacket steps into the square of light. He's wearing a baseball cap and the light catches the gold of two earrings. He doesn't recognise this man but the other two men stand aside and stare at him with new interest. 'Fuckin' Marty,' he says. 'Where you been hiding yourself all these years?' He rakes off his cap and pushes his hand through the ginger stubble of his hair. 'Hope I don't look as old as you do, mucker,' he says smiling but worried that he won't be recognised.

'You look good, Jaunty,' he says, stepping forward to shake his hand. 'It's been a long rime.'

'What you doing with yourself? Rob says you've been workin' in the museum. Thought he was pullin' me leg. The fuckin' museum!' he says, looking at the two men who smile with him as if it's some kind of joke. 'Marty and me go a long way back,' he says to them. 'Used to be a bit of a hard man.'

He just wants to find where Rob lives, doesn't want to stand here talking to someone whose memory is like a bad smell. 'I need to find Rob,' he says. 'We've got out of touch. Need to find him.'

'Out of touch with Rob? Don't know why you want to change that, Marty. No offence, but he's still the useless bastard he always was. But suppose you know that better than anyone. Rob – what a fuckin' weight to carry all your life. It's him should be in the museum – stuffed and nailed to the wall.' He puts his cap back on and the two men snigger, exhale smoke in a jerky stream. 'Come inside and I'll tell you where you'll find him.'

He doesn't want to go but sees no way round it so he follows him through an outer waiting area and into an office. As soon as they're inside it Jaunty sits behind the desk which has a computer and printer sitting on it. Opening one of the drawers, he takes out a bottle of whisky and some glasses, pours them both a drink. 'So you really work in the museum?' he asks.

'That's right,' he says as he feels the slow burn of the whisky on the back of his throat. 'This is your business?' he asks.

'This? This is small stuff,' Jaunty says, leaning back on his chair. 'Run it more as a service to the community. I'm into business now, range of interests. If you ever need a job I could use someone like you to manage some parts.'

'Thanks,' he says, impatient to learn Rob's address.

'We had some wild times, Marty,' he says. 'Lucky we survived them.'

'Yeah,' he says. 'We're lucky we survived them. So you've done well for yourself?'

'Can't complain. Thinkin' of buying a couple of places in Florida next month. Rent them out when they're not bein' used. Put any money you have in property, Marty, you can't ever lose.'

'I'll remember that.'

'Sometimes it'd do your fuckin' head in though. Every five minutes someone's phoning you up to get you to decide about something. Drive you mental after a while. So what's it like workin' in a museum, Marty?'

'It's a job,' he says, staring at the glass his hand holds.

'So what do you do exactly?'

'Watch over things, check no one steals anything valuable.'

'Here Marty, remember in first form when they took us to Old Trafford to see the game and Hendy tried to rogue the shirt from the shop? Old Watson had to spend the whole afternoon in the police station with him, never got to see a minute of the bloody game. He kicked the shite out of Hendy on the boat on the way home. Took a total psycho. Hendy said he thought he was goin' to throw him overboard.'

'I remember,' he says, pretending to smile.

'Never saw a moment of the game and the old goat was United crazy. He could have stayed home and watched it on *Match of the Day*. We had some laughs all right. Here, have another drink. I'll get one of the boys to taxi you home.'

'Listen, Jaunty,' he says, 'it's good to see you and thanks for the drink. After all this time like. But I need to find Rob now. Family stuff.'

'End house, street behind the community centre. Got a red van parked outside. Tell him to come and see me soon. Might have some work for him.'

He says his thanks and turns to go. The voice calls to him. 'Any time you need a change of job, give us a call, Marty. I could use a sound man in a lot of things. The world's full of thieves, always need people I can trust.' In reply he lifts his arm and lets it fall again, but doesn't look back as he gets in his car. Already, he's asking himself why he's come, why it matters about Rob. It feels like he's stepping back into a sewer and then he tells himself that this is part of the price that has to be paid and he knows, too, that there will be worse than this.

The community centre's roof is circled with barbed wire and on the tiles in large letters someone has painted U.F.F in white paint. Some kids stand smoking in the doorway. He finds Rob's street, sees the red van and parks a little way from the house. The wooden fence is broken and a dog sniffs round the patch of uneven grass. There is a satellite dish jutting from the chimney. He wonders if Rob is still with Angela, if they have any kids, how he is. What he will say when he tells him. Again he wonders why he's come, considers starting the car and driving away. Rachel was still in primary school the last time he saw her – she never knew him as an uncle. She never knew much about any of his family and after a while whatever natural curiosity she might have had slipped away.

As he walks down the path to the door, the dog turns briefly to inspect him then returns to its sniffing. There is a light on in the living room but he can't see a bell or door knocker so he raps with his knuckles. The wood feels cold and damp against his skin. A hand shivers the curtain and a few moments later the door is opened by someone he thinks is Angela. Her hair is blonde now, not brown, and she has rings in her eyebrow and nose. The smell of cigarette smoke and cooking engulfs him so strongly that he blinks his eyes as if trying to clear it. She stares at him without speaking and it's clear she isn't sure who he is.

'Is Rob in?' he asks. 'It's Martin, his brother.' She doesn't take her eyes off him or say anything to him but shouts for Rob and when he doesn't appear she shouts again, and each time her voice is louder and more insistent and it mixes with the blare of the television. She's wearing a black blouse with tracksuit bottoms and nothing on her feet. Her feet are small, blue-veined and ragged in the nails. He stares past her and in the kitchen he can see a basin on a table with washed clothes piled into it. She doesn't ask him in or speak, except to call for Rob, and finally she turns to go and get him.

It's his last chance to go. To go and never come back. But he forces himself to stay because now he knows there is nowhere to go. Nowhere that is better than this. He touches the frame of the door, lets his finger trace the peeling strip of rubber. There is a child's pram protruding from under the stairs. A curly-headed doll on the floor between the wheels. Rob never told him. Never told him about a child.

'She's dead, isn't she?' Rob asks. He comes down the hall and he doesn't look any older than how he remembers him – only a lightly lined tightening round the eyes and a thinning of his hair at the temples mark the passage of time. He's scared now though; that, too, is familiar in the way his body locks itself into a tight angular frame, the way his hands suddenly seem stiff and clawed as if they're looking for something to hold on to. 'She's dead isn't she?' he repeats.

'Yes, she's dead,' he answers and hates him for making him use the words.

'I knew you'd come some day to tell me that,' Rob says. They're still standing on the doorstep. He watches him shuffle a little, turn a half-circle then unclench his fists. What does he mean, he knew he'd come?

'I can't come to the funeral – I'm sorry, Marty. I've already decided that whenever it happened, I wasn't going to go to Ma's funeral. I'm sorry. I'll do anything else but I'm not going.'

'Ma's not dead, Rob. It's Rachel who's dead. It's Rachel, Rob.' And he wishes with all his heart that what Rob thought he was coming to tell him was the truth, that with a sleight of hand, some reshuffling of the dealt cards, that it might become the truth.

'You're jokin' me, you're fuckin' jokin' me,' Rob says and then at last he stretches out his hand and invites him in. Rob repeats the words to Angela even though she's been standing at his shoulder, then wanders into the living room ahead of them both as if they're no longer there. When they follow him into the room Rob is staring at the television, and doesn't turn his head to look at him when he speaks. 'I thought it was Ma, Marty. I'm sorry. I just thought when you came, it would be to tell me she was gone.'

Angela stands in the doorway, still staring at him. No one turns the television volume down. Neither of them hear how loud it is. He has to talk over it, tell them what he has to tell them, about the funeral arrangements, his voice merging with the laughter and applause of the game-show audience. Rob only sneaks glances at him, as if someone has told him that he's not to look. He wants to get up and rip out the plug, grab Rob by the throat and make him look him in the eye. Every word he uses now spills a little more of himself, rubs the memories raw and suddenly he thinks of the pram in the hall and asks about their child. But it is Angela who speaks and tells him that Corrina is four years old and that she's from a previous relationship. And part of him wants to say that they don't deserve her, wants to take her from them, give her to people who will take better care of her and love her more. But then he thinks that even in this house, in the middle of this estate, even here with Rob, they're taking better care of her than he did of Rachel. So he tells them of the arrangements, lets Rob know he can come or stay away as he wants, and then he's hurrying to the car and trying not to be sick.

*

She holds it to her nose – mint, arnica, witch hazel – but nothing can sweeten what she smells now. The sourness of loss clings to every part of her skin, clammy and heavy, and even if she wanted to, she knows she can't ever shake it off. It clogs her pores, coats every strand of her hair and as she watches the rain fall against the glass, she wants something that will wash it away. Something that will lighten and lift what she feels – even for a moment, even for a single moment. But she feels only one thing sharply now: the constant stab of a fine steel blade that is unrelenting in seeking out some new spot to pierce. It finds it in Rachel's clothes buried in the pile of ironing, the letter which arrives from some university she had asked to send her information about courses, the yoghurts that only she liked, creeping past their sell-by date in the fridge.

She feels only one thing now and everything else is muffled and rendered vague and undefined. Nothing else touches or impinges on this thing, not the hands of the clock, not food, not even the need to wash or brush her hair. Everything that constituted her former life is drained away, diverted into some channel which sluices it all off. Sometimes she wonders how she even remembers to breathe because everything else has been forgotten – how to sleep, how to walk further than from one room to another, how to talk to the people who come to the house to pay their respects. Maybe it is the tablets which cut her off from her self, maybe it is the sedatives which leave her feeling nothing but that sharp stab of pain. She wants herself back because she needs her memories now more than anything else and when she tries to make Rachel alive in her head, the images are shrouded and out of focus like some photograph which hasn't been fully developed. She's even scared to summon those moments which are precious to her because each time they form in her consciousness, they seem to have travelled an ever greater distance and be more insubstantial than the time before. So as she stands watching the falling rain slant against the glass, she is filled with a dull ache of fear that soon there will be nothing left upon which to draw.

The yoghurts are past their sell-by date. It's stupid. She takes them out of the fridge and then puts them back. She irons the clothes and puts them in Rachel's drawer. She props the letter against the lamp on her desk. What did her hair feel like? Why didn't she touch it when she had the chance? Why didn't she say all the things that now seem important? Why did she put off everything to some future date? Now there is no future, only a past that is slipping slowly through her hands. She looks for a cigarette but knows there aren't any, remembers that she hasn't smoked since she was a teenager.

She puts her hand to her hair, is repelled by what she feels. She lets her head rest on the coldness of the glass, lets her face wear the mask of the falling rain. Not even to know your own child. She thought she had a daughter who knew so many things, when after all she knew as little as anyone else and maybe even less. She hates the stars now, blames them for deceiving her, for stopping her being the mother she should have been. They stole her daughter from her and now if she could, she would take them and throw them into the darkness. Her breath steams the glass and when she wipes it clear, the prints of her fingertips whorl it before fading into nothing. More rain falls. She wants to be clean, to be wakened to her self again, and so she opens the back door and goes outside.

*

He pauses before he gets out of the car, momentarily unwilling to re-enter the round of his life. But the funeral is soon and there are still things to be done. When he opens the front door, the house feels empty and strange. As he walks down the hall, he can hear Tom's footsteps in his room, but there is no sign of Alison. He calls for her and looks, asks Tom, but there is still no sign, then coming down again to the kitchen, he notices that the back door is slightly open. A little shift of rain has glistened the vinyl. He opens it wider, feels the damp breath of the night brush his face – the rain is heavier now, coming down in fine riddling slants and he stands on the step and calls her name. There is no answer but somehow he knows she is out there. Suddenly he gets frightened, wonders where she is and what she's doing, startling himself with the thought that perhaps loss is not singular but when it comes it can flow and flow until whatever you once had is washed away, until there is nothing left. As the rising wind shivers the light, he calls again and steps out into the frittering span of yellow from the kitchen, pauses momentarily at the wall of dark and then passes through.

'Alison, are you there?' he calls, but even in his cry his voice is soft as if he's shouting to some creature that might flee in fear of his approach. 'Alison, Alison.' He hears her now, knows she's down the end of the garden where the couple of apple trees are. As he gets closer he hears her crying but it doesn't sound like her crying. It's dried up, used up as if it's only the dregs that are left, so it's a thin and reedy quaver in her throat as if something's stopping her breathing properly.

'Alison, what are you doing? You're getting wet.'

Her back is pressed against the trunk of the tree. In the matted tangle of grass he feels the press of its rotting crop underfoot. Hardly bigger than horse chestnuts, bitter to the taste. The tree's good for nothing except for the children to climb in its branches when they were younger. She doesn't answer. One of her arms holds a branch; even in the darkness her hand is pale against the blackness of the bark. Her hair is plastered to the knob of her skull and her face, which doesn't look at him, is swollen and seeped as if her drowned body has been pulled from a briny sea. He doesn't try to touch her but grasps the gnarled branch in his hand. It feels sapless, ready at any moment to snap under the squeeze of his fingers.

'Do you remember the time I tried to make a swing?' he asks. 'Out of a wooden box and the clothes line. I thought it was really good but neither of them would get into it. Said it wasn't safe.'

'I don't blame them – it didn't swing straight and they got splinters from the wood.' She lets go of the branch, wipes her face then runs her palms down the sides of her head. 'It was a death trap.'

They both flinch a little and he kicks his foot through the tangle of grass. 'Let's go inside,' he says, 'you're soaking wet.'

'In a minute, in a minute.'

'I'll make you a hot whisky,' he says.

'I can't with the tablets.'

'Sorry, I forgot. I'll run you a bath. A real hot bath.'

'Martin, I can't face the funeral.' There is the same rasping quaver in her throat. 'I can't leave her there, can't walk away and leave her there all on her own.'

He tries to hold her but her body resists him. It feels like the branch of the tree and if he holds it too tightly, it too will snap. He lets one hand cup the wet splay of her hair. He knows there must be things that can be said to ease her pain, knows that there must be some soft chorus of words that will give her something to hold on to, but he can't think what they are, so he pushes through the stiffness of her body and presses the dampness of her face into the cushion of his shoulder and tells her that they'll get through it, that they'll help each other. That they'll get through it, that everything will be all right, as if the repetition of the words will create a spell, an incantation that will protect them both.

*

The policewoman sits on the edge of their settee and tells them they're very hopeful, that they'll make a break-through before long and she's confident they'll make an arrest very soon.

'That's why publicity is so important,' she says. 'Seeing you both on television could be the thing that stirs somebody's conscience, encourages someone to come forward. There's people out there who know who sold those drugs. If we get their help we can crack this case.'

As she talks, tells them how important this case is, how high a profile they're going to give it, how many resources they're allocating to it, she looks at her hair. At her perfect make-up. And as she gives them her sympathy again, she looks at the clear polish on her slim fingernails. Her shoes and clothes are elegant, expensive; she looks as if she's spent a long time on her grooming, on her appearance. She's not like a police person at all – her presence makes her feel grubby and unkempt, threadbare in her own home.

'I know it's going to be difficult for you but you have to do it. You have to do it for Rachel and for all the other young people whose lives these people put at risk. The TV people have a lot of experience – they know how to handle it. Sometimes it's just like talking to a friend and if at any point it all gets too much then we can stop it and take a break.'

'We'll do it,' Martin says. 'We want these people caught.'

He's started to talk a lot about those responsible being caught, about their being brought to justice. It seems to have some meaning for him that she can't understand. What difference will it make now? Just a lot of noise and shouting and then a slap on the wrists. And when they come back out of prison they'll start right in again. And the life they're given in prison is like luxury compared to where they come from. But she'll do it, let the world see how it feels, let the world be discomforted just for a moment in the cosy safety of their living rooms. And if they think she must have been a bad mother, she doesn't care and maybe they'd be right, so let them look at her and feel her shame at not having saved her own daughter from the world.

'You must have some leads,' Martin says. 'The girls she was with from school must have told you names.'

Let them stone her with their eyes – she doesn't care any more. She'd been a fool to think that the stars would protect her child, that they meant she was immune from harm. So she'll go on television and share her shame. Do it for Rachel. Do it to say she's sorry.

'We're following several leads,' the policewoman says. 'Drugs and the people who deal them are links in a chain, and the chain always leads back to the paramilitaries. Getting names isn't as hard as getting the evidence to convict in court.'

'So you're saying that you don't think you'll be able to convict anyone?' Martin asks, his voice flecked with rising anger.

'No, I'm not saying that. I'm saying we're going to do our very best, that we're going to make every effort, but I would be misleading you if I let you think that it was going to be easy.'

Martin sits back on his chair and a little deflated stream of air pushes through his lips.

'The television appearance will help. I've no doubt of that,' she says, glancing at her watch. 'It'll be hard but you'll be helping us and maybe helping other parents who have teenage children. They'll want to have a good photograph – one in her school uniform would be best. Most effective.'

She watches her scanning the room looking for the most effective photograph of Rachel and wonders how someone who's supposed to spend her time investigating terrible things, who's bound to meet the city's scum every day she does her job, can have so much time to spend on her appearance – how she can sit there and bear no trace, no stain of the world. She remembers the smell of food that plaits her own hair, the tiredness of her limbs and wonders how it can be done. Does she wash it off every night and then anoint herself with sweet-smelling scents and expensive clothes? 'Call me Joan,' she says. How can it be done then, Joan? What's the secret? Share it with me. She's looking at her watch again, she's impatient to go. She fiddles with the broad band of her wedding ring. Her knees are neat and sharp like little points of light. Does she have children of her own? Does she touch their hair at night? Her mobile rings and she goes out to the hall before she answers it. They hear her voice but not the words as they sit and look at each other. Martin's face is shiny as if he's just washed it. There is a little patch of red on his throat like he's just shaved. While Joan talks in the hall it feels the house is no longer theirs. It feels like being visitors in their own home. She thinks of the photograph they will use – the one that was taken for the school magazine on prize day, holding the cup. The one Rachel hated, wouldn't let them get framed or put on display because she looked 'swotty' in it. Because her hair wasn't right. Because it wasn't cool. Martin goes to say something but stops and looks towards the hall. She's coming back, one hand slipping the mobile into her pocket. Smiling, as if that's an answer to some question they've asked her.

'I have to go now,' she says. 'I'll stay in touch and you have my number if you remember anything or if you want to get in contact. Doing the television appeal is the right thing – it'll bring new publicity to the case, stir a few consciences. Bring us a bit closer to the lead we need.'

After she's gone her scent lingers in the room. Martin speaks to her outside the front door. He's talking about catching those responsible, about punishment. She hopes they never catch them and that she never has to look at their faces, doesn't understand why anyone would want to see the faces of those responsible for their child's death. Rachel's face is already blurring, her memory unable to focus on it as sharply as she wants, so she doesn't want to have it replaced with the faces of those who killed her.

'What do you make of her?' Martin asks when he returns. But she only shrugs her shoulders in reply. 'I'm not sure,' he says. 'She talks a good game but I'm not sure. You don't see many women doing her job.'

'You think she's no good,' she says, 'because she's a woman.' Sometimes even an argument feels as if it might bring solace, transfer the pain for a little while, distract, even for a fleeting moment. 'She wouldn't be where she was if she wasn't any good.'

'I don't care about her being a woman. All I care about is her catching them. I don't care if she's from outer space so long as she puts the scum where they belong.'

'What good will it do?' she suddenly asks, indifferent to the voice telling her she shouldn't say it. 'What good will it do?' She watches as her words scratch at him. She wants to hurt him, is desperate to strike some flame of feeling from the friction. 'It'll not bring her back.' Why should he be able to ease his pain with thoughts of punishment of the guilty? Why should he find something to hold on to? The only person she wants to punish now is herself. Let them put her in the dock, lock her up. Throw away the key.

'We owe it to Rachel,' he says, his voice high and thin, fraying at the edges like a wind-blown flag. 'We can't let them do it to some other family. They've got to be stopped.' He shakes his head. He's talking someone else's words. He doesn't know how to go on. His hand fastens on his throat as if he's trying to squeeze it free from some obstruction. 'We owe it to Rachel.'

Owe? How will this pay back? What will she ever know about this? How can this transaction ever balance the books? She looks at him and thinks that he doesn't understand, that she's married to a man who is stupid and she hates him a little because he wants to make this thing, that is more terrible than anything she's ever known, into some small boys' game. A game of gangs and tit for tat. When she was a child in primary school they used to play chain tig. When you were caught, you joined the chain, became a hunter. She doesn't want anyone to come to the funeral. It's none of their business, it's got nothing to do with anyone except them and because he no longer sees what's important, she's on her own. Just her and Rachel. No one else. She doesn't want to be part of a chain, to have someone hold her hand. This is private and she needs that privacy to speak to Rachel. She needs the silence.

*

The funeral is all wrong. It's not how he wants it to be. Even the wreath is wrong – all garish colours and the words 'From Mum and Dad' puffed up in white petals. He knows Rachel would have hated it. And somehow everything feels like a secret, something that has to be hushed up. He doesn't even know half the people here, people who shake his hand or put their hand on his shoulder. Those he knows least are the ones who say the most and sometimes he'd like to stop their mouths with his fist. Those he knows best, like the people from work, skirt the circumference of the mourners, huddle in tight little groups and when they approach him no one knows what to say and so they shake his hand in a slow procession as if he's become a dignitary and they're being introduced. He stops speaking, just nods his head at each of them. They wear their green blazers. They look strange against the black. Part of him wants to run away and find the most silent corner of the museum. His hand wants to touch something solid – the stone axes, the cold glint of machinery – not this soft slither of endless palm on palm. Alison is always somewhere else. They should be together, shoulder to shoulder. Tom, too, is always on the periphery of his view. But he's never seen him look so well. Alison has bought him a new black blazer and trousers that fit him. He looks older, less of a child. Soon he'll try to talk to him – he's put it off for too long. Things should get fixed, not put off to a future that might never come. He'll work harder at it than he's ever done.

The minister talks about waste, about tragedy, about the evil men who prey on our children. He calls them 'vultures', prays that God will bring them to account. And if it doesn't happen in this world, then it will surely happen in the next. For God is not mocked and those who have done this thing out of their lust for money and the things of the flesh must face their maker on the Day of Judgement.

At the graveside Alison almost faints against him and he has to hold her close to his side. He looks through the minister's interminable words to the rim of the crowd and sees a group of girls huddled close to the cars. He recognises some of their faces but doesn't know their names. Rachel's friends – perhaps the friends who took her to the club, the friends who gave her the tablets. For a second he wants to go to them and ask the questions that rattle round his head, press them for the truth that will help him understand how this thing happened but Alison slumps into the hollow of his side and the minister's prayer is slipping to its terrible conclusion. This is the moment when they give her back, let her go. It's the thing that Alison said she couldn't bear. And now he understands because how can they walk away, get back in the cars and leave her here? Leave her on her own with the cold, clotted clay and the already wind-blasted wreaths? How can they return to the warmth of the house when on top of her casket they'll pile this mound of earth? When she was a young child on holiday and they stayed in a little cottage in Donegal, she differentiated their permanent home from the cottage by calling it 'Home sweet home'. Now she's taken that name with her and he never wants to go back to the house, never wants to climb the stairs and see her empty room. The room that's just as she left it. Suddenly Alison falters towards the lowering coffin and she's trying to shake away his arm but he pulls her back and locks her into him with the stiff brace of his arm. Her whole body is trembling inside the ring of his arm but he keeps it taut and rigid until her struggling subsides into the quiver of her sobs, keeps it locked there until all the faces and the final tumble of words have faded into silence.

'WE CAN'T GO ON like this, Marty,' Rob says, his agitation unravelling. 'Something's going to happen to her. Something bad.'

At first he can't believe what he's hearing. He doesn't think he has the patience any more to play these games.

'I don't think she can live in that house on her own. She'll fall or burn herself. It's not right, Marty.'

'So what do you think we should do, Rob?' he asks.

'We'll have to get someone to look after her full-time or get her in a home or something. She can't go on like this.'

It's as if after all these years of zero contact, he's allocating blame, accusing him of neglect. It's Rob. All these years later it's the same old Rob. He wants to say, 'Fuck off, Rob'; the words are on his lips, he wants to say it for all the times in the past he should have said it. The words are on his lips but he stares at his brother's face, the tightening frame of his anxiety and he hesitates.

'She'll hurt herself, Marty, maybe fall and break a leg. We have to do something.'

He's not quite ready to assume his familiar role, so he says out of spite, 'Maybe she could go and live with you, Rob? Maybe you could look after her.'

Rob blinks. It's not something he's ever considered so he blows a little wisp of air through the tight purse of his lips and his face furrows into a pained simulation of thought. 'We haven't got the room, Marty. Not with Corrina getting bigger and everything. I'd like to but I can't see how we could do it. Know what I mean?'

'Sure Rob, you haven't got the room. No problem.' He watches his brother's relief, the smoothing of the furrows, the untangling of his clenched hands. 'I'll speak to the doctor again, try and get things speeded up.'

'That's good, Marty, that's the right thing to do.'

He watches his brother walk away just the way he's always walked away from things. For a second he envies the sudden, easy, lightness of his step, his ability to transfer what has weighed him down to someone else. He watches as he gets into his red van, the one that used to be a post office van and on whose side the covered-up letters gleam faintly visible through the paint, listens as the exhaust spurts into a gravelly, throaty churn. Watches as it makes its way to the end of the street.

'Fuck off, Rob,' he says. 'Fuck off.'

*

It's bound to make a difference. They'll all know why he's been off school so it's bound to make a difference. He's lost his sister. The whole school will know for sure. It might even make a big difference. He stops at a shop window and looks at his reflection. He probably even looks different. His reflection isn't sharp enough to see his expression but he pushes his face into what he thinks must look like sadness, lets his shoulders droop and his bag sag loose on his shoulder. He thinks he should have been allowed to stay off longer, calls up, as evidence, the names of those who have stayed off for much longer, with less cause.

He's a little late so there are only fellow stragglers about and a couple of younger kids who've already decided that they've had enough and are heading in the opposite direction. None of them pays him any attention. At the newsagents he goes in and buys himself some sweets then splits them into handfuls and secretes them in various pockets and the fluff-filled, ink-stained corners of his bag. There is a sudden hollow squirm of nervousness in his stomach – it feels like it did on his first day when his head was filled with stories of initiation ceremonies and having your head flushed down the toilet. But he survived it then and he thinks he can again and he tells himself that he knows so much more now, that he's learned stuff, that he can ride whatever waves rise up and not be engulfed. And it's different now, too, because he is someone he wasn't before; he's the victim of a tragedy that's been on the news and in the papers. His steps take on greater urgency, if he hurries he might just make registration, but maybe it would be better to be a few minutes late, come in when everyone's already there. He rehearses it in his mind. He'll not speak to anyone, just nod his head, not let anyone see what he's thinking and he'll not rush to his seat like he normally does, but walk a little slower, drop his bag to the floor as if he's not bothered about what's in it.

The bell has already gone when he enters the school but people haven't yet reached their form rooms so the corridors are a stream of counterflows and changing currents of bodies. People see him but there is no sudden sweep of silence, no collective fixing of gazes on him and he has his first tremors of doubt. Snuffling his glasses back on the bridge of his nose, he sifts the sweets in his pocket through his fingers as if they are gold coins, talismans of good fortune. There is a knot of his classmates at the foot of the stairs which lead to his form room. They look at him now. They're looking at his face.

'All right, Tom?' a voice asks. It's his name. It's his name they're using and he almost smiles at how strange it sounds in this place but he only nods and keeps on walking. The echo of his name seems to bounce off the walls of the corridor and ricochet round the walls and tiles before it gets slowly absorbed in the scrimmage of more bodies and the voices of teachers telling people to get to their form rooms. All right, Tom? Just for a moment he feels all right. He remembers the ice-hockey players, their puffed-up, parcelled-up bodies balanced on the thinnest of blades, and the way they sped across the ice, scoring only their lightness into the flurry and squeak of its surface. So cold and light. Light as air. 'All right, Tom?' another voice asks and this time he stops on the stairs and blows the thick quaver he feels sliming his throat into a clean breath of air. But he doesn't speak and instead nods his head while turning his face away from them. Then he hurries up the stairs and opens the door of his form room.

Mr Benson hasn't arrived yet and there are hard-edged huddles of boys strung round desks and perched on radiators. A few heads turn towards him as he makes his way down the first row towards his seat but he stares at the back wall and doesn't meet anyone's gaze. As his bag hits the floor, he kicks it under his seat and flops down on the chair, then stares at his fingers as if there's something sticking to them. He starts to pick at a bit of loose skin, pulling at a little whitened corner. The new skin is pink and smarting. Just for a second he wonders if it might be possible to peel away layers of yourself, slither by tiny slither. He eats the slither of skin he's detached, playing it first between his teeth and the tip of his tongue. There's someone standing at the edge of his desk but he doesn't raise his eyes to see who.

'All right, Fat Boy?' asks the voice he recognises as Chapman's. He watches the hands he recognises also prise free a strip of the wood veneer which bevels the edge of the desk before they let it smack back to its original position. The classroom door opens and Mr Benson enters, simultaneously kicking it closed behind him and ordering everyone to their seats. 'Enjoy your holiday, Fat Boy?' Chapman asks, while briefly and very lightly patting him on the back before strolling to his seat. The roll is started, the names barked out, and the owners respond with weary and studied indifference. His own is called and he has to speak for the first time. He says 'Here,' and he knows it's true, knows that he's here again and that nothing but nothing has changed.

Afterwards he doesn't follow the rest of the class to assembly but slips under the stairs and squats where the shadow curtains the corner. His fingers find one of the sweets and he takes the paper off without removing it from his pocket. Then he says sorry to Rachel.

*

The lights make the room unbearably hot. He's squeezed up beside Alison on the settee, their bodies positioned by the man behind the camera. It feels as if all her nervous heat seeps into his body, intensifying his own, choking the breath out of him. A girl has already wiped his forehead once and puffed and dusted his skin with powder to try to stop it shining like glass. They know where to look, they know what to say. It's all been rehearsed and the interviewer has told them what is good and what will be most effective. She's been gentle, like a minister or a doctor handling someone who's fragile, like a teacher helping a young child. 'I know this must be very difficult for you,' is what she says in between the advice and the directions. 'Very difficult.' Sometimes, when she looks at the photograph Alison has to hold, she says things like, 'She's a lovely looking girl,' or 'You must have been very proud of her,' and it almost feels as if she really cares. But when he sees her speaking to the cameraman with her eyes, or looking at her reflection in a small hand mirror, he knows that she's only doing a job and that doing it right is more important to her than anything else.

'Mr and Mrs Waring, this must be a particularly painful time for your family. Would you like to tell us about Rachel? What sort of girl was she?' she asks, leaning towards Alison with her face open and inviting, almost like she's asking the question for the first time and hasn't heard the answer a dozen times before. It's Alison who must answer this and so he hears her speak about 'a good girl', 'a girl devoted to her studies who worked so hard', 'a girl who never missed a day of school and who never gave a moment's trouble', 'the best daughter anyone could have'. He knows it word-perfect by now – it sounds like a nursery rhyme to him as he anticipates the cadences of his wife's voice.

The proudest, happiest day he had with Rachel was when she came that Sunday morning to the closed museum. It felt as if he owned it all and that it was within his power to give her everything inside its walls. The empty galleries were laid open for her private inspection, and when she wanted to know things about the exhibits, he was able to satisfy her with what knowledge he had. It was probably the last time she asked him for answers. And in her child's eyes his job wasn't a mundane, repetitive nothing, but something special and important, as if he had been personally entrusted with the guardianship of this valuable treasure trove. He tried to remember what she had liked best but it's started to blur in his memory. She wouldn't look at the mummy – he remembered that.

Wouldn't look at Takabuti's wizened, black scab of a face on her own, even though like all the other children it usually drew her like a magnet. Had he teased her about it? Had he made a joke? Already it's slipping away and then he shivers as he remembers where they have left her.

Alison's elbow is pressing into his side. The interviewer is nodding her head in encouragement. His mouth is dry, the palms of his hands damp. He doesn't know if he'll be able to speak. What is it she's asking him? What is it he's supposed to be talking about? 'She was very gifted academically, wasn't she Martin?' Alison prompts him again. 'Oh yes,' he says, blinking his eyes and trying to find his focus. And then he talks about the stars and prize day and the cup they gave her. Talks about Oxbridge. Talks about the future she was going to have.

Even though Martin is sitting pressed against her, his voice sounds as if it's coming from somewhere far away. And it sounds strange so that she struggles to recognise it. What is the point of speaking of the future when everything is permanently consigned to the past and locked up in some heavy trunk that can't be opened? All she has now of her daughter are the photographs, the ones she clings to more and more as in their finger-printed surfaces she tries to feel some moment of true memory, to get her child whole and real even for a second. To pull her complete from the rushing slew of her own half-formed and unfocused images. And all the precious photographs which have started to bruise and smear with the moist press of her fingers, wouldn't she trade them all, every last one, for the most fleeting touch of her daughter's hair? She thinks of all the wasted opportunities and she stiffens with anger at herself and at Rachel for what they have denied themselves.

'So, Alison, what would you say to young people out there, possibly thinking of experimenting with drugs?'

He'd say let them take it, let them take it all, only give him back his daughter. Let them all die but not his child. 'We wouldn't want any other family to go through this pain,' Alison says, but he doesn't care about anyone else's pain and he'd see them feel all of his if he could have her sitting beside them now. Squashed up between them like she did as a child, when they would sit on this same settee and watch television. He's too warm and he tries to blink away some of the heat of the lights. The rhythms of Alison's voice falter a little and he moves his arm against her, wanting to tell her that the script is almost over, that all they have to do is the final appeal for information 'to stop this tragedy happening again', 'to take these people off the streets before some other son or daughter is snatched from their family'.

'Snatched from their family': it makes it sound as if Rachel was kidnapped, that some ransom note of cut-up newspaper letters will be pushed through their letter-box. She feels the unexpected flurry of her anger. For all the stars and the books, for all the cups and prizes, she was a stupid, foolish, selfish girl who didn't think of her mother or anyone else when she did what she did. 'The selfish little bitch,' she wants to say to the camera, tell it about all the times she climbed those stairs to her room and took nothing away, not even the briefest touch of her hair. Tell about every day she stands in that canteen with the noise breaking over her and the smell of cooking and grease that coats the very strands of her hair. Then the surge seeps away and she longs for that ransom note and knows to pay it she'll stand there every day for the rest of her life, that she'll take nothing ever for herself, but pay with every minute of her life and, if it's what it takes, not even try to wash the smells away with sweet-smelling scent.

'So we'd just appeal to anyone out there who knows anything about the people who pushed these drugs to come forward and help the police with their enquiries. Any little bit of information might make all the difference,' the interviewer says finally. Suddenly he notices the camera is focused on his hands. He's seen it before. The camera wants him to speak with his hands, to replace his stumbling inadequacy in words with the silent, eloquent revelation of gesture. It wants a glimpse into his nervous, secret pain, a poetic symbol of what he feels, like a rose on a Valentine card. He slowly clenches his hands into fists, then watches as the camera's gaze returns to his face.

*

Nothing happens. No calls, no leads. The phone calls and visits from the police fade to nothing. It's time for him to go back to work and at first the prospect seems like a relief, a potential escape from the claustrophobia of the house but soon he understands that it will bring no relief. All the things that before were solid and familiar take on a new amorphous shape, moored to nothing and drifting on the rise and fall of whatever flows through him. The other staff tiptoe round him, their every communication couched in unfamiliar extremes of politeness. He looks at the sixteen polished axes and sees nothing but wood and stone and now he knows that he's the one who is on display, pinned open in a glass case, and in the whispers and suddenly aborted conversations which greet his arrival, he feels the intrusive gaze of the world. It frightens him when he thinks about what they might see.

Some of the very things he drew comfort from conspire now to taunt him. So when he arrives for work each morning the first thing he sees is the stone sculpture called *Mother and Child*, with its cold grey faces layered and linked. Nothing can ever separate them, or split the grain of the stone. And he will do anything to avoid Level Four. There's only another week and the exhibition will be taken down.

On his first Sunday afternoon back he watches children dropping coins into the water and even that makes him angry. Why should they have luck? Why should they have what he's never had because a coin splashes into water? He watches the single fathers with their children borrowed like a weekend video, and remembers all the times he thought this was the worst thing that could happen and now he hates them because they don't know how good the little they have really is. And he thinks about what he would give if he could only stand in their shoes. Sometimes he feels so angry that he wants to hurt someone and more and more he believes that hurting those who did this thing will take away some of his pain. He's started to let the reel run in his head, little snuff movies where always he's the executioner, the one with his finger on the trigger. But he knows it would be better if there was a face at which to fire the bullet and it's started to eat him up that no one's found that face.

On the way home from work he calls at the police station but the officer at the counter doesn't recognise him or his name. When he tells him that he's the father of Rachel Waring he stares at him blankly and then tells him to have a seat. There is a woman with her son, a boy of ten or eleven.

'Don't you try and act the big man,' she says to the boy.

'Who's acting the big man?'

'You just listen to what they say and don't give them any buck lip.'

'I didn't do anything, anyway, so I don't know why I'm here.'

'Listen, Gerard, you're friggin' lucky they're just givin' you a warning, so don't make it any worse. I know you, you'd argue black was white but if you don't get your act together, you'll end up in Hydebank.'

'What do you know? I'm too friggin' young for Hydebank and it couldn't be any worse than livin' at home.'

The woman looks over at him and rolls her eyes. For a second it looks as if she is going to speak to him but he turns his eyes away, wants no invitation into her world. To one side, two lads sprawl on the plastic seats. They both wear identical blue Nike hooded tops and baseball hats. He watches one of them take a black marker and write on the back of a chair while the other leans back and tilts his seat on its back legs. The one with the marker can see him watching while he's drawing under the writing but he doesn't care. Up at the counter the officer is hunched over something he's reading. The woman tries to brush her son's hair with the palm of her hand but he shrugs it off and squirms further away from her. The boy with the marker sits back for a second to inspect his work, then adds some embellishment, smiling at his own joke.

'Don't do that, son,' he says, says it before he knows he's going to say it. The two lads angle their heads to look at him. The woman and her son stare at him. Only the officer at the counter appears not to have heard him speak. The two boys look at each other before the one with the marker asks, 'Do what?'

'Don't draw on that seat.' His voice is calm and quiet.

'Are you a policeman then?' the other boy says, lowering the legs of his chair to the floor.

'No,' he answers, part of him telling himself that he shouldn't have spoken, but another part glad.

'So what's it got to do with you then?' the boy with the marker asks.

Suddenly he feels himself swept along on the rip tide of his anger. 'Because I paid for that chair and all the other chairs in this room and if you don't stop writing on my chair I'm goin' to stick that fuckin' pen down your throat.'

'Here,' his friend shouts to the desk, 'did you hear him threaten us? Is he a fuckin' psycho or something?'

The officer looks up from his reading, gazes round the room and straightens himself.

'Watch your language, son, or you can wait for your mate out on the street.'

'He threatened us – are you not goin' to do anything about it? How can you get threatened by a psycho inside a fuckin' cop station?'

'I told you to watch your language. Now the pair of you piss off and wait outside.'

The boys stand up with the sullen practised defiance of the oppressed and one kicks a chair on his way to the door. He turns and looks back at him. 'Fuckin' psycho man!' he calls before they bang the door on the way out. 'You can't talk to them anymore,' the woman says and he knows she feels vindicated in her judgement, that what her son does is not her fault because there's nothing you can say that will make any difference. He doesn't answer but feels his heart beating faster. He sees the officer at the counter looking at him. He drops his eyes under the unbroken gaze, hears him say, 'When we need extra help with security we'll let you know.'

It's another half an hour before someone comes to speak to him. It's Roberts, one of the detectives who has been working on the case.

'Hello, Martin,' he says, shaking his hand. 'What can we do for you?'

'I was wondering . . .' He glances at the woman and her son watching them both and hesitates. 'I was wondering if I could have a word with Joan?'

'Have you got some information for us? Something you want to tell us?' Roberts asks, but makes no effort to take him anywhere.

'Can we talk somewhere?' he has to ask before Roberts leads him to an office. It's a small room with one desk and a computer that's stained with fingerprints and badged with yellow notes. There is the remains of a takeaway in a tinfoil dish on his desk and a can of Coke. The whole room smells of Chinese food.

'Sorry about the mess,' he says, clearing away the remnants of the meal. 'Not good for the ulcer but beats canteen food. So how are you goin' then?'

He doesn't know how to answer this so merely nods his head. 'Is Joan here? She told us to call her Joan.'

'No, Joan's not here. In fact we got a postcard from her today.' He holds it up as if to confirm what he's just said. 'It's from Tenerife – says it's really hot.'

'She's in Tenerife? So who's in charge of the case?'

'Well, she's still in charge.'

'So is she followin' some lead in Tenerife or what exactly is she doin' there?'

'She's on holiday, Martin. Everybody's entitled to a holiday, even the police.'

He looks at Roberts, looks at the computer. One of the yellow notes says 'Phone home', another, 'Collect the tickets.' There is a sticker for the Belfast Giants on the side of the monitor.

'Are there any new developments?' he asks. 'Are we any closer to finding who killed Rachel?'

'I know it's hard, Martin, but no one killed Rachel. No one made her take that tab. There was nothing wrong with the tab – other people took them. It was one of those freak, tragic things that happen.'

'Are you saying it was an accident?' He can't believe what he's hearing. 'Are you telling me that Rachel's death was an accident, that no one's to blame?'

'Oh there's people to blame all right and we're doing our best to find the people who supplied the drugs. But it's not easy and I'd be deceiving you if I let you think that any day now we're going to see someone in the dock for this.' The phone rings and he excuses himself before engaging in a long conversation about a missing car. While he waits, he looks round the room, looking for what he's seen on television, a picture of Rachel on a board, surrounded by names and clues, photographs of suspects, allocation of responsibilities, but there are none of these things. After the phone call Roberts apologises and when he starts talking he says it's off the record and it's as if he's trying to help him understand.

'Here's what we know, know without having to ask anyone or be Sherlock Holmes. All drugs go through the paramilitaries: some do all the importing and dealing, others take a percentage cut from those they allow to operate. Either way they control the market. Freelancers, or anyone who gets greedy, or thinks they can exercise their own franchise, tend to get a head job as they sit in their four-wheel drives. Now the Troubles are over, everybody has to make a living from legit crime – drugs, protection, counterfeit goods, moving fuel over the border and all the rest. It's what they think of as the peace dividend. You know how it works.'

'Rachel,' he says, his impatience undisguised.

'The drugs that killed Rachel were supplied through Loyalist paramilitaries, operating out of the estate closest to those hotels and clubs in that part of the east of the city. You and I both know where that is. Who dealt the drugs on that particular night is more difficult. Sometimes, but not ordinarily, their own players do it, sometimes it's younger runners, and sometimes it's nobodies earning the price of a fix. A name and a face is entirely possible for us to find eventually. Getting someone to stand up in a witness box, well, that's a lot more difficult. Being a tout is a dangerous profession in this part of the world.'

'So no one's going to be called to account for my daughter's death? Is that what you're telling me?'

'I'm not saying that won't happen but I'm trying to be honest with you. I know how you must feel. If it was my daughter, I wouldn't feel any different.'

He can't listen any more to what Roberts has to say. He stands up and mumbles something that makes little sense even to himself, hears Roberts encouraging him to stay in touch. But already he knows he won't come back here and as he leaves the station he wants Roberts to phone home and hear his beloved daughter has been diagnosed with cancer, that she's slit her wrists in the bath. Let these things happen and then he'll know how it feels. Let him really know how it feels and then they can talk, maybe find some comfort in what they share. But not until then, not until he knows what this feels like. Not ever.

*

It's great to have a mate and Rob's the best mate he could ever have. He's not what he imagines an uncle should be like – he's more a mate, a real laugh and he's always saying that they have to make up for lost time. He's already been out with him three times – once to the pictures, once to his house and once, a drive in his van to Bangor. He thinks Angela's all right too – maybe a little strange, but he likes the tattoos she showed him. Rob says she's dead on and Rob seems to know a lot of things.

The thing he likes best of all about Rob is that he doesn't seem to notice his weight problem. He's never mentioned it, never stares at him like some people do as if they're weighing him with their eyes. He never stops talking, but you never need to worry about anything he says because he never says anything that's serious or that needs you to think about an answer. The other thing Rob never mentions is Rachel. Maybe it's because he never really knew her; maybe that's the reason he never says her name or refers to what happened.

One night he takes him to see a band parade. Afterwards as it breaks up they sit in the van and eat chips.

'I almost went to Australia once,' Rob says.

'Australia?'

'Yeah, the other side of the world. It was your dad stopped me at the last minute. Talked me out of it like.'

'He didn't want you to go?'

'No, he thought it was better we stuck together. Maybe he was a bit scared of being left on his own. I don't know.'

'Do you wish you'd gone?' he asks.

'Sometimes I think about it, wonder what it would be like. But then if I'd gone to Australia I'd never have met Angela and Corrina.' He crumples the chip papers into a tight ball, takes a slug of Coke and then burps out of the corner of his mouth. 'Sometimes things work out for the best.'

'What would you have done in Australia?' he asks.

'Don't know. Anyway. I didn't have a passport or visa or something and you probably need them to get in.' He scrunches the ball of paper more tightly until it's the size of a tennis ball. 'Maybe some day we could go for a holiday. Do you fancy it, kid?'

'That would be so cool, Rob. Do you think we could really go?'

Rob doesn't answer as he watches a knot of bandsmen filter across the front of the van. Some have taken their tunic jackets off and their white shirts flap in the wind like flags. A green bottle is passed like a baton from hand to hand. One of them comes to the side of the van and knocks on the glass. He's still wearing his plumed beret and as he rests his flute on the sill of the opened window and crouches down beside it, there is a smile on his face.

'All right, Postman Pat?' he says. 'Any letters in your bag?'

'Not tonight, Earl,' Rob answers. 'I'm with my nephew,' he says, indicating him with a jerk of his head. Earl smiles at him but it's the sort of smile he recognises and it makes him squirm a little into his seat.

'Postman Pat and his black and white cat,' he says before walking away from the van.

Rob says nothing for a while then takes another slug from the can, wipes his mouth with the back of his hand then drops the ball of paper out onto the pavement. 'Earl,' he says, pretending to laugh, 'the light's on but no one's in. Know what I mean?' On the way home Rob doesn't say much but as they reach his street he starts to sing:

Postman Pat, Postman Pat
Postman Pat ran over his cat
All the guts were flying
All the kids were crying
Postman Pat, Postman Pat
Postman Pat and his black and white cat.

*

All the women are kind to her. There's lots of hugs and hand-holding and in their morning break they gather round her like children and everyone wants to sit beside her. But their words sift through her consciousness like some fine wind that rustles and stirs only a momentary memory of her old life before everything settles and hardens once more into the concrete shape that feels fixed for ever. She doesn't speak much, tries to get through her first day by concentrating on the work and that alone takes all her energy. It's as if she's forgotten it all, has to pause to remember which cupboards hold which utensils, sometimes has to ask where things are. And through everything runs the feeling that she's separated from her previous self by some gauze or mesh that filters out the things that made her who she was. She tells herself that it's the drugs, tells herself that she's going to stop taking them. Stop them soon so she's able to find something of her old self again. Stop them soon.

The women think it will make her feel better if they

share their own memories of suffering. So as she slices open the bags of frozen chips, Annie comes and helps her, standing close, almost touching her shoulder and her voice is soft and confidential, the voice she uses to pass on important gossip.

'We nearly lost Janine once. It was the worst time of my life. She got knocked down in Templemore Avenue. She just ran out in the road without lookin' and a car clipped her. He swerved at the last moment and that probably saved her life. But she was in a coma and we didn't know whether she was going to make it or not. Touch and go for a while. Worst time in my life.'

There are glittery spangles of ice on the bags. She feels the coldness of it against her skin, thinks of the first time Rachel was old enough to experience snow. She was wearing a red coat and red wellies and a red hat. All trussed up like a parcel. Snug as a bug. Kicking up flurries with her feet. Not quite sure about it. Afterwards she cried because her hands were cold so she had to warm her own at the fire, press Rachel's together as if she was teaching her how to pray, then hold them inside the oven of hers.

'She still has a scar on the back of her head. You can't see it with her hair but it's about two inches long. The doctor said we were lucky she didn't end up with brain damage. It was the worst time of my life, sitting at the bedside waiting for some sign that she was going to pull through.'

They shuffle the chips across the baking trays straight from the bags, then use their hands to space the layer evenly. She doesn't want to hear any more stories about other people's suffering. It can't be shared – they can't share hers, she can't share theirs. If it could, she would give them all the tiniest little sliver of it so that what was left could be borne. But there's no way to do it. As she bends down to slide the trays into the oven, a sudden flare of heat masks her face and she blinks her eyes and wonders why Martin never touches her any more. She doesn't want to do anything – it wouldn't seem right but maybe if he would just touch her or take her hand . . . Why don't the women tell her different stories? Good stories like the miracles in the Bible where Lazarus rises from the dead as if he's only been sleeping, or about the woman going to Christ's tomb and finding the stone rolled away.

So when she starts to pour the soup powder into the canister and Jo is telling her about her first stillborn, she wants only to hear of a child brought back to life with a gentle breath; of death falling away at the touch of a kiss on tiny lips. Let their whispers speak of miracles and reversals, of time wound back to when everything was all right. Let just one of them tell her about such things and she will believe it possible with all her heart.

'There's not a single day I don't think of her. All these years later,' Jo says. 'Sometimes I wonder what she would have looked like?'

The coldness of ice freezing over her make-up, her lips blue-washed, her eyes closed, the little vein on her lid like the scribble of blue ink, livid under the strip lighting. Her best clothes smothered under the sheet. Not a child, not a woman. It was her last chance to touch her hair. Reaching out her shaking hand, pulling it back, frightened of what she would feel.

'What flavour is this soup?' she asks Jo. Suddenly it seems important to know.

'It's supposed to be vegetable but they all look the same. Probably taste the same as well. Don't suppose there's many vegetables get anywhere near it. Put more water in – I think it looks too thick.'

Why does Martin never touch her any more? Sometimes she thinks he's started to blame her and maybe he's right. Someone must be to blame. Things like this don't just happen. The more she thinks about it, the more she thinks that she didn't know her child at all and that's a failing. Not to know your own child or what goes on in her head. And all the time she thought she was such a good mother, it was an illusion and maybe she deserves all of Martin's blame. Sometimes in the bed they're like tight knots on a rope, stretched taut to its edges, entangled only with whatever it is that fills their heads in the moments before sleep.

'How long have we got?' she asks.

'Another twenty minutes before the bell. Though if that new teacher lets her class out early again, they'll be here sooner. How are we doing?'

'It's heating up. Are there enough of those cups?'

'No, I mean you.'

'Fine,' she says. It's the word she mostly uses now, gives it with a quick imitation of a smile. 'Fine, thanks.'

'Maybe not in this world, but some day we'll understand why such things happen. You've got lots of people here to talk to, people who care about you.'

'Twenty minutes? Better get a move on.'

Twenty minutes and the doors of the canteen will be thrown open. Twenty minutes and the whole place will be flooded with children and every one of their faces raw with life and none of them Rachel.

*

He stands at the door of her bedroom and looks in. Just like he's done a thousand times before. Everything is just as she left it. There are still books open on her desk. The only person who comes in now is Alison, to clean the thin sift of dust that seems to drift insistently into the unfamiliar silences and spaces of the room. He doesn't want to, but it has to be done and so after a final moment's hesitation he steps inside and closes the door. He feels like a thief come in the night, an intruder, because everything is redolent with her presence and every step he takes, every movement that disturbs the settled stillness, seems to be an intrusion into her privacy. But he tells himself again that it has to be done and that now there is only him and no one else who can do what needs to be done. So he starts by looking carefully at everything, and then checks the book-rack, his hand tracing the spines of the books, before he moves to the desk-top and lets his gaze take in the open books and the essay she was working on.

He can't see what he needs to find so he starts to look in the drawers of the desk. It's there in the second one, underneath an old scrapbook, a school magazine and writing paper – a thin red-backed address book that he's seen once before when she was writing Christmas cards at the kitchen table. He knows it's foolish but he's started to feel frightened by the thought that somewhere in this room might be the key to a world she lived in and of which they had no knowledge, so he handles the book nervously as suddenly it might open doors that are best kept shut. But he remembers his visit to the police, the postcard on the desk and his anger stirs again as he flicks the pages, trying to match his memory of first names with faces and identities. He copies names and addresses and then searches the school magazine until he finds the class photographs and is able to put faces to the names. Some of them are familiar, others he struggles to remember from the funeral but it's a start and the feeling of doing something carries him and he tells himself that there was no other world than the one they saw every day and that what took her from them was the outreached hand of scum who have to be made to pay.

The first address is only a few minutes' drive away and as a fine spray of rain begins to fall, he sits in the car and looks at the house. There's more money than they have and there is an expensive car in the driveway. He sits for a few moments then walks to the door. The bell chimes loudly in a climbing fanfare of notes, then through the dimpled and coloured panes of glass he sees the shadowy approach of a woman. He shakes away some of the rain from his face as she starts to open the door. At first she doesn't recognise him, her face passive.

'I'm Martin Waring, Rachel's father. Could I speak to Joni, please?'

'Come in, please,' she says, her face suddenly animated and her hands springing into welcoming gestures. She leads him through the hall with its wooden floor and prints on the walls to a room that extends into a conservatory and a view of the garden beyond. 'Please sit down, Mr Waring,' she says directing him to a chair which places his back to the throw of light that invades the room despite the rain.

'I'd like to speak to Joni.'

'Yes, of course. I'll just get her for you,' she says before pausing and turning again towards him. 'I'd just like to say how sorry we all are about Rachel.' She goes to say something else but the words falter and are replaced by a shake of her head.

He hears her footsteps on the wooden floor in the hall and her voice calling to her daughter. There is no reply. His eyes travel round the room, taking in nothing but the overall effect of money and what he knows is considered good taste. It makes him wonder if Rachel was ever ashamed of her home. He couldn't blame her if she was, because in comparison to this it suddenly seems tawdry and threadbare and he can't remember many times when she had girls from school round. Not in the last couple of years at least.

'Joni will be down in a few moments,' she says. 'Could I get you a cup of tea or a drink of something?' she asks. When he declines she sits down in a chair that feels very far from his. 'They're always hidden away in their rooms,' she says, then looks at her hands. 'How is everyone coping? It must be the most terrible time for your family.' He doesn't answer, merely nods his head. 'Joni's taken it very badly. She has a few problems of her own and this has been a real setback for her.'

He looks at her but she doesn't meet his gaze and then she's apologising for how long it's taking for Joni to appear. She asks him again if he'd like a drink and then excuses herself and he hears her feet hurrying on the stairs, the opening and closing of doors and muffled voices. When she returns, she uses the palm of her hand to smooth her hair and stands behind the chair on which she has been sitting.

'Mr Waring, Joni's not feeling well at the moment. Could I get her to ring you later on? If you could tell me what you'd like to speak to her about?'

'I want to speak to Joni,' he says. 'It won't take long.' He anchors himself in the chair, stretches out his hands and tightens his grip on the arms.

She doesn't know what to say at first, whether to argue with him or apologise again but he doesn't help her by speaking and his only movement is the slight splay and drum of his fingers.

'I know you're very upset and you've every right to be, but Joni hasn't been well. As soon as she is, you can talk to her.'

'I'm not upset. But I'm not going until I've spoken to her. I only need ten minutes of your daughter's time.'

She hesitates, kneads the back of the chair with her hands, then leaves the room. As he waits and looks more carefully round the room he tells himself that for all their money and their style, every day he stands closer to more beautiful things than these. Real things, preserved in time and not to be owned through the cheapness of money. And now it's two sets of feet coming down the stairs, the one the lightest echo of the other and when they enter the room she is completely hidden behind her mother.

'Hello Joni,' he says. 'I'm Rachel's father and I need to ask you about a couple of things. It'll only take a few minutes.'

Suddenly she steps from behind her mother's body and he sees her for the first time. Almost as tall as her mother, the same blonde hair, but there's nothing else there. Her face is hollow, and even through her clothes he can see that her body is stick-like, fleshless. Only her eyes are big. He's not sure anymore. Not sure what he's doing there or is going to say.

'I'm sorry,' she says, 'very sorry about Rachel.'

'Thanks.'

'Rachel was a nice girl.'

'Yes, she was. Can we talk about what happened?'

'Joni told the police everything she knows,' her mother says, resting her hand lightly on the raised ridge of her daughter's shoulder.

'It's all right,' she says to her mother, then walks past him like a shadow towards the conservatory. He follows her and the fall of her hair looks brittle and thin. The rain has stopped and outside the garden looks green and quickened into life. Joni sits down on one of the cane chairs and pulls her knees up in front of her. The brightening light washes against her face but seems only to draw out what little colour there is, so only the blue of her eyes is sparked with life. Her mother stands watching but makes no attempt to join them.

'You were one of Rachel's friends?' he asks.

'Yes, not special friends, but friends.'

'And you were with her that night, weren't you?'

'Yes, I was with her,' she says, threading a strand of her hair through her fingers, which look like the thin blades of scissors.

'I need you to tell me the truth now, Joni, and I'll accept the truth whatever it is, but I just need it to be true. You understand?'

She pulls her legs up more tightly and lowers her head towards them so only the blue of her eyes is visible. In the growing flush of light it's difficult to see where the paleness of her skin meets the seam of her hair. He looks at the twigs of her wrists and the tight little knobs of her ankles. The folds of her trousers flap loosely around her legs.

'Had Rachel ever taken drugs before?' he asks, the words shivering in his throat in fear of the answer.

'No, Rachel hadn't ever done it before.'

'Are you sure?'

'I'm sure. It was her first time.'

'And you took a tab too, didn't you?' he asks, trying to keep his voice gentle.

She looks over his shoulder into the garden, lifting her face up over her knees. He notices the ragged edges of her fingernails, the way she's coloured the hollows of her sunken cheeks, which look now like the lifeless dregs in the bottom of a teacup.

'Yes, I took one. The police know I did.'

'Who gave you the tabs? Who gave Rachel hers?'

'We just had them.'

'But they must have come from somewhere.' He leans towards her. 'Tell me where they came from, Joni.'

'One of the girls had them, I don't remember who it was.'

'I need to know Joni,' he says, lowering his voice. Part of him wants to stretch out his hand and grab the stick of her wrist, twist it into the truth. Instead he says, 'It's important. Rachel didn't deserve what happened to her. You can help fix this thing, help put it right.'

She hesitates for a long time, pulls a strand of her hair through the slow splice of her fingers. 'If I say a name, you won't say you got it from me?' He agrees but she makes him swear. Even then she doesn't say the name but sits blinking at the sharp spears of light piercing the glass, before shielding her eyes with the slow salute of a hand.

'Andrea had them. I don't know where she got them.'

He already knows the second name. There are a few more questions he wants to ask but he can sense her mother deciding whether his time is up or not. There's not much time left.

'Why did she take it?' he asks.

'Because we all did, because we thought it would be all right, I think. I don't know why,' she says. 'I'm sorry, really sorry.'

She's crying now. A little smear of light on her cheeks. The tears mean nothing to him. He knows there are things he could say but he has nothing to say to help her and instead stands to go. Her mother comes to comfort her, telling him that it would be best for him to leave and there is a new, insistent strength in her voice. He leaves them without speaking and when he glances back sees her almost hidden in the folds of her mother's arms.

*

Already the first pupils are rushing through the doors to get to the head of the queue, ignoring as always the admonitions of the supervisors to slow down. She's on serving and as the metal lids clatter off the containers, she feels herself tense. The smell of food flurries up round her and for a second she feels as if she's going to be sick but she steels herself against it and stares at the boy who's leaning across the counter to get a better view of the contents of the trays.

'A burger and a half chip,' he says, starting to eat the chips with his fingers as soon as she passes the polystyrene dish to him. The chips are too hot and he blows on them as he puts them in his mouth, then sucks air noisily.

'Stop pushing or you won't get served,' Annie says to the squirming, flopping line.

'He's bunking in! Tell him to get to the back!'

'Take your turn or no one'll get served.'

'A hot dog and a chip butty.'

They hold on to the shoulders of the person in front, lending and borrowing money, shouting to friends, or abuse at enemies behind them in the queue. In the space of a minute the queue takes up one whole side of the canteen and the rising noise has started to fill the hall. She's too hot, the coagulated steam and smells from the food snaking up through her fingers and body before garlanding her face. Her skin feels damp, brushed with the moist and bloated plaque of heat.

'I didn't ask for a burger,' the girl says. There is exasperation in her voice. 'I asked for a slice of pizza and a baked potato.'

'I'm sorry,' she answers, looking for the tongs, as already the next voice shouts its order.

'Stop pushing and it's good manners to say "please",' Annie insists.

'What flavour is the soup? What's the meal of the day?' a boy asks.

She stares at him, the thinness of his voice lost in the flaring blaze of noise as each voice gets subsumed into what feels like a forest fire spreading through every inch of the room. He asks again but it's as if his voice is coming from somewhere beyond her hearing.

'Vegetable,' Annie says, 'and it's on the board!'

'He can't read, him. He's dyslexic. Aren't you, Johnny, son?'

'He could read it if it said everything was free,' Annie answers, serving two girls at once. 'He could read it then all right.'

'I'm not dyslexic,' the boy says. 'I've never even been to extra reading. A burger and chip.'

She serves him and he looks at her as if he's noticing her for the first time. Does he know who she is? Did he see her on television? The food disgusts her, she wants to tip it out of the heated trays and spill it all on the floor, let them wallow in it like pigs at a trough. There is the sound of breaking glass from somewhere in the hall and the usual ironic cheer. It feels as if the noise is irresistible, as if it's tightening round the little firebreak she's tried to clear in her head. She needs a drink of water but there isn't time.

'A salad and pasta, please,' one of the teachers asks. She doesn't recognise her face. Maybe she's a student. She looks very young, hardly more than a child herself.

'Miss, have you marked our test yet?'

'You only did it this morning,' she says, balancing the plate and her purse carefully in her hand.

'It was hard, Miss.'

'Wouldn't be so hard if you paid more attention in class, Brian.'

'A burger and chip.'

'Please,' Annie says.

'A burger and chip, please.'

'Are you all right, Alison?' she asks.

'I'm fine,' she says; straining to hear what the next child has said. Silence was always what was important to her. Tread gently, don't disturb anything. Don't make a fuss in case it breaks her concentration, because it must take enormous concentration to be able to remember all the things she needs to know. And the food had to be simple and clean. Just a round of toast, a piece of fruit or a couple of biscuits. Sitting at her desk, her head bowed over the books, the light almost touching her hair. 'How's it going?' – that's all she would say before she went out the door.

'A soup and a hot dog please.'

She opens the lid of the soup and stirs it with the ladle. It feels thick and heavy but she tries to fill the polystyrene cup carefully so that none spills over the sides.

'And a hot dog, please.'

She nods her head in apology. The rush of the fire roars in her ears. Everything flees before it. It's harder and harder to breathe. Sparks shoot from tree to tree, igniting a strung necklace of flame. There's sudden cracks of noise like guns being shot and as she stares down the hall, she thinks there is nothing she can do to evade the flames' all-consuming path.

*   *   *

There's an unspoken deal with the RE teacher. He sits on the edge of the desk and talks about whatever takes his interest and if they don't interrupt, he doesn't give them work to do. It's the period after lunch and after its exertions most of them are tired, so they make little cushions of their heads and soon the drone of his words is replaced by their own daydreams. The air is heavy and stale, laced with the sharp tang of sweat. Under the shoes of those who have been playing football, little worm casts of grass settle which have freed themselves from the ridges of their identical shoes.

Tom thinks the RE teacher doesn't believe in God because for the last term he has discussed the miracles in the Bible and given scientific explanations for each of them. The Red Sea was parted by an earth tremor; the water that turned into wine merely fermented; the witnesses of the resurrection experienced a collective hallucination. Tom doesn't believe in God either and as he looks round the class he sees only a variety of slumped forms, heads propped in hands, eyes staring at nothing. Under his own desk there is no grass but a little pile of screwed up golden paper like the droppings of a golden sheep. He silently pops the toffee eclairs into his mouth like a trout gulping flies. His tongue rolls and prods them until they bob about his mouth, a boat in a swell. When they are soft and pliable his jaws chomp and masticate them meticulously and all the time his mouth never opens.

In the absence of inspiration the teacher begins to read from the Bible. It's the story of Christ being taken by the Pharisees to the brow of a hill that they might cast him down, and how he passes through their midst as if he is invisible to them. The story interests him and he listens carefully to every word, trying to work it out in his head, to understand how it might be done. Something distracts his concentration. He glances sideways to see Chapman smiling at him. For a stupid, mindless second he goes to smile back and then watches as Chapman contorts his face, screwing his mouth, letting his tongue snake and loll, making his eyes bulge. Then Chapman's smiling and nodding his head at him, enjoying his joke, enjoying his joke about Rachel. He can't look any more so he grips the side of his desk and stares at the teacher, but it doesn't stop him hearing Chapman whisper, 'Fat Boy's sister was a smack-head.'

He thinks of going home, for the briefest second thinks of telling someone, but knows he has to stick it out. Like he always does. He prays to the God he doesn't believe in that he, too, might wear a cloak of invisibility, that he might pass through his tormentors and not be seen, but later in the changing room there is no hiding place. He takes his normal spot which is the peg in the corner closest to the showers, tries to change as quickly as he can after the games period.

'Great tits, Fat Boy,' Rollo says. 'Better than Jordan's.'

'You should be on page three of the *Sun* with tits like that,' Leechy laughs.

'Why don't you borrow your ma's bra?' Rollo asks, flicking the mud from the soles of his boots at him.

He takes even longer than usual to take off his kit in the hope that he'll be able to leave while they're in the showers. He pretends he has a knot in the lace of his boots, keeps his head lowered and doesn't react to anything that's said. As his fingers fiddle with the knots, they're pressing keys in his head so now he's running and his feet are carried on wings. Down the corridors, running, jumping into the arms of the air and never looking back or feeling fear. So let the dogs leap from the shadows, let them snarl and arch their backs ready to spring, because he can blast them with the explosive power in his hands. Give them back their own fear so they can taste it in their mouths.

'Tits, you never told us your sister was a junkie,' Chapman says, suddenly walking towards him. He's just come out of the shower and has a towel wrapped round his waist. The words make the changing room silent. He knows everyone is looking at him. No one is laughing. 'Must run in the family. For you're a bit of a junkie yourself – always shovellin' shit down your throat.'

For the first time he looks up, then takes his boots off and holds them both in his hands. Chapman has stopped and is watching him. The silence is terrible in his ears. He thinks of tiger eyes, the way fire burns in them, knows that he can never be invisible, that there's nowhere he can run.

'Shut your face, Chapman,' he suddenly says in a voice he doesn't recognise as his own, so he's not sure for a second whether it's his or someone else's he hears.

'What did you say, Fat Boy?' Chapman asks, cocking his head to show he needs to hear the answer, that he's doing the decent thing. Giving him the chance to make a public apology, by saying 'nothing'. Maybe if he says it, he'll let it go, make a joke of it.

'I said, shut your face about my sister.' He stands up, still clutching both boots. He doesn't care anymore. He takes off his glasses and puts them in the breast pocket of his blazer. They all know what the gesture means. The room is bleary, smeared featureless – even Chapman's face is soft-focused. He can't see the expression in his eyes, in the silence has to listen for what is going to happen. So before anyone else does, he hears the door of the changing room open and the slapping, squeaking feet of the PE teacher.

'Tom, get yourself into those showers, splash some water round yourself. And the rest of you lot get changed and out of here. There's a first-eleven practice starting in five minutes.' He collects sick-notes from non-changers and a set of school rules given as a punishment, then borrowing someone's newspaper, flicks the pages. 'And Tom, don't be using all the school's hot water on that beautiful body.'

He stands in the showers on his own. In the distance a bell rings. Someone turns off showers but he doesn't move, standing perfectly still as the droplets from the shower heads drip on his body, until the only sound he hears in the changing room is the gurgling of the water as it runs down the great sucking mouth of the drain.

*

Rob's there acting as if he's in charge, as if he's been her lifetime carer. She sits in the chair at the hearth and sometimes her hands pluck at her dress and make throwing movements towards the fire. Although she isn't eating, her mouth moves and sometimes she pushes out the side of her cheek with her tongue. Rob hovers about her like a good angel, slipping a cushion behind her back, at regular intervals kneeling at her feet and squeezing her hand, talking to her all the time.

'Are you all right now, Ma? Your boys are here to look after you now. We'll see they take good care of you.'

He watches her eyes as she looks at Rob and smiles, but it's the same smile she uses for everyone. She nods her head at him while her skittering hands pluck at invisible threads and throw them in the fire. There are still little smuts in her hair and one on her cheekbone. The smell of smoke wreaths the whole house even though he's opened every window.

'It's for the best, Martin,' Pat says. 'It's a miracle she didn't burn the whole place down and herself with it.'

'It's lucky you looked in when you did. If those kitchen curtains had caught and it'd got a hold, I don't know what would have happened.'

'Is there any sign of the ambulance?' Rob asks. 'It wouldn't take it to be a matter of life or death.'

'They're goin' to check her out, then give her an assessment, the doctor says,' he tells Pat, even though he's told her already.

'It's for the best, she couldn't go on like this. The doctor told me he didn't think she'd be coming back. She's gone down pretty quick over these last few months.'

Rob kneels at his mother's feet again. 'It'll be all right now, Ma, they're goin' to take good care of you.' He tries to remove the smut from her cheek with his finger but only smears it across her skin. Pat comes and wipes it clean with a tissue. 'We'll see you get the very best of everything,' Rob tells her. Then while still kneeling he looks up at them. 'It should never have got to this. She could have killed herself. I knew something would happen. I told you Martin, you know I did. Knew it for sure, didn't I?'

'That's right, Rob, you did. You told me.'

'Where's my bag?' she suddenly asks, starting to get out of the chair.

'I'll get it for you, you stay there,' Rob says.

'What ambulance?'

'It's just to give you a wee check-up, see if the smoke got in your lungs,' Pat tries to assure her, as she hands her the bag.

'What smoke?' she asks. 'Has somebody been smoking? They're not allowed to.' She fumbles in the bag until she finds her purse, then takes some pound coins from it and hands them to Rob. 'For your birthday, Martin. I nearly forgot.'

Seeing his confusion, he says, 'Take them, Rob.'

Putting them in his pocket, Rob goes back to the window and looks for the ambulance. 'Where is it?' he asks, his voice edged with anger. 'If she was suffering from smoke inhalation or a heart attack it'd be a right mess by now. Did they get the right address?' he asks.

'They'll be here soon, Rob, why don't you go to the end of the street, make sure they know where to come?'

Rob nods and hurries outside. He goes to the chair opposite hers and sits down. She gives him the same smile she gave to Rob.

'I almost forgot about your birthday,' she says, looking in her purse again. 'I have some money for you here, you can buy yourself something.'

'You've already given it to me. My birthday's not every day.'

'I'll put the kettle on,' Pat says, disappearing into the kitchen.

He watches his mother's eyes start to dart about the room, her hands grow more animated, more desperate in their plucking and now she's looking at him, almost looking through him. When she speaks her voice has dropped to a whisper.

'You're not allowed to smoke,' she says, 'but I won't tell him. I won't tell him you've been smoking.'

The words course through his being, freezing every-where they touch. He tries to calm the rush of his heart, stop himself stepping through the door of the past. It's a while before he can bring himself to speak.

'You'll be better off out of here,' he tells her. Then watching her eyes, says, 'You should have left long ago.'

In the kitchen he hears the spurt of water and the kettle being filled, and because there is a voice in his head telling him that he'll never see her again, he whispers, 'You should have left years ago. Should have packed a bag and gone. Taken us with you. Why did you never do it?' She looks at him but it's as if there's a fine film coating her eyes through which she no longer sees anything as it really is. She reaches for her handbag again, searches intently for something, then takes a comb out and runs it through her hair. Her tongue is pressing against her cheek again, probing and pushing it. The kettle comes to the boil, there is the rattle of the teapot lid.

They should be in bed but they're too excited to sleep. Rob keeps asking how long it is until the morning. They've only been sent to bed an hour ago and in the kitchen they can hear her working, getting the turkey ready for cooking. It's just been delivered to the door, the voice of the butcher rumbling in the hall as he wishes her Happy Christmas. Rob wants to see it, keeps on asking him to come with him and sneak a look. They know he's out of the house, that there's no chance of him coming back until his drinking money is spent, so eventually they get out of their beds. With ex-aggerated slowness and delicacy, their extended spider arms and legs feel their way down the stairs. There is the smell of bacon being cooked and the sizzling kitchen is already veiled in steam and heat. Rob pushes him forward and he stumbles. She turns her head, sees them freeze-frame but only smiles and they know it's all right, so they walk towards her. A pot containing more potatoes than he's ever seen is cooking on the ring. She splashes salt on the bubbling foaming water. But now they only have eyes for the turkey. It's huge, its flaccid, goosebumped skin humped loosely on a giant dish, daring them to touch it. Rob goes first, gently pressing his finger into it, then squirming away with revulsion. He goes next, then jerks his hand away with fear and pleasure. She laughs at them, reminds them that they're supposed to be sleeping but he can tell that she's pleased they're there. She gives them little nibbles of the bacon and after they eat it they wipe their greasy fingers on their green paisley pyjamas. But it's not over yet because she lifts the plate with the turkey on it and advances towards them, stepping slowly, her eyes wide with pretend menace. They squeal and walk backwards but she keeps coming and then they take to their heels and she chases them down the hall. They do it again and again, until she tells them that it's enough and the turkey has to go in the oven. Afterwards as they lie in bed their hearts pump like pistons and then as calm slowly claims them, he tries to follow her movements from the noise she makes, until he slips into a soft and easy sleep.

He takes the comb from her hand and combs her hair, removing the filament of smut. Her hair feels wiry, spots of black spangling the grey like a monochrome photograph. She holds her handbag on her lap and sits as if he does this every day. It was the only time he can remember when there was fun in fear.

'Who was smoking?' she asks. 'Tell them the man says they're not allowed to smoke.'

'I'll tell them,' he says.

'Takin' up hairdressing Martin?' Pat asks.

'Gettin' the smoke out of her hair,' he says, slipping the comb back into her bag and taking the cup of tea she hands him.

'I've had a word,' Rob says as he leads the ambulance men into the room. 'It should be all right now – I've explained everything.'

'That's good, Rob,' he says as one of the paramedics kneels at his mother's feet. His face seems familiar but he can't place him and then suddenly he is shaken by the thought that perhaps he was one of the crew who carried Rachel to the hospital.

'So you've had a bit of a fire, luv,' he says, placing his hand on hers.

'You're not allowed to smoke,' she says. 'Someone's been smoking.'

'Very bad habit, smoking. Gave it up years ago myself. Do you think you can stand up?'

She smiles back at him but doesn't reply.

'We'll help her,' Rob says. 'Won't we, Ma?'

'No need,' the paramedic says. 'Geordie, get the chair. We'll soon have you out of here, luv, get you to hospital for a wee check-over. Soon have you as right as rain.'

He was told she was dead when she arrived at the hospital. Perhaps he was with her during the final moments. Maybe this man shared her last living moments. Maybe she said something to him. He wants to blurt out his questions but stifles them and turns his head away for a second.

'You've been having a fire, luv,' the paramedic says. 'And it's not even the Twelfth of July.' Then, turning to them, asks 'Did she inhale much of the smoke?'

'No, I don't think so,' Rob answers, 'we got her just in time.'

Pat looks at Rob and then at him but he avoids her gaze. Geordie returns with a wheelchair and working together they slowly lift her into it while Rob hovers around them as if he's directing the operation.

'Careful now,' he says, walking backwards and holding the door wide.

Maybe if they'd got there quicker they could have saved her. Did they even understand what was wrong with her? Maybe she was just another young girl who had drunk too much, the type they must see every night of the week. Did she say anything? He wants to ask but it's too late now as Rob climbs into the ambulance and the doors are banged shut. As it drives off he thinks he sees a face pressed to the darkened window but isn't sure if it's his mother's or Rob's, or just the way the light slants and skirmishes against the glass.

*

He's never been in an ambulance before, so he waves to Marty to let him know that he's with Ma and everything's all right now because he's there to look after her. As they drive away he thinks his brother has started to look old and as if he doesn't know all the things he thought he did. It's to do with Rachel and he's sorry about that but maybe it's good for him to realise that he doesn't know everything.

'All right, Ma?' he asks. 'Rob's here with you now. Rob's here to look after you.' He watches her eyes but they don't look at him and his words, finding no one to receive them, filter back to him in the silence. None of them ever listened to him – he has a whole storehouse full of his unheard words. Sometimes at night in the spaces before sleep or when he walks on his own, high in the fields above the estate, they sift out from where they're stored and drift about his head like thistledown blown on the frittery worry of the wind.

'All right, Ma?' he asks and touches the sleeve of her coat. 'I'm here to see you're looked after proper.'

Marty, big man Marty, who always thought he knew best, didn't even know how to look after his own mother.

166

Anyone could see that she was going to hurt herself. Anyone with half a brain could see that it would end in a mess. Hadn't he warned Marty only five minutes before it happened? It should never have come to this and if Marty's supposed to be looking after things then he's making a right mess of it. But that was always the trouble with Marty. Always the bloody expert even when he knew frig all and what he doesn't realise, is that he's not the Rob he once was. He's not some snivelly kid, frightened of every shadow that flits across his face. He can work things out in his head for himself, doesn't have to be told everything like he's some kind of idiot. Didn't he see what was going to happen to Ma? Didn't he tell Marty before it happened? No one can say he didn't. And Marty doesn't like that, doesn't like someone else knowing more things than him.

Like the smicks. 'You couldn't catch a cold,' he'd said. But up in Orangefield where the thin little river flowed under the bridge and round the boundary of the park, he'd proved his brother wrong. In his bare feet, the green streamers of slime and silt pushing up between his toes, he's shown him what he could catch. Sticklebacks, dark darts of smicks, as quick as the blink of his eye, quivering into the shadowed edges of stones beyond the stretch of his arm. Like they knew you were coming, like they read your thoughts before you thought them. And then getting so close that one brushed the tips of his fingers.

Her eyes are slow, moving round the ambulance as if she's not sure where she is, as if she's looking to make herself remember. 'All right, Ma? Not long now,' he says but she looks at him only for a second before her eyes start their slow trawl again. Couldn't catch a cold. So what did mighty Marty know about fishing? He wanted him to be there to see it, knew he wouldn't believe him unless he was able to see it for himself. He finds two empty paint tins and it doesn't matter that his clothes are splashed, or his feet are cold as he scoops the smicks up in one tin, then transfers them to the other. Now it's as if they're begging him to catch them and sometimes he catches two at a time and the sun is warm on the back of his neck even though his clothes are wet and his feet beg to be taken out of the water.

'We'll soon be there, Ma,' he says. She was the first to see them when he arrived back in the yard, the metal wire of the full cans cutting red weals into his palms. 'What are you going to do with them?' she'd asked and then he didn't know what to say except 'Show them to Marty.' But she'd given him a plastic bucket and he'd poured the catch in, then sat and watched them swimming. Sat there until Marty came home and saw them. Saw every last one of them swimming in the yellow bucket.

'All right, Ma?'

She looks at him for the first time.

'I haven't given you anything for your birthday, Martin,' she says and her hands start to pluck at her bag.

*

It's clear his visit has been expected. Andrea's father stands in the doorway of his expensive house, making himself big, inflating his existing obesity with an additional puff of stiff determination. He blocks any view of the house inside and his hands rest on both sides of the door frame, a barrier to potential entry.

'Andrea's not here,' he says without any introductions. 'She's staying with her aunt at the moment.'

'Can you give me the address, Mr Finlay?' he asks.

'No, I can't do that. Listen, I know how you must be

feeling but it's not a good idea to talk to Andrea right now. She's already spoken to the police and she'll say everything she has to say at the inquest. Now it's best if you leave it at that for the moment.'

'Fair enough,' he says, as if to go, then turns back and with his left arm pushes Finlay back against his door, brushes past him and up the hall. The door hammers against the wall, vibrating in piercing tandem with Finlay's shouts.

'Here, you can't barge in here like this! Leave right now or I'll call the police!' His wife comes out of the kitchen, a phone in her hand. 'Will I call them, Terry?' Her finger is poised over the numbers, stiff and frozen, in the air, like an icicle waiting to melt. She is as small and thin as he is large. She wears a light-blue tracksuit and there is a lattice of gold at her throat and dangling from her wrist.

'Go ahead,' he tells them. 'Go ahead and I'll tell them that Andrea was the one who gave the girls the drugs. That she's the one who handed them out.' He watches them look at each other, sees the hesitation in their eyes. 'So go ahead if you want.'

'What do you want with Andrea?' Finlay asks.

'Andrea's never taken drugs before. She swore to us this was her first time,' his wife insists. 'And we're really, really sorry about what happened to Rachel.'

'It could have been any one of them,' Finlay says.

'But it wasn't, was it? It was Rachel. It was my daughter.'

'What do you want with Andrea?' Finlay asks again.

'I need to talk to her, ask her about where the drugs came from.'

'I know you've had a terrible loss – we feel for you, we really do and you've every right to be angry,' Mrs Finlay says, 'but will it make any difference to anything where they got the drugs, when according to Andrea there's people dealing them on just about every street corner?'

'Yes, it'll make a difference to me,' he answers, looking round the room for any trace of Andrea but there's only the sweep of leather and wooden floors and colours that are supposed to be cool and easy to the eye. 'And you're right, I am angry, so tell me now if she's here or not.'

'You need to go,' Finlay says, trying to impose himself again on the situation.

He looks at him, tries to subdue a growing desire to punch him in the sagging folds of his stomach, to cut off his supply of air, to silence the stupid words that come out of his mouth. To choke her with the gold hanging from her neck because he thinks it is their money that helped kill his daughter.

'I'll go as soon as I've spoken to her. It'll only take a few minutes.'

'But she's not here,' her mother insists. 'He was telling you the truth – she's staying with her aunt for the present.'

'Is that right?' he asks. 'Then I'd better go.' He can feel their relief at his words as he walks back down the hall but when he reaches the front door he suddenly turns and makes for the stairs.

'You can't go up there!' Finlay shouts. 'Jean, call the police! Tell them we've an intruder.'

He climbs the stairs, two at a time, his anger leaving him indifferent to the beep of phone numbers being pressed, pushes open the doors of rooms until he reaches one which is obviously her room. She's not there. He has to peer into it – the curtains are closed. The walls are dark purple and covered with posters – the type that Rachel has, but the room is different, too. There's no desk or books, nothing that makes the room anything more than somewhere to sleep and it's a mess, with clothes strewn everywhere, including the floor, as if simply dropped at the point where they were discarded. It makes him pleased for a second when he compares it to Rachel's room, knows that for all their money they're nothing, nothing at all. And then he's gone, turning only once to look back at the house before he spits on the pavement, trying to expel what lingers like a bad taste in his throat.

The next day Roberts calls to see him at home. Alison thinks he's come with news about the case but when she calls to the living room to announce his arrival, there is no excitement or expectancy in her voice. It's started to annoy him that she seems to have no interest in finding out who supplied the stuff, or anything to do with what happened. She doesn't even stay as Roberts picks the room's most comfortable seat but instead makes the excuse of getting tea to take herself off to the kitchen.

'So you've some news for us?' he asks, not bothering to hide the cynicism in his voice.

'You know why I'm here, Martin.'

'Mr and Mrs Finlay squealing down the phone then?'

'That's right. Not making a formal complaint or anything, very understanding of what you're going through but concerned that you don't upset Andrea, or try to contact her.'

'Upset her? Do you not think it's a bit late for upset?'

'Like all the girls, apparently she's been very fragile since . . .' He pauses and skims his gaze round the room, but doesn't finish the sentence.

'She gave the drugs to the girls, she was the one who passed them on,' he says as if he's playing his trump card and locks his stare on Roberts' face.

'You don't know that, Martin.' His face reveals no surprise or shimmer of shock.

'I know it because it's true.'

'It may be true but none of the girls are going to come out and say that. Right now they all want an equal share of the blame. Maybe they need it to feel better.'

'I don't care about them feeling better. What they feel is of no interest to me. And if you really want to know, I think you seem to be more concerned about the girls and their families than you do about this one.'

'That's not true – you know it isn't true.'

'From where I'm sitting it looks true to me.'

'From where you're sitting right now, Martin, nothing much in the world must look fair or right. I understand that.'

'How can you understand that?' he asks, desperate to throw off whatever lifeline of sympathy is going to be thrown to him because right now he feels as if he's drowning and he doesn't want either the illusion or reality of escape. 'How can you understand that, when you haven't lost a daughter to the scum who deal this shit?'

'No, you're right, I haven't lost a daughter but I have lost people who were close to me, people I cared about. For what it's worth, I've lost a guy I went through training with – best man at my wedding. He'd just come off duty, was collecting his daughter's birthday bicycle. They shot him three times in the head. We got the guy who did it – a cold vicious bastard who killed a lot of people – managed to pin it on him in court.' He pauses, looks at his feet for a second then looks him in the eye. 'They let him out of the Maze a year ago with all the others. I see him from time to time – he always makes sure to smile and wave, asks me how I'm doing. You know how that feels, Martin?'

He doesn't answer, just nods his head.

'And I'll tell you something else. They say he's going to put a suit on soon, become a politician, make decisions about how the country should be run.'

'So what are you going to do about it?' he asks.

'What am I going to do about it?' Roberts asks. 'There's sod all I can do about it, Martin, except do what everyone else with any sense is doing – take their package and get out.'

'So maybe you're retired already. Maybe this doesn't matter to you any more,' he says. He is full to the neck with other people's consoling stories of suffering. He is full to the gills with their insistence that they understand. 'You couldn't pin Omagh on anyone – twenty-nine people and two unborn babies – so what's one seventeen-year-old girl?'

'I'm not retired until the day I leave. And until that day comes I'll be doing everything to bring this case to a close. Believe me in that.'

Roberts is standing up when she enters with the tea. She can see that he's angry, knows that it must be caused by something Martin has said. She holds out the cup for him to take and he hesitates for a second as if he's thinking of going, before he takes it and resumes his seat.

'How are you doing?' he asks her. His voice is flat but contains no trace of anger.

'Fine,' she says, offering him a plate of biscuits. He takes his time before making his choice.

'That's good,' he says, balancing the biscuit on the saucer. Silence settles for a few moments. 'So how're you doing?' he asks her again.

'Fine,' she repeats. The cup looks small in his large

hands. She worries that the biscuit might be soft, can't remember how long they've had them. The fridge and cupboards are half-empty – she'll have to do a proper shop soon, try to get back into some rhythm. They can't go on like this, living from day to day, hand to mouth, running out to the shop at the last minute for things they need. There isn't any fresh fruit in the house, the toothpaste has been squeezed completely flat. She thinks of Rachel's yoghurts in the fridge. Maybe it's time to try once more to re-enter the round of their lives and just maybe if she can clutch those old rhythms, their mechanical routines and rituals will help deaden what she feels. And she's going to stop the drugs soon because she doesn't think they help any more, only make her feel the same things in different ways.

'So you're back at work then?' Roberts asks.

'Yes, I've gone back.'

'So how's it going?

'Fine,' she says, offering him another biscuit.

'Have to watch the waistline,' he says, 'before it gets too late. Someone told me that in Turkey they say a man without a stomach is like a house without a porch.'

'Where's Joan?' she asks. There is a little sprinkle of crumbs on his lapel.

'Joan's in Tenerife. On holiday,' Martin answers. 'I told you that.'

'She'll be back next week,' Roberts says, placing his cup and saucer on the hearth.

'That's good,' she says. She remembers Joan's hair and perfect make-up, the shine of her nails and her polished shoes. She wonders what it feels like to have the heat of the sun on your skin, to have your body brushed with oil, to swim in a warm sea. She lets her hand trace the line of her own hair. She thinks she'll get it cut soon. Better to keep it as short as possible, easier to keep clean. Her fingers start to comb it but she stops as she imagines someone else touching it and feeling nothing but the thick tangle of grease and food. She pulls her hand away as if it's been burnt.

'I'd better be going now,' Roberts says, standing up. Martin stays seated and doesn't look at him or say anything.

'Fine,' she says, standing up too. 'Fine,' she says again, trying to remember how to smile. As Roberts moves to the door she watches the thin spray of crumbs fall silently to the floor. She wonders again if the biscuit was soft. Outside he pauses at the gate to say something to her but she doesn't register the words and in her head starts to make a list of what it is she needs to buy but when she tries to repeat it to herself, can't remember the items with which she started.

*

He's watched the house for three nights in a row. There's no sign of her. Then he goes round on his afternoon off work and just when he's started to think the Finlays were telling the truth about her going to stay somewhere else, he sees her come out of the driveway and head off down the tree-lined avenue. He follows her in the car at a safe distance. She looks older, heavier than he imagined. She's dressed in a hooded top and jeans and once, as she walks, she pauses to put a mobile phone to her ear. He drives by, then pulls the car to the kerb and gets out.

'Hello Andrea,' he says, 'it's time to talk.' He sees the panic in her eyes, the frantic internal debate about whether she should turn and run. 'There's no point running away like a child – I'll only come after you. Get in the car and we'll talk.'

She stands perfectly still, her body stiff and rigid, the mobile phone held out from her body at waist height, as if it's a gun she's been ordered to drop. 'I've been told I'm not to talk to you,' she says, her voice trying to hide its uncertainty.

'And you always do what you've been told?' he asks. 'Get in the car – I'm not goin' to hurt you. I just want to talk.' She doesn't move; still weighing up her options, her eyes starting to skitter about in search of possible escape routes. He doesn't move either because he knows that a sudden movement will panic her into flight. 'I just want to talk,' he repeats. 'We can just sit here in the car – we don't have to go anywhere.'

She looks at the mobile phone, then puts it in her pocket. Her top lip bites the bottom one. She still isn't sure. If he moved quickly he could grab her by the hood of her top and drag her but he tries talking to her again.

'I'm not goin' to hurt you. I just need to talk, that's all,' he says, trying to keep his voice neutral, drained of any trace of threat.

'I'm really, really sorry about Rachel!' she says, bursting into a high-pitched, staccato sob. 'Really, really sorry. We didn't think anything like this would ever happen. We never, never meant for anyone to get hurt.'

'I know that,' he lies. He'll say anything to get her in the car, to have his chance to talk. He takes a step backwards to show that the choice is hers. She's holding her hands to her eyes as if to staunch her tears but in them he sees, too, the constant calculation of what she could do to get away from him. He holds his arm out towards the car in a final silent invitation. She puts her fingers to her lips, plays with the zip of her top and then walks round the back of the car and gets in the passenger door.

As soon as she gets in he starts the engine and drives off, ignoring her protest. 'We'll just park round the corner,' he says to reassure her, trying to calm her rising apprehension. 'Just a couple of minutes and then we'll talk.' He drives into the nearby shopping centre and parks as far away from the other cars as he can.

'So you're Andrea,' he says, hardly wanting to look at her.

'We never meant any harm to come to Rachel,' she says. 'It could have happened to any one of us. It could have been me.' He doesn't answer but stares at the recycling banks with their different colours and instructions. 'Honest, Mr Waring, honest to God, we never thought this would happen.' But already he knows there is nothing that is honest in her. He sees it in the flick of her hair, her spew of childish sincerity, the controlled shake in her voice. He grips the wheel with both hands, hunching himself over it. 'We all loved Rachel, we all thought she was great. Really smart and good fun too.' He watches a woman post a tatty bundle of old newspapers into one of the containers. One of them will carry his child's photograph, her story.

'You're the one who gave the other girls the tabs,' he says, still not looking at her.

'No, I didn't!' she says, her voice rising into sharp peaks of indignation and hurt. 'I swear to God I didn't. Ask anybody, they'll tell you the same.'

'I have asked,' he says.

'It wasn't me, it definitely wasn't me. I swear it.'

There is the clank of glass bottles being tipped into their container. He can't bear her voice, the stink of her perfume, her sitting so close to him. He winds down his window as if somehow that might help him escape the terrible totality of her. He's made a mistake, been foolish to think that the meeting will bring him closer to anything other than more of his anger. He wants her to go but he gives it one last try.

'So if it wasn't you, then where did the stuff come from?'

'We all got them, it wasn't one person. We all did it.'

'And Rachel?'

'She was there with everyone.'

'And the drugs? They didn't drop out of the sky, they didn't just appear in your hand. Where did they come from?'

She hesitates, slips into her little-girl-crying voice, pouring her supposed remorse all over him. 'It was just some guy who was at the club – I don't know his name or anything.'

'You don't know his name?'

'I swear, I don't know his name. I only saw him the once.'

'What did he look like?'

'I'm not sure, I'm confused when I try to remember it.'

'Remember!' he shouts, suddenly banging the steering wheel and looking at her for the first time. His voice is fierce, breaking like a wave against the confines of the car, his sudden spray of breath misting the glass.

'Young, maybe twenty, about your height, short black hair,' she says, the words tumbling out. Only fear cutting through to her quick, only fear reaching something closer to truth. 'Blue eyes, grey Adidas top, didn't say much. We only saw him for a few moments. He was nervous, jumpy. That's all, honest, that's all I remember.'

He wants to stretch out his hand, grab her by the throat, let her know what real fear feels like. He wants to put his hand in the fall of her hair and turn it into a slowly tightening knot. But she's lucky because as strong as his desire is to hurt her, his feeling of repugnance at the thought of having to touch her is even greater and throbs inside his head and slimes the lining of his throat. He winds the window lower.

'Get out of the car,' he says, so low that she doesn't hear what he's said. He says it again, 'Get out of the fuckin' car.' She goes to say something but he silences the words by holding his hand in front of the side of his face like a shield and then all he hears is her fumbling for the handle and the door clunking shut.

*

He's giving it one last try, narrowing and squinting his eyes into the sharpness of razor blades, shrinking his body to nothing but the merest vibration of space. Trying to be invisible. Moving like a shadow across the buildings, leaving nothing in his wake but a stir of the air. But there's something inside him that he can't shrink or diminish and it's pressing against his head, trying to burst out into words. He feels the weight of it in every step, clogging his breathing and slowing his journey – it's the fury he feels at himself for what he's done, for answering back, for not being able to take a joke, for not bending when the wind blows. He can't hold it in any longer and he curses himself with the litany of his names. Fat Boy, Tits, Fatboy Slim, Willie the Whale, Cheesy, Flubber – on and on and when he runs out of names he invents his own, stringing them together like beads on the thread of his anger. He spits out the words and the anger slows him down, dissipating his invisibility, pulling at the edges of the cloak he's draped about himself. It's falling off his shoulders, dropping off him like leaves off a winter's tree. He passes two boys who look at him, who see him. He opens his eyes and blinks as

179

if he's been swimming under water. It hasn't worked – there are no miracles in this world.

He stops at the corner of the science building and lets his hand feel the comfort of the pitted, flaking brick, then digs out a tiny bit with his thumb. In the buildings and tombs there are always doors, choices to be made, obstacles to be crossed. Maybe now if he can only find the right door he can break through to where he wants to be. If he were to go right home and get his school books out and begin to study really hard then he could be clever, pass all his examinations and do what Rachel did. He could follow in her footsteps and some of what his parents felt for her could be given to him. And if he's going to take that road then they could find another school for him, transfer him out of this place. One day he'd be here, his name on the roll and then the next an empty desk and only silence when it's called at registration. A clean break and a new start, where all that people would know him as would be his name, a school where everyone wears neat uniforms and does their work and goes home.

'Tom! Tom!' Andrews calls, tugging him by the sleeve. He tries to shrug off the intrusion but the smallest boy in the class keeps tugging; only his eyes are big, his voice sing-songy like a bird's. 'They're waitin' for you at the gates. Don't go that way, clear off home through the park. Chapman says he's goin' beat the shite out of you.'

He pushes the boy's small hand from his sleeve. He wanted to be invisible, to have no body so now this insistent touch is bitter in its disappointment. 'Let go,' he tells him.

'They're goin' to give you a kickin'. Frig off home the other way before they see you,' Andrews urges.

He should be grateful for his help but something

despises it, doesn't want shared membership of this club. 'Let bloody go, Tich,' he says. 'And mind your own business, will ya?' He sees the hurt in the boy's eyes and it pleases him that the hurt is spread around a little. He watches Andrews – Handy Andy, pocket-size – slip away, fading away from his consciousness as other images of Chapman rush in and take his place. Everything inside him feels as if it's collapsing, like a tent where the poles have been lowered to allow it to wallow slowly to the ground. He feels weighted and stalled, as if his feet have become great inert blocks and even though he tries to conjure up memories of the skaters, their bulked-up bodies balanced on the fluid, flowing lightness of their skates, there is only this growing sense of paralysis. And he's trapped now in the closing net of his memory, of fights he's seen – sudden convulsive frenzies of fist and head, or a flurry of feet – fights where there are no rules and the only ending is the arbitrary but requisite infliction of pain and the spilling of a seemly amount of blood. He wonders what will appease Chapman, what will atone for his crime and suddenly he feels alone and very frightened. He looks around for Andrews, feels sorry for how he treated him, but sees only the empty playground, where inky smudges of crows blot the concrete as they scavenge the discarded crusts of sandwiches and peck at crisp packets.

Maybe this is the time to tell someone, to go back inside and find the first face that looks friendly and let it all spill out. To sit in the counselling room with its cheery little posters and slogans – 'Big shots are only little shots who try harder', 'Best friends come in all shapes and sizes', 'Be a friend to make a friend' – and try to explain it all. But then there'll be the who and when and where, the names of witnesses and he'll have to sit and speak his names in front of someone who'll nod and disguise their disgust at him with sympathy. He thinks again of his names, tells himself that they're like badges he's been given to wear, that they don't mean anything, that they're funny really and that he'd be crazy, a total and utter dick to give them up and exchange them for a new set. He can hear them now, the same ones he's heard given to others who go down this road – Tout, Snitch, Supergrass, Blabber Bake, Squealer – and if he has to choose, and this is the moment he has to do it, then he'll keep his own badges, rather than wear these new ones.

He tries to stifle his loosening fear by telling himself that it'll probably be over in a matter of minutes, that he doesn't represent a worthy opponent to Chapman. That he might just make a joke of it, clown around with him a little, be content with a few slaps or spilling out his bag. He's not going to fight so there won't really be any point to it – it'll all be a stupid waste of time, a little circus act of laughter. He might even clown round a little, make them laugh by being ridiculous or mock heroic. If he could do it well, make them laugh, they might even think he was all right, let him be one of them; and even if it's worse but he shows he can take it, then just maybe they'll respect him, think he's finally paid the admission price.

He forces himself out of the paralysis threatening to trap him and starts to hurry through the gates and along the road to home. It's even possible that Andrews got it wrong – always chirping too loudly, wanting to be someone by being loud – and that by now they're on their way home or shoplifting in the centre, or doing one of a hundred other things. His feet start to scurry and skip, his bag slapping against his back in syncopated rhythm and he can smell his own sweat, feel the fire of his feet. He scrunches his glasses repeatedly with his nose and as he hurries, little smudges of mist start to smear and bevel the lenses. His tongue feels thick and leathery and he starts to convince himself that the fear swilling about his stomach is nothing but hunger and imagines what he'll eat to fill it when he gets home. And there is Lara, too, waiting for him, desperate for the touch of his hands. So the pained awkwardness of this hurry, the breathless tightness in his chest will soon be replaced by the lithe speed of her limbs, the wingless jumps across chasms, the streamlined dives into water and the only sound needed will be those little puffs of breath, half pain, half pleasure, as her sure feet find their next temporary resting place. He hurries on, for a moment travelling on the slipstream of her image and his hands drop to the holsters of his pockets.

'Fuckin' marathon man,' Chapman says. 'What's the hurry, Fat Boy?' They're standing at the railings of the park, behind a van and in the penumbral shadows of the overhanging trees, where their black-blazered thinness makes them almost bars in the railings. He lets his hands slip into his pockets but finds nothing but emptiness.

'Trying to put a hole in the pavement?' Rollo asks, his hand caressing the top spike of the railing.

'You need to get a sports bra, Fat Boy,' Leechy says, his face full of pretend sincerity as if he's offering a friend advice.

'And a nappy because you're shitting yourself now,' Chapman says, stepping off the railings. 'So all of a sudden you're gettin' lippy, Fat Boy, and just because somebody mentioned that your sister was a druggie.' He comes closer to him and pulls his lapel. 'And it's not as if it isn't the truth, is it Fat Boy?'

He doesn't answer but stares at a point in the distance

and tells himself that he's not worthy of Chapman's anger, that in the face of his passive silence Chapman will soon get bored and the three of them will melt away. But Chapman tugs his lapel again and asks 'She was a junkie wasn't she? Couldn't handle the stuff.' Still he doesn't answer and then he slaps him hard on the cheek with his open palm. 'Wasn't she?'

'Yes,' he says, forcing himself not to place his hand on the stinging sear of his skin. Rollo takes his bag off his shoulder and starts to rifle though it.

'That's right, she was,' Chapman says. 'A sad smackhead.' Then as a car goes past, he drapes an arm over his shoulder and says, 'All right, mate?' before turning it into a fist-closed thump when he car has gone. 'And she was supposed to be a real brainbox. Doesn't sound such a smart arse to me.'

'Livin' with you, Fat Boy, probably put her head away,' Rollo says but he still looks only at Chapman and sees that he's not laughing and there's a narrowing of his eyes as if he's scrutinising him and he knows that he's deciding where to hurt him and he wonders why he hates him so much. There are fat flakes of rust blistering on the railings. He wants to peel them off with his fingers, see what's underneath, and then he tells himself that if it's personal he must deserve it for something he's done, something he is.

*

After she gets out of the car he sits a while with the window down, trying to sift out her presence. He turns on the radio but the music is too loud and hurts his head. Only a few people visit the recycling banks and he thinks no one looks at him or notices his presence because they're so intent on what they're doing for the world, concentrating on their different parcels and getting them in the right place. He wonders what becomes of the things they leave, what journeys they go on and then he doesn't know where to go or what to do. The car feels cold and after a while he thinks of Tom and decides to collect him at the end of school, surprise him with a lift home, even talk to him about things, how things are going. He's neglected him, hasn't spoken more than a dozen words to him in the last week, needs to give him more. But why does he always find it so hard?

When he gets to the school he's just missed the final bell and only a few stragglers are lingering at the gates or waiting for lifts, so he follows Tom's path home, scanning the footpath for him. At first he doesn't see the group under the trees until a bag being tossed in the air catches his eye and then he sees him. He's with his mates. He almost drives on – if he's with his mates let him be, he gets little enough company. Didn't even know he had mates. Something about the tight huddle of bodies and the overhanging branches of the trees makes him forget it's the wrong time of the year and for a second he imagines they're playing conkers. A boys' game. But as an arm swings down he gets a closer and clearer view and in seconds he's braking hard and is out of the car. Rollo sees him first and tries to run but he grabs his collar and throws him against the side of a van, his back and then his head thudding hollowly against its side panel. Leechy has already gone, his black-soled trainers weaving in and out of the parked cars and the traffic. Chapman alone doesn't move or flinch, but arranges his blazer as if he's just noticed it's untidy. With an almost gentle press of his palm, he pushes Tom back out of his face just as if he's accidentally stood on his toes.

'You all right?' he asks his son as he sees the red weal on the side of his face for the first time.

'I'm all right,' Tom says, pushing his glasses on his nose and blowing a stream of breath like he's just finished a race. But he doesn't look at him, staring at the pavement as if searching for something he's dropped. When he goes to touch him lightly, he shrugs it off and tells him again that he's all right. Behind them there is a sudden burst of movement and the slap of Rollo's feet on the pavement as he, too, takes his chance to run.

'You don't look all right, son. Were these guys givin' you a hard time?' Tom meets his eyes at last and then glances at Chapman and shakes his head. 'Looked like it to me and it looks like someone's just hit you in the face.' He turns to Chapman, who's got a thin smile seaming the frozen fix of his face. 'Did you do this?'

'Yeah. He was slabberin', mouthin' off,' Chapman says calmly, without any show of concern.

'Is that right?' he asks Chapman gently and then slaps him hard on the cheek, making his head almost jerk off his shoulders.

'Dad don't, please don't. Let's go home,' Tom begs and in his son's voice he can hear all his fear and he understands everything about what's happening. 'It's all right, son,' he says, holding on to Chapman's lapel.

'Fuck off!' Chapman shouts, trying to twist and tear himself free like a fish on a hook. 'Fuck off! Get your hands off!' But every twist and thresh only screws his grip tighter, and he keeps the boy at a rigid arm's length.

'So you've been givin' my son a hard time, have you?'

'Everybody gives Fat Boy a hard time,' Chapman says before suddenly flailing a blow at him. He moves his head backwards and avoids it, feeling only the swish of air on the side of his cheek.

'And I bet no one gives it better than you,' he says,

shaking him back against the railings. 'Well I've something to tell you.' He pushes him some more as if he's trying to push him through the railings.

'Dad!' Tom cries again and he feels his hand gripping his shoulder, pulling him back but he ignores it.

'That's right, Fat Boy, get him off or you're dead meat.'

'Dead meat? Is that right now?' He slaps Chapman on the face again, this time with the back of his free hand. 'The only person dead round here is you because if you shoot your mouth off once more I'm goin' to tear your fuckin' head off.' It's the first time he's seen the flicker of fear in the boy's eyes, the first chink in the armour.

'I'm gettin' my da – you're a dead man walkin'! He'll break your legs!' Chapman shouts. He's got him pulled tight as a knot and though the boy gives one more spin of his shoulders to try to free himself, he holds him in the same position, his arm an iron rod. Then when Chapman least expects it, he releases him, causing him to stumble for a second. But almost immediately he takes him again, grabbing his throat in the vice of his hand and pins him against the railings.

'You do that, son, you do that. And then you know what I'm goin' to do? I'm going to kick the shit out of him for havin' brought such an ugly little shite like you into the world. Do you understand?' He tightens his fingers on Chapman's throat. 'Do you understand?' Chapman nods, his fear-flushed eyes big and flashing like new coins.

'Dad, please – it's only goin' to make things worse,' Tom says in his ear.

'No son, it's goin' to make things better, much better. Isn't that right?' he asks Chapman, 'Isn't that right?' There is another nod, repeated and insistent this time. For a second he tightens his grip again, thinks that he could squeeze the very eyes out of his head, pop them like corks out of a bottle, but then slowly and reluctantly releases him. Chapman slumps to the ground with a whimper, and wheezing, sits crumpled on the pavement like a wizened balloon, his breath coming in wallowing gulps.

'Let's go, Dad, he's had enough,' Tom begs again.

'I think he has,' he answers, 'but we need to be sure.' He kicks Chapman in the side, making his body spume up as if shot by a bullet, then squats down beside him to whisper in his ear. 'If you ever go near my son again or even look at my son in the wrong way, I'm goin' to find you and kill you. Do you understand?' Chapman nods once more. 'I can't hear you, I need to hear you.'

'Yes, yes,' Chapman says in a whispery voice that is soft and crumpled like paper.

'That's good, that's good,' he says. Then he looks up at Tom and says, 'Kick him.' Tom stares at him as if he hasn't heard. 'Kick him, kick the shit! To help him remember.' Tom doesn't move. 'Do it! Do it!' he's shouting over and over at him, 'Do it! Do it!' He can see the fear in his son's eyes, his reluctance to come any closer so he grabs him by the arm and pulls him over to where Chapman huddles on the pavement by the railings. He pummels his son in the soft folds of his back. 'You can't just stand there and let someone like this little piece of shit piss on you. Show the little cunt that you're not goin' to take it! Stitch him!' He sees Chapman turn his head away with the pain of shame and the heave of his chest as if he's going to be sick. Tom kicks him with the slow shuffle of a foot before stepping away again.

'No! No!' he shouts at his son. 'Like this!

'Kick the little cunt like this!'

IF HE COULD, HE'D build a wall round his house, a high wall with razor wire on the top, build it to keep the world out and away from his family. He has no time or energy for talking any more. He doesn't have the words and he should never have gone on television and tried to use them, knows that he can never find them and that even if he could, out there, there's no one listening. No one's ever going to listen to the likes of him or what he has to say. It's all over, they want it to be over, to forget it ever happened, so they don't want someone like him coming round to remind them. He remembers the school's embarrassment, thinks that after a couple of months have passed, they'll probably write them a letter asking for their cup back, so they can give it a polish, award it to the next pupil who wins the stars. Maybe they'll just forget to engrave Rachel's name on it, pull a discreet curtain over the year. He remembers the postcard from Tenerife lying on Roberts' desk, thinks of Rachel's photograph yellowing in a discarded pile of newspapers and a fork of anger shoots through him.

And Rachel wasn't enough for them, so now they'll pour their shit on Tom, and shame fuses with the anger because he's let his children down, hasn't protected them from the scum that floats on the surface of the world. He hasn't taught them how to defend themselves or guard themselves from what it wants to do to them. And he's been a fool to think that a job and a house of their own on a different road would be enough to carry them beyond the reach of what's out there. He remembers the fear in Tom's voice, his insistence every morning that he won't go back to the school and he thinks of Rachel. It isn't about words any more, it's gone beyond that and he can't defend them with weapons he doesn't understand. So he knows what it is he has to do now and the knowledge gives him a sense of direction, something he can hold on to, something to give shape to the chaotic flux he feels spinning inside himself. He has to go back to being a soldier, to stand on the walls and protect what they have left, because if he doesn't, they'll take the rest bit by bit, then spit their venom in his face. He was a soldier once but he was fighting in the wrong war, didn't understand who the enemy was. Then he was young and foolish, pumped up on the lies and loyalties, trying to prove himself to win the approval of older men, running like a dog after whatever sticks they threw for him to chase. But there were things he learned during those years and even though he came to despise them and buried them with the rest of his past, he starts to dig them out of his memory, slowly unwrapping their rusted, twisted remnants.

He drives over to see Rob and everything has started to tighten into a focus. It's the best he's felt since it happened. Things are starting to make sense in his head. He's a soldier, without a uniform or an army, but a soldier who's only taking orders from the anger at the core of his being and he has no fear any more and that makes him feel cleaner and lighter. And there's only one thing these people understand, it's the only currency they deal in – there is no other form of exchange or barter, nothing that can persuade or touch outside its power. It's the language, the greased rails on which everything moves and as he drives he tries to remember the lexicon, flicks the pages of what he's seen and heard all those years ago. And into his memory comes the image of a man on a doorstep, delivering a message that can't be laughed off or ignored. A man walking away, while he buttons his coat against prying eyes and the coldness of the night.

Rob opens the door. There's no sign of Angela or Corrina. The house looks like it hasn't been cleaned or tidied for days. 'All right, Bro?' Rob says, the way he's started to greet him each time they meet. They sit in the kitchen where tangled piles of washing sit in a basket and on the boards. The sink is full of unwashed plates and there is a mangled mix of smells that he can't untangle. A still lit, half-smoked cigarette smoulders on a saucer.

'How's Tom?' he asks. 'I'm worried about him, Marty. I think he might be gettin' a hard time at school.'

'Has he said anything to you?' he asks quickly.

'No, it's just a feeling I had. One or two things he said.'

'Why didn't you say something, tell me?'

'It was only a feeling like – he never really said anything. So you think he has been?'

'It's sorted.'

'Did you go up to the school then?' Rob asks.

'No, I sorted it myself.'

'Best way,' Rob says, reaching for the cigarette but putting it back.

'Where's Angela and Corrina?' he asks.

'Her ma's not well, they've gone to stay with her for a while until she gets better.'

'You'll need to clear this place up before she gets back. Don't want her coming back to a mess,' he says as Rob nods and reaches again for the cigarette.

'Do you want a smoke?' he asks, holding it out to him.

He shakes his head and then he understands what he's being offered and he's on his feet and grabbing Rob's wrist, shaking it so that he drops the cigarette on the table.

'What the frig, Marty?' Rob shouts, jumping up.

'You're offering me this shit?' he shouts, taking the cigarette, dropping it on the floor and stubbing it out with his foot. 'You're offering me this shit!'

'Take it easy, Marty, for God's sake – it's only a bit of dope.'

'How long have you been doing this?' he asks, leaning over the table towards his brother. 'How long have you been smoking this shit?'

'For God's sake take it easy, Marty – it's nothing but a smoke. It's not heroin or something you stick in your veins. The whole world smokes it, for frig's sake.'

'Do you do other stuff?' he asks, staring at his brother's face.

'No, Marty, honest to God. I hardly even smoke – just now and again, when I feel a bit uptight.' He rubs his eyes with his knuckles as if he's just woken up and is squirming the sleep out of them. 'You gonna hit me, Marty?'

'Hit you? I never ever hit you, even when you deserved it!' he shouts, but his fists are clenched and the wave of his anger flows to the very tips of his fingers.

'Just the once – you hit me once.'

'That's right I did,' he says, collapsing back on the chair and into silence as if broken by the power of the memory.

'Listen, Marty, don't lose the head, but maybe it would be good for you – help you through things – know what I mean?'

'I don't need that kind of help,' he says. 'I don't need any help.'

'Okay, Bro,' Rob says.

'Don't ever have that stuff around me again.'

'Okay Marty. Okay Bro.'

He wants to tell him to stop calling him that but instead asks him to put the kettle on and make them a cup of tea, tries to calm himself.

'Tea's addictive,' Rob says. 'Caffeine's a drug, too, Marty.'

'That's right, Rob. Don't make it too strong then.' He watches Rob fill the kettle, at first letting the column of water hit its rim and spray against the wall. The droplets shine against the dullness of the wall like spots of fresh paint.

'Why do you never go and see Ma in the hospital?' Rob asks without turning round.

'I've been busy and anyway she's got you now.'

'You should go and see her,' Rob says. 'She's been saying it's your birthday, she has some money for you.'

'Same five pounds she's being giving to me and I've been giving back to her for the last six months.'

'I think you should go and see her,' he says placing two mugs on the table.

'I will,' he says. 'It's good I've got you to keep me right, Rob. Now tell me what you know about Johnson.' He watches his brother masking his silence with the pretence of concentrating on pouring the tea.

'Jaunty?' he says after a few moments.

'Jaunty,' he repeats.

'You used to run with him, Marty – you know him as much as me.'

'That was twenty-something years ago, Rob. I want to know about him now.'

'What do you want to know?'

'I want to know everything you know. I want you to tell me, Rob. I want you to tell me now.'

Rob sits cupping his tea in both hands as if he's scared he might drop it, then blows on it to cool it. 'I don't know what to tell you,' he says. 'He's the top man – everybody knows that. What else do you want to know?'

'Where does his money come from?'

'Well, he has the taxi business, a couple of pubs, a chippy and he'd something to do with those new apartments they built off the carriageway and probably other things as well – things you know about as well as me. I don't know nothin' except he's loaded. They say he has a place in Spain, but I don't really know, Marty.'

'Does he live on the estate still?'

'He has a house here but he's another place along the coast. It's supposed to be worth seeing, big gates like Stormont. But why do you want to know?'

'Want to know what he's made of himself, that's all. He runs the drugs as well, doesn't he Rob?'

'I don't know anything about drugs, Marty. And with a guy like Jaunty, it's better not knowin' too much or asking too many questions. Know what I mean? It's best if you stay away from him.'

'Maybe I should ask him for a job.'

'Don't be crazy, Marty, you've got a good job in the museum. You don't want to get involved with someone like him.'

'But you work for him, don't you?'

'I just drive a taxi now and then, when they're short, or one of the regulars has gone on a bender, that's all. And if I had any better offers I'd be out of here like a flash. It's not a good place for kids, for Corrina.' He sips his tea then places the mug on the table. There is a chip on the rim. 'Do you remember the time we were goin' to run away to Australia? Maybe we should have. Maybe we should have cleared out when we were young and had the chance.'

'You didn't know where Australia was. You were goin' to stow away on a boat that would have taken you to the Isle of Man.' Rob smiles, shakes his head at the memory. 'So Jaunty's the big man now?'

'Top of the tree. Always has a tan, always just back from a holiday.'

'It's well for him. Who would have thought that the same guy would have ended up top of anything? We were in the same class in school. He couldn't beat the deck.'

'He's in a class of his own now,' Rob says.

'And he's never been inside?

'Did time on remand once but it never came to trial.'

There are other questions he wants to ask but he can work out the answers for himself. Just like she was able to do from the time she was no age at all. He looks at his brother and wonders if he even knows what the stars mean. She always had questions, dozens every day and then they all started to take the same form – what would happen if? What would happen if this or that were to occur and if he tried to palm her off with half-baked answers, she'd come right back until she got what she wanted. And then before he knew it, she worked out where to go to find her own answers and she was too old to ask or to hold his hand any more. He thinks of the photograph where she's trying to look at the world through the lens of the camera, trying to look at the world which gave her life and then took it away again. She's wearing a blue dress with white and yellow flowers. No shoes on her feet. What did she wish for on that last birthday? Maybe if he had thrown coins into the water, made good wishes . . .

'You all right, Marty?'

'Yes,' he says, standing up to go.

'But you haven't finished your tea,' Rob says.

'Things to do, lots of things to do,' At the door he pauses, 'Don't smoke that shit, Rob – it's no good.' And then he touches Rob on the shoulder, but without saying goodbye hurries out to his car.

He drives the short distance from Rob's house to the club. He's sat in its car park on many nights, watching the people going in and out. The club is to one side of the main building, approached by its own path and lit by purple lights and neon graphics. Young people spill out of packed cars, the girls pulling at the hems of skimpy skirts that have ridden up, the boys doing elaborate stretches with their arms. Lines of swaying coloured lights link the trees and garland the doors. He watches night after night as groups of girls laugh and move towards the doors in tight phalanxes of bare arms and legs, their tight clothes brief transfers of colour on the dark skin of the night. Unwinding the window he listens to the excited descant of their voices which climbs above all the other noises in a kind of discordant harmony. Sometimes he catches the call of their names which suddenly shoot up like startled birds and fly, released on wings of anticipation and laughter. After they've gone inside, their voices linger in the car, echoing round his head, sharp-edged and alive, pressing their reality into the soft spaces of the night and then tightening into a sudden and renewed sense of loss.

He tries to remember the sound of her voice, to pluck it from the swirl and chaos of what he remembers but it's indistinct and unformed, spiralling ever further away as he struggles to reach it, subsumed into the static of the present, overwhelmed by the climbing rip tide of these young voices which are flecked and white-tipped with life.

Alison looks at photographs all the time but there is no photograph that contains the sound of her voice, no tape or recording to preserve it. He tries to hear it when she was a child asking him all the questions but even though he has her words, they're voiceless, formed only by his own thoughts. So now as he struggles, it is the lilt and squeal of these other voices he hears, the squeak and stutter of high heels, the bullish bravado of the boys that's fired by a sense of freedom and what the night might bring them if they're lucky.

He feels old, his being corralled by the creeping confines of time. The car is airless and small so he gets out and leans against it, watching over its roof, breathing deeply, squinting at the neon until it becomes one seamless smear of light. On the doors of the club are two bouncers, their shaved heads colour-washed by the neon above them, their animated faces flickering screens of light. A coach arrives in the car park and there is the clatter of feet on metal as it empties. It's a birthday party and some of the girls carry red heart-shaped balloons. One of the balloons escapes and floats into the night sky, pursued by squeals and laughter and then their pale moons of faces tilt upwards, watching until it disappears.

He stands for a long time until the growing cold tells him it's time to go. A car arrives and parks under trees at the far end of the car park. When no one gets out, he thinks it's a courting couple, keen to delay their arrival at the club for a few more moments but the headlights of the car are left on and when someone eventually gets out, it is a young man in a fleece and baseball hat. He stands at the tail of the car and makes a call on his mobile phone, then gets back in. A few minutes later two youths in white shirts come out of the club and get into the car. They only stay a few moments

197

before getting out and walking back to the club, the breeze infiltrating and puffing their shirts and making them shiver and lower their heads. Their steps are synchronised, strident, keen to get back to the heat.

He grips the steering wheel with both hands to steady himself before slipping out of the car and quietly closing the door. He takes the long way round, keeping a screen of shrubbery between himself and the car, moving slowly, stooping where there are gaps, then walks directly to the driver's door and opens it. The driver is putting an elastic band round a tight wad of notes and the shock on his face is illuminated by the light. He wants to see all his face so he knocks the cap off, then pushing him over towards the handbrake, forces himself in beside him.

'What the fuck?' the lad says, stuffing the wad of notes inside his fleece.

'Shut your face!' he orders, staring at him, taking in everything he can. He's not yet twenty, skinny, the skin on his chin and cheekbones purple-tinged with acne scars, his eyes dark as his hair. There is a lightly bruised blue circle under his left eye that's beginning to fade to yellow.

'Are you the police?' he asks, trying to straighten himself.

'No, I'm not the police – I'm worse than that. Where's the stuff?'

'What stuff?'

'Tell me!' he shouts, swivelling his body and punching him on his cheek below his eye.

'Jesus!' he cries as he throws both hands to his face. 'Honest, mister, I don't know what you're talkin' about.'

'Tell me where the stuff is or I'm goin' to break your fuckin' arms!' There is something rattling at his feet – it's a crook lock. He picks it up and it rattles in the shake of his hand. 'Tell me where the stuff is now or I'm going to beat your head to a pulp,' and he clatters the metal against the dashboard.

'Listen, listen,' the lad says. 'Please listen. You take this stuff and we're both dead men.' He's started to cry for real, his shoulders heaving in rhythm with the struggle of his words. 'You don't know what you're dealing with here – it's not mine, none of it is mine. It belongs to people who'll shoot my kneecaps off and give you a head job as soon as they find you.' He wipes his face with the back of his hand. 'You understand what I'm saying? Take this stuff and you're dead when they get you.'

'Tell me now,' he says quietly then suddenly leaps astride him pressing the lock across his windpipe. 'Tell me now while you've still got a voice.'

'Jesus! Jesus!' he screams. 'Don't hurt me, Boss, please don't hurt me. It's there, in the front. But do this and we're both dead men walking!' It's the second time in days someone has said this to him. Dead man walking. For a second he thinks he sees a flicker of recognition in the boy's eyes. He lifts himself off and opens the glove compartment. He doesn't know what he expected but what he sees is something that looks like nothing more than a polythene bag full of sweets. He stuffs it in his pocket.

'If none of this is yours, then who owns it?' he asks, glancing back at the club.

'You can kill me if you want but I'm not goin' to say any names.' He's holding both hands to his face like a child who doesn't want to watch a scary film. He sees that no fear he can spark in the moment will cancel out the boy's permanent and ingrained fear, so when he speaks it's almost gently.

'I know that you work for Jaunty, so all you have to do

199

is nod your head when I ask and then I won't have to hurt you anymore. Do you understand?' The boy nods, still holding his face in his hands.

'You work for Jaunty, don't you? This stuff comes from him doesn't it?' Without looking at him and almost imperceptibly the boy nods his head, then asks, 'Who are you? Who you workin' for? Are you the police?'

'No, I'm not the police. It's not the police you need to worry about.'

'What you goin' to do with me?'

'I'm goin' to kill you if I ever see you again with this stuff. Do you understand?' he says, dropping the crook lock to the floor, then getting out of the car and walking towards his own. He knows already that the boy is on his phone but doesn't hurry and as he starts the engine, he sees the two bouncers coming towards him from the doorway of the club, the speed of their movement hampered by their weight and the tight stiffness of their suits. They're scampering towards him but he has the car in gear and he's moving away before they can do anything more than thump the boot with their flailing, white-cuffed fists.

*

She's off the drugs. She had to do it and she has. Her head aches and sometimes she has to stop the shake of her hands but she's off them. It feels like the worst hangover she's ever known and some days she thinks her head is filled with a swirl of drowsy fog which will never let her focus or see anything clearly again. When there's no one else there she'll shake her head as if she's being tortured by flies, or splash her face with water. And there's another thing she's decided – they're going out together as a family. Going out to do a shop and then for a drive and maybe something to eat. She doesn't care what they say, they're going to do it, because they can't go on like this, crumbling away, bit by bit, like some shore slowly eroded by the sea. She can't stand the silence, the way no one talks to anyone, the way the only voice in the living room belongs to the television. Martin and Tom hardly look at each other, avoiding each other's path as if they're side-stepping a stranger and Martin doesn't seem to care what his son does any more – what he eats, when he goes to bed or how long he plays on the computer. They can't go on like this and it's up to her to pull it all together.

They look at her as if she's speaking a foreign language when she tells them, start to shake their heads and make excuses but she brushes them aside and she can see they're shocked by her insistence, the show of energy that finally leaves them acquiescent if unenthusiastic. She can't fathom either of them any more, thinks that what has happened has carried both of them to places she doesn't know. But she's going after them, because if she doesn't there won't be any family left, only three people vaguely connected by name and a common past, three people who move about and through each other like ghosts. She's started already with Martin, reaching her arm across to him in bed and letting it rest lightly across his shoulder, ignoring the tight knot of his body, the way he stations himself at the edge of the bed as if he's guarding a borderline, touching her only by accident in his broken sleep. Ignoring the way he places his hand under the pillow and pushes it tight against his face for comfort – sometimes so tightly it looks as if he's trying to smother his head in its folds. When they both lie awake she's started to speak to him, talking on even though he pretends to be asleep and when he does talk it's sleep talk, the words screamed out on the rack of his dreams.

There's talk of Tom getting a home tutor, she doesn't know what to make of it but if it's only for a little while then maybe it wouldn't be a bad thing, might even help him get himself together. She's already seen him with his books out, looking as if he's revising for something, so that must be a good sign, and she's decided that she's going to clear out his wardrobe and take him out soon and buy him new clothes, clothes that fit and with which he's happy. She understands the importance of his happiness more than anything else and she's not going to neglect it, or take it for granted any more.

On the Saturday morning they try again to resist the idea but she won't have it, showing them the sandwiches and flask of soup she's made, injecting her voice with a jolly determination she no longer feels. She's made a list of the shopping they need and as she waits in the kitchen for them to get ready, she opens the fridge but there's no need to clear spaces for what's coming because it's almost empty. She stares at the yoghurts, hesitates and then lifts them out, finds a plastic shopping bag and with her hands shaking a little, places them in it and ties a knot with the handles of the bag. She carries it outside, blinking at the sharpness of the morning sun and lifts the lid of the bin but at the last second she can't do it. She tells herself it has to be done for the rest of the family, that she has to do it if they are to survive, but the inside of the bin is dark and putrid with the smell of decay and she lets the lid drop. Walking to the edge of the garden she lets the fresh smell cleanse her. The grass is still sheened and glittery with dew. Fine filaments of whispery web tremble on plants and branches of the trees. She thinks of work, of the heat, feels it start to seep into her consciousness, flushing her memory and leaving her unsure, but she's not going to let it and so she shrugs it away and, kicking off her slippers, walks on the wet grass in her bare feet. Walks down the garden, feeling the sweet coldness on her skin, pauses a second to smooth her palm over the grass, then gently pats her face with the droplets. She feels them on her tongue. It has to be done.

She's reached the apple tree. Sometimes she's not sure if it's alive or dead but this morning it stands strong in the sharp definition of light, and its leaves are green and limed with dew. As a child Rachel always wanted it to be bigger, the branches wide and strong enough to build a tree house. She'd just watched *Swiss Family Robinson* on television and wanted Martin to build her one. They could see her from the kitchen window, climbing in its branches and sometimes knocked on the window to signal her to be careful but she never fell; through her whole childhood she never really had any accident worse than a skinned knee. In some other garden a bird sings, shrill and insistent. She steadies herself by holding one of the branches, then kneels on the grass and opens the bag. One by one she peels back the lids of the yoghurts and fixes the cartons in the forks of the branches.

In the supermarket Martin and Tom trail in her wake. She tries to involve Tom by tempting him with food, asking his opinion about whether she should buy this or that, but he shows no interest and always there is a space between the three of them as if they're a convoy of ships, bound to keep a requisite distance. But she won't give up and keeps talking to them both, asking them questions, ticking things off her list, handing them things to look at, getting them to make decisions. She pauses – she's in the dairy section and she suddenly finds herself looking at yoghurts, almost about to reach out for them – but hurries on, getting what they need, adding new things she's just remembered. Afterwards she tells them she's tired and sits in the car, leaving them to pack the bags in the boot, the closest they've been all day.

When they've finished Martin says, 'Maybe we should go home now, if you're tired.' But she tells him she's fine and looking forward to their day out. She tells him that she wants to go to Bangor, that they haven't been there for years and they can go round the coast and find somewhere nice to have a picnic. She opens a bag of sweets she's bought and passes them round, tells Tom to take the paper off his father's, but when it's done he passes it to him without either looking at the other or speaking.

It's where they used to do their courting but she hardly recognises it any more. Now there's a marina and they park and set out along the walkway and look out at the sleek lines of moored boats. She makes them pick their favourite, the one they'd like to own, the one they'd like to sail away on. The boats feel like bookmarks on the pages of different types of lives, where people who have money skim over the waves, travelling where they choose to go, coming to rest in a safe harbour like this.

'You'd hardly know the place, Martin,' she says.

'Everywhere's different now,' he says.

'It's where we used to come before we were married, Tom. Walk along the front to Pickie Pool, get an ice cream or a chip.' Tom only stares out to sea. She looks at his feet and thinks that the first thing they have to get him is new trainers. The ones he's wearing are scuffed and battered. She looks at the bright paint of the boats, sees the way everything looks new and expensive, tries to read their names and thinks that her idea has been a failure.

They walk on round to where there is a miniature railway, a kids' playground and a pond with pedal swans.

'This is good,' she says, gives Tom some money and tells him to buy himself something at the shop. When he's gone she turns to Martin. 'Martin, I know this is very hard but I want us to clear Rachel's room. We can't keep just leaving it, it has to be done now.' She sees the shock in his eyes, the way his body bridles with a silent refusal. 'We can't go on like this, we have to keep going or everything's going to fall apart so bad we won't be able to put it back together. We have to clear her stuff and in a little while, when we're all ready, I want Tom to have it, to have the extra space.' Still he doesn't speak but shuffles his foot over a tiny stone. 'Speak to me, Martin.'

'I don't know what to say.'

'You could tell me that you love me.'

'I love you,' he says but his voice is flatter than she's ever heard it.

'Look at me, Martin, and say it.'

'I've something to tell you,' he says, finally looking at her. 'I want you to go to your sister's in Scotland. I want you to go tomorrow night, take Tom with you.'

'Scotland?'

'I've it all arranged. I've spoken to her and she really wants you to come. It's all arranged.'

'What about work?' she asks

'They'll understand – I'll sort it. Don't worry – just go, you need the break.'

'What about you? Will you be all right?'

'I'll be okay. Please go, Ali.'

It's the first thing he's said to her that contains anything of himself, or his feelings, and because of that she has no choice but to agree. She sees Tom coming back from the shop, there isn't much time.

'I'll go,' she says, 'but there's two things you have to do for me. I want you to clear Rachel's room, pack up her things so we can decide what to do with them when I get back.' He nods. She pauses.

'What's the other thing?' he asks.

'I want you to take Tom and get on one of those swans.'

'You're joking,' he says.

'No, I'm not. Do it for me, Martin. Please.'

Then she sits on the bench and gets out the sandwiches, opens the flask and lays everything out ready for the picnic, glancing up from time to time and smiling as her husband and son pedal slow laps of the pond in a white swan.

*

When the phone rings at intervals he doesn't answer it – he doesn't want to talk to anyone, has already decided that words only get in the way, hinder him in his path to what must be done. But he's glad Ali and Tom are safe. He takes one final walk round the empty house, going into every room, sometimes touching things as if storing their memory through the gentle brush of his fingers. He pauses at the foot of their bed. He never meant to betray her, to deceive her. She treated him better than anyone ever had, she deserved better than the little she got. The truth was she deserved better than him. He feels a surge of deep remorse and part of him regrets that he won't have the chance to explain to her, to thank her for everything she gave to him but to tell her that it was no use, that he couldn't be saved, that inside where even she couldn't see, he was damaged beyond her power to heal. Then he gets in the car and drives, great looping circuits of the city that are without purpose except to kill time. Once, on impulse, he stops at a garage and buys some flowers, then drives to the hospital where his mother is being assessed.

It takes him a long time to find the right building, a longer time to find a parking space but he doesn't mind because now he's got time to spare. There is no smell from the flowers and as he looks at them for the first time he thinks that they don't look like the colours of real flowers. Never in his life has he given her flowers and as he pauses at the entrance to the building, clutching his cheap garage bouquet, he wonders why he's come at all. A couple of smokers huddled to the side of the door glance at him and for a second he thinks of dumping the bunch but it's too late and he strides past them, not looking at their faces.

Inside, nothing is as expected. There are none of the elements he has constructed in his imagination, things that, when combined, created the impression of a home rather than a hospital. But the smells, the sounds of rattling metal and echoing footsteps, the shiny slime of gloss paint on the walls that looks as if it would feel damp if touched, all bear the indelible mark of a hospital. He remembers the name of the ward and searches for the signs, then shares a lift with an elderly man who carries a plastic bag that reveals a bottle of cordial, some apples and a pair of slippers. They do not speak to each other, or acknowledge each other's presence in any way, until the man suddenly says, 'For the wife.' He nods his head in answer and then there is silence again.

When he's left alone in the lift he sets his flowers down in a corner and leaves them. A nurse greets him as he tries to establish where he's supposed to go, then tells him that his mother is in a day room at the end of the corridor. As he starts along it he thinks she's watching him, wondering why he hasn't visited before, or perhaps she's recognised his face from the television. Either way it's enough to force him on and stop him from turning round and heading back to the car.

He first looks into the room through a glass window. There are three women in the room. Two sit close to the yammering television; his mother further back, slumps in a plastic-covered, high-backed chair that dwarfs her and makes her look like a child.

'All right, Ma?' he asks, sitting in the chair beside her.

'Why am I here?' she asks after a long silence, her eyes focused on the television.

'You're here for a check-up, for some tests, that's all.'

'I don't like it here,' she says. 'I want to go to my own house.'

'When you get your tests done. When they get everything checked out.'

'They don't treat you properly in here. They steal your money.'

'They don't steal your money, Ma,' he says, looking at her hands which grip the chair's armrests. They are small, the skin a waxen, stippled parchment. The veins are raised like a blue tributary printed on a map.

'They steal your money,' she insists. 'They stole your birthday money.'

'You gave me my birthday money, give me it every time you see me.' He wants to touch her hand because already he knows he's going to leave. Tells himself that he's plans to make, things to take care of. The hands look so small now, shrunken into themselves. 'I'll tell them to take good care of you.' He goes to touch the back of her hand but stops at the last second. He wishes he'd brought the flowers.

'I have to go now, Ma,' he says, standing and looking towards the television.

'Right, Martin,' she says. 'I'll have your birthday money for you next time.'

'Thanks, Ma.'

Outside the room he stands for a while and watches her through the glass. What was she thinking that night she watched them in the yard? Once he almost goes back in but then he's gone, using the stairs because he can't bear the idea of being shut with someone in the confined space of the lift.

His stomach feels hollow and he realises he hasn't eaten anything since the day before, tells himself that he has to keep his strength up, so he drives to the university area and eats in one of the cafés close to the museum that has tables and chairs out on the pavement. He sits inside and orders a bowl of soup. The place is filled with young people but now it helps him to see them, to listen to their laughter and watch their unthinking and complete embrace of life. Some are with their parents – it's the middle of the graduation ceremonies – everyone dressed in their best suits and dresses, some of them wearing wispy, broad-rimmed hats. Their laughter spills out like the champagne they drink and mixes with the clink of their glasses and the scrunch of ice in the metal buckets.

Behind the counter, a man he thinks is the owner complains to one of the waiters. 'This policeman comes in and says we'll have to move the tables because they're blocking the pavement. Some hick from down the country by the way he spoke.

'I tell him he can't be serious, that it's what cafés do in the summer. And do you know what he said, what he actually said to me? "This isn't Paris you know." Can you believe it? This isn't Paris. Paris – I wish!' They both laugh as they look out over the counter. 'I felt like saying if he'd nothing better to do he could take a stroll five minutes down the boulevard to Sandy Row and ask the drinking clubs to show him their licences, open their books for him to have a look. I can't believe it: "This isn't Paris you know." ' They both laugh again and then the owner straightens some glasses on the bar and as he moves them they splash with light.

After he's finished his soup he orders a coffee and moves his seat to the window. He can see the roof of the museum, the tops of the trees in the park where it sits. After he's paid he enters the park by a side gate and stares up at it from a distance, separated by shrubbery and trees. When he got the job there, put on his uniform for the first time, she was so pleased and proud, as if he'd become a general in the army and even if the pay was no good she never complained, always understanding that he felt safe there. Strange to feel safest from the past in a museum. He doesn't fully understand it. He moves a little closer, wanting an uninterrupted view, when he realises someone is speaking to him, offering him something.

'I'm sorry to trouble you,' the man says, 'but would you be so kind as to take a photograph for us?' He's holding out a camera to him. Behind him stand his wife and his daughter who's wearing her graduation gown. He takes the camera and nods his head. 'You just press this button here,' the man says pointing. They go and stand on the grass in front of a flower bed. 'How does this look?' they ask.

'Good,' he says, looking through the camera as they push up close together. The camera feels small in his hand, not big enough to capture the smiles spreading across their faces. They drape their arms round the shoulders of their daughter, sharing possession of her equally. His hand shakes a little and then he presses the button and they're thanking him but he doesn't say anything and hurries back to where he's parked the car and drives and drives. He drives the roads and streets, cut off from everything he sees, the people, the other drivers in cars. He's in his own world now, separate and soon to be complete, and he feels calm and in control, steering himself on his chosen course.

He ends up in the hills above the east of the city, finds a parking place usually occupied by lovers, climbs into the back seat and falls into a shallow, dreamless sleep. When he wakes he looks at his watch and knows that it's almost time. Already the city below is dressing itself in neon, stirring and defining the network of roads with expectant garlands of light. His mouth is dry and his throat a little sore – he should have brought a drink. The best he can do is to open the window and let the night air stream in against his face. There is the smell of cut grass from the fields on either side of the car and birds that look like swallows swoop and pulse through the darkening sky. From the airport below he sees the lights of a plane slowly climbing, seaming the clouds with red. It's time to go. It's finally time.

He takes the most circuitous route he can find and parks a couple of streets away, leaving the car outside a gospel hall. Putting on a baseball cap he pulls the peak down as low as he can and makes his way to the house, walking casually, trying not to draw attention to himself, but checking all the time that no one's watching him. The streets are almost empty with only a couple of boys in identical Rangers' tops kicking a ball against a gable wall and some teenage girls in a doorway smoking, passing the one cigarette round between them. One of them steps out from the group and does an elaborate little dance routine, holding her hands in the air as if praying while her feet shimmy in loose, sliding movements. She's joined by another who mirrors her movements, their bodies almost touching. When they see him, the first girl stops and stares and he lifts his hand in a wave as he quickens his steps, is glad when she resumes her dance.

He crosses a patch of waste ground at the end of the street that is pitted and blackened from some previous fire. Coiled metal springs, shards of green glass and the twisted knots of beer cans litter the scabbed and blistered ground. A skinny shake of a dog sniffs its way from the shadows and follows him for a while until he chases it away. On the derelict end wall of his row there is a mural with a portrait of Michael Stone and the slogan 'His only crime was loyalty,' disfigured by daubs of green paint. He wonders what it was all about; a world where the tribal heroes have the names of animals: King Rat, Mad Dog. All the houses except his mother's are boarded up, blinkered and sleeping, waiting in a decaying line for demolition and now she's gone, the wait will probably be a shorter one. He pauses, pretends to look at his watch while checking again for prying eyes, then walks quickly to the front door and opens it with the key he has ready in his hand. Inside he locks the door behind him and without turning on the lights goes to the front window and searches the street, standing where he can't be seen at the edges of the frame and moving the net curtain slightly before checking both ways.

He suddenly feels a pulse of panic and the need for light as the damp coldness of the house brushes against his face like a web, but he forces himself to resist and instead switches on the torch and points it to the floor where the whorl of light becomes another yellow-headed rose in the brown of the carpet. He's not yet ready to climb the stairs so he slumps into the chair by the hearth and after a few moments feels strong enough to switch off the torch. It's the chair where his mother sat on her final day in the house, the chair in which he combed her hair. He wishes there was a fire in the grate now, a warm fire shooting flames into the thick-sooted blackness of the chimney that would take away this coldness which feels as if it's seeping into the very marrow of his bones. Opposite him sits the high-backed settee on which as boys they watched television, squabbling over who would sit at the end closest to the fire, engaged in the perpetual argument as to whether your place was forfeited if you went to the toilet. He lets the light from the torch play over it, exploring the soiled brown brocade, the lumpy, misshapen seats with their cushions sunken in the middle and curling at the seams. He should be climbing the stairs by now but there is a lethargy gnawing away at him, brought on by an unwillingness to step further into the heart of the house.

He shines the light on the arm of the settee nearest to him, knows without seeing it that it wears a shiny skein of grease and wear. It's where his father would lay his sleeping head, where he saw it resting that night he came home from nothing but one more endless evening standing on a street corner. He was cold that night as well – it must have been the middle of winter. He remembers that but can't remember where Rob was and why he wasn't with him. But there was no heat in the house – the fire was a collapsed smoulder of ash and the only sound his father's grunts and snores. He smells the drink that seeps from his pores, the stagnant, mingled odour of sweat and work and he sits in this same chair for a few moments and talks to him in a whisper. 'Hello Piggy,' he says, 'havin' a little piggy sleep? Oink Oink Oink.' His father stirs and snorts. 'What's that you said, Piggy? What's that you said in your little piggy sleep?'

He hears his mother upstairs. It's early for her to be in bed. Maybe she's gone in disgust. He leans forward to whisper, 'Oink, oink, oink,' this time more loudly and he contorts his face into what he thinks looks like a pig.

After a while he goes upstairs and sees his mother's bedroom door open. She tells him to get himself some supper, that there's a new loaf and he can do himself some toast, put some cheese on it. She's sitting on the bed, fully dressed, with her back to the door, and something makes him go in and even though she turns her head away he can see the dark cowl of bruising already thickening round her eye. Without him having time to ask she tells him she banged it on a cupboard door in the kitchen, that it served her right for being so careless, that it'll be gone in the morning. He stands for a few seconds but says nothing then goes back downstairs. There is an anger breaking loose in him and it's almost impossible for him to suppress it, but he walks as quietly and slowly as he can to the kitchen and opens the drawer. He's pulled it too hard and the cutlery rattles angrily against itself. He lifts out the bread knife, hears his mother's voice telling him that there's a new loaf, that he should make himself some toast, and then he goes back to the sleeping figure of his father. He's on his side, facing him, his head resting on the pillow of his two hands and raised on the arm of the settee. The first three buttons of his shirt are open, his neck exposed, black chest hairs like tumbleweed rising and settling on the heave of his open-mouthed breathing.

Like killing a pig he tells himself. Just like killing a pig. Slitting his throat from ear to ear, the blood spilling out like the gush of water. Like killing a bastard pig and the world a better place for it. He moves closer, feels the weight of the knife in his hand. He thinks of the Shankill butchers, those loyal cutters of throats, and shivers. What if any of his father's blood were to splash on him? He can't bear the thought. Splash on his face, on his eyes, in his hair, on his mouth? To be contaminated by the splash of his blood and not be able to wash it away. But he tightens his grip on the knife, holds it perfectly still by his side to find its balance.

'What you doin,' son?' his father asks, one eye squinting up at him and then both.

'Gettin' some toast for supper,' he says, letting the knife slip behind his leg.

'Do some for me,' he says, 'and get me a cup of tea – my mouth's parched.'

When he brings them, he sits upright, rubs his mouth with the back of his hand, licks the palms of his hands and washes his eyes. Taking the tea and toast from him, he clears his throat and then says, 'Good lad, good lad.'

He switches off the torch and sits in what light edges into the room from the street lamps. Almost the closest he's ever come to taking a life. Maybe even closer than when good luck was all that saved him and someone he had never seen before, nor since. They said he was a Provie but he doesn't believe it now, or anything else they told him. One of a team of three – his first big job, the chance to prove himself. He remembers it all: the fear rolling in his stomach that mixed with adrenaline; the stupid pride at being chosen, at being blooded. And afterwards, when a change of routine, an unexpected delay, a chance meeting or some other stroke of good fortune saved someone he didn't even know from a rendezvous with death on his own doorstep, he felt nothing but a secret, unexpressed relief that carried him back to the edges of it all and eventually his involvement petered out, obscured and unnoticed in a gradual change of leadership.

But it's time now to climb the stairs. He can't put it off any longer. And he's feeling colder and colder as if he has ice at his core, so he thinks that if he doesn't move, his whole being will be frozen into inertia. He lights his way with the torch, the boards squeaking their familiar complaint and the handrail installed for his mother smooth and polished to the touch. As boys they could go up and down silently, their feet picking the right places like mountain climbers on a precipice. Now it seems as if the tiny house gulfs above him like some great hood that threatens to fall over his head and trap him in its airless prison. On the landing he avoids looking into his parents' room and only goes into his old room long enough to lift out the chair he needs. He places it squarely in the space between the bathroom and the bedroom, tests it with his hand, then stands on it and slides back the square of wood which leads to the roof space. Reaching his arms up, he pulls himself through the narrow space and sits on one of the boards which stretch across the rafters round the opening, until he can switch on the torch. Beyond this circumference of board there are only bare rafters and from everywhere rushes a musty dampness that feathers and brushes his skin. He can taste it in his mouth as he shines the torch round the detritus which circles the entrance – an artificial Christmas tree, a biscuit tin with silver tinsel lolling from under the lid like a furred tongue, a birdcage, offcuts of carpet, an old red box mono record player, cardboard boxes filled with junk. Then he stands up and, shining the light on the water tank, starts to slowly make his way towards it, balancing his feet on the rafters and bending over to avoid bumping his head. The tank is rust-blistered and the light from the torch seems to soak into the metal without giving back a reflection. He starts to hurry a little and his foot almost slips off the thinness of a rafter, then as he stops to refind his balance he thinks he hears something but tells himself that it's only the passing of a car, the slamming of a door, the wind scuttling below the slates.

He squeezes behind the tank with more difficulty than he experienced as a younger, thinner man, and his heart is beating faster the closer he gets. So many years have passed, so many things have happened, that he wonders for a second if his memory has played tricks on him, or if he's following the confused hallucination of some half-remembered dream. But then its physical reality is confirmed by his fingers as he reaches as far under the tank as his arm will stretch. He pulls the tightly taped, plastic-wrapped package free and the light shone on it reveals a thick scurf of web but as he scrapes it clean, the black plastic still glints in the light. It's not the time or the place to open it so he carefully slides it into an inside pocket.

He freezes motionless again – he's sure he's heard something this time and then it comes, a dull thud against the front door and then another and another. In a few seconds he knows it will burst open and they'll be inside, so stepping the rafters two at a time, he scurries hunch-backed to the entrance. There is the sound of breaking glass from the back door – they've come team-handed. Holding on with one hand, he swings as low as his balance allows and just manages to grab the top of the chair and swing it up beside him and as he hears the final surrender of the -front door, he slides the square of wood back in place, its noise lost in the clamour of shouts and stamp of feet. As he steps silently backwards he can hear them on the stairs, in the room below, moving through the house and their voices which call out to each other are fired by curses. He doesn't want to, but he has no choice, so he switches on the torch, shielding as much of the light as he can with his jacket, and starts to open the package, stripping away the taped layers until it rests cleanly in his hand. It feels smaller than he remembers, the bullets he loads in the chamber like part of a child's toy, and his fingers fumble a little. As soon as it's done he switches off the light and slowly lies down on the rafters, his body stretched across the supports in an X-shape, his face turned towards the opening, the gun held in his right hand. And all the time he's asking himself if it still works, after all these years wrapped in its shroud, if it still works.

The angry shouts have collapsed into a low undertone of indistinguishable conversation, a kind of constant hum like the refrigerator makes in the late night kitchen. He feels his body tense as he imagines the door being thrown open and the first of their faces breaking in but he tells himself that they can only come singly through the opening. He looks again at the gun – in the darkness it is a black smudge against his skin. At the time of the supergrasses, when the organisation was riddled with informers and self-doubt and the first flush of panic set in, they spread round a cache to prevent its seizure. No one asked for it back and when the new faces took over the reins, he no longer wanted to remind them of who he was or his past involvement, so he decided to let things be until someone came for it. Now it's been resurrected, awoken from its sleep and in his hand it feels balanced, a snug fit and the safety catch releases smoothly as he listens to what is either the thin threading of the wind or the whisper of voices. But nothing happens. Perhaps they're looking for steps or arguing that he's not there. He doesn't know and so he hangs on the rafters, the wood pressing against his flesh and his face close to the layers of web and black-spotted mould.

The voices have dropped lower until he's not sure if they're there at all and sometimes he thinks the whispers he hears come from inside his head. Someone must have seen him, or maybe they were watching the house all the time. If he has to, he will take them with him and not give it a second thought because it's time for someone to pay and if they get in the way of what he has to do then it makes no odds. But nothing happens and although pain is stirring in his arms and legs from the strain of his position, he knows he can't move without making noise and giving confirmation of his presence. He tries to tells himself that maybe it's just a bunch of kids who're taking advantage of an empty house to turn it over, thieving everything they can carry away, so if he waits a little longer he'll be able to make a getaway. But as he shifts his weight and raises his face in search of fresher air, he hears the shout of excited voices and names called to each other. Perhaps they've been waiting for reinforcements or the arrival of guns, or for someone who will tell them what to do.

'Why don't you come out now, Marty?' a voice suddenly calls. It's loud and clear and must come from someone standing on the landing. He doesn't recognise the voice. 'Why don't you come out and we can talk about this man to man?' He doesn't answer but tightens his grip on the gun. 'We haven't got all night, Marty and patience is runnin' out. So why not stop skulking up there like a rat in a pipe, give us back what doesn't belong to you and we'll call it quits?' He still doesn't answer. 'Marty, speak to me – we're reasonable people, we understand you're not thinkin' straight but this isn't gonna help anybody, especially not you.' He kneels on the rafters and points the gun at the entrance which he expects to see flipped open at any moment. 'This is your last chance, Marty, no shit Marty, this is your last chance, for some of the team aren't as reasonable as me. Know what I mean, mucker?' For all their talk he knows that none of them is keen to be the first to thrust his head through the entrance, that they have already understood the vulnerability of that position, how exposed they would be in the moments it would take to hoist themselves up into darkness, a movement that would require both their hands.

'Okay Marty, have it your way,' the voice calls and his words are followed by silence again. He stands up and moves towards the water tank, driven by a fear that they might shoot up through the ceilings, maybe pepper them with a shotgun. His right leg is numb but he squeezes into the gap between the tank and the outside wall. No shots come, just a new whispering rush of voices and sounds he doesn't recognise which filter up in distorted waves. He strains to listen but can't make any sense of the activity below until finally he hears it and understands. There is the raking, breaking surge of a fire taking hold and a snarling crackle as it starts to consume the dried-up kindling of the house below. He knows now that they've sprinkled petrol, thrown in a match, intend him to burn in it. The first slow puffs of smoke are already beginning to seep into the roof space and he doesn't want it to end like this. He hasn't finished what he has to do and he won't be cheated of it like this. There is little time left for him, he has to get out, so he goes to the door and feels its first flush of heat. He slides it no more than a inch and that's enough to see that the very heart of the fire is on the landing below and the crazy, convulsive fury of flame will soon reach ceiling height, so he drops it back in place and retreats, his face wearing a tight print of heat. He shines the torch round, lets it slide across the roof, thinks of forcing his way out through the tiles but despite the furious press and batter of his hands they remain securely in place. The angle is wrong and standing on the rafters restricts his movements. The smell and taste of the smoke is in his throat now – he knows the door will go on fire soon and when that happens a surge of flame and smoke will shoot through the funnel of the opening.

He scampers across the rafters to the wall that joins the house to the next in the row, shining the light on the red partition of brick. The mortar is smeared thinly and flakes away at the skim of the torch. The terrace row of houses is over a hundred years old, built to house the army of shipyard workers, and he knows now that it's his only chance, so he steadies himself, finding a balance by holding on to the trusses above his head, and kicks the wall again and again, concentrating on the same spot where the bricks run down to an edge, until it suddenly gives way in a dust-filled collapse. He shines the torch through into the next roof space to see the mirror image of where he stands and then with his hands pushes enough bricks out of the wall for him to scramble through. But he doesn't follow his first impulse and go to the entrance, instead moves to the adjoining wall and repeats his actions until he's broken his way into the third house. It's here that he removes the door to the roof space and drops down to the landing. There is a scurry of a rat at his feet at which he kicks out, but it vanishes into the thick shadows of one of the rooms. Making his way down the stairs without the use of the torch, his eyes by now attuned to the darkness, he stumbles his way through to the kitchen. His foot scrunches something metal. The door and windows are boarded up and he has no choice but to switch on the torch to search for an opening, and as he does so the light catches the litter of beer cans and polythene bags. It's somewhere kids have been using to drink and sniff glue. The walls are paint-sprayed with their names and everywhere there is the acrid smell of piss. As soon as he puts his hand to the back door it flops open like a turned page in a book and when he steps into the yard he gulps deeply, trying to expel the taste of the smoke.

He's still too close to his house so he climbs the wall into the next yard and on and on until he reaches the end house of the derelict row. Only there does he look back to see yellow spurts of flame vaulting from the upper windows and a black spiral of smoke beginning to coil up from the roof. In a short time the whole house will be engulfed and for a few moments he feels transfixed by the sight, wants to stay and watch it to the very end. A smile spreads across his face. There is a snap and the crash of something collapsing in on itself and the sound seems to shake him free, so he opens the door to the entry quietly and peers back down its length but it's empty, and hugging the darkness coating the walls, he hurries away and back to where his car is parked.

The gospel hall is lit up now and as he gets into the car he can hear hymn-singing. His mother came here from time to time, once tried to get them as boys to go to the Sunday school but they miched off, spent the collection money on sweets. There were times like that when they were cruel to her, doing what they wanted, secure in the knowledge that she would never tell him and so they exploited her silence. He checks his rear-view mirror to make sure he's not being followed and drives off, and for a little while before the car's engine and the tight grid of roads impose themselves, he carries the memory of that chorus of voices and wonders what his mother's voice sounded like when she sang.

*

She stands at the stern of the boat and watches the tumbling plume of water weave itself into a foaming, briny braid. The fine, salt-laden spray mists against her face but she doesn't look away, can't take her eyes off the spinning wake. She won't go inside to the heat and the other passengers – this is where it feels right. It's the cleanest she's felt in a long time and even though others come and stand for a few moments, or the length of time it takes to smoke a cigarette, then scrunch their shoulders and retreat to one of the lounges, she stays, sitting on one of the narrow wooden seats. She's never seen anything that looked so cool and clean as this but is glad that she didn't see it when she felt the way she did, because she knows that she would have climbed the rails and given herself to it, plunged without fear or hesitation into its arms. But those moments have almost gone and for the first time she can lift her head and think that if it is the past she sees tumbling away, then there has to be some future. For her, for Martin, for Tom. She's left Tom playing the machines and is glad when she thinks how pleased he was when she gave him Rachel's mobile phone, the way he treated it with respect, the way he understood what he was being given.

She touches her hair and feels the sheen of moisture, then ploughs her hand back through it, letting her fingers run across her scalp. When she's at her sister's she's going to get it cut, try to force some shape back into it. When they were girls they must have spent hours combing and grooming each other, plaiting and enjoying elaborate experiments. Making each other beautiful. Parading down the hall like models on a catwalk. She wonders if she can ever be beautiful again, or if it's gone for ever, unravelling and fraying with the forward roll of time. She wonders if a man will ever look at her again and smile, taking her in with his eyes, if Martin will ever reach across the emptiness of the bed and pull her into his arms. She watches the furrowed sea buckle and swell again, its surface reforming in the distance and she wonders, too, if there are unseen parts of her which have died with her child. Sometimes she thinks she feels an emptiness in the heart of her womb, a pain in the quick of her being, but tells herself that it's in her head and not her body. She slips her hand through the folds of her clothes and lets it rest on her stomach, kneads and smoothes the round looseness of her skin, then softly hums some half-forgotten lullaby to herself, as if soothing a child into sleep.

A few things are clear now. She knows she's not going back to work in the canteen. Too many smells, too much heat burrowing into her, too many faces of other people's children pressing against her. She thinks she'd like to go back to education and take some night classes, get better qualifications and look around for a different type of job. She smiles as she wonders whether, if she worked really hard, she could come close to getting a star. That would be something. Really something. Then perhaps she might get some kind of office job where she had her own desk and chair, where there wasn't a scream of voices constantly shouting, where she didn't have to brush up food trodden into the floor. Maybe it's only a foolish dream but she wants it to happen and in that moment it exists on the horizon like the dark bevel of land she can see with its steady, beckoning blink of light away to her right. The boat's wake breaks and froths in a foam-filled trench of white. She'll have to go and check on Tom soon. But not just yet. So she sits on, tilting her head to the sky and the beaded mist of spray, her hidden hand still resting on her stomach and her lips moving in a silent song, calming her child, stilling her beautiful lost child into the safe waters of sleep.

*

The machines are no good – stupid, boring card games where you bet on luck but the spinning cogs of the machine's memory systems always allow it to win in the end. He hates it, too, when the boat sways and his feet have to struggle for a new balance. He thinks those seconds feel the way it must at the start of an earthquake when the earth shifts and searches for a new settlement. When it happens he clutches the sides of the machine and leans his weight on the controls, feeling them press into his stomach. He thinks about luck a lot but still has no answer as to why it should give itself to some and not to others. Just like this machine he plays, he tells himself there has to be some system, some programmed pattern of numbers that even when it seems random, has to be based on something. Perhaps even luck could be based on deserving, parcelled out only to those who have done something to deserve it. Over his shoulder he hears the laughing chink of money being paid out and he glances round for a second but sees nothing in the winner that distinguishes her from anyone else.

There is the smell of fried food from the cafeteria – he's already seen people tucking into big happy plates of cooked breakfast where the yolks of sun shine and the sausages curl like smiling mouths. But he's not going to be tempted because his stomach is queasy with the lurch of the sea and in the last week he's started to feel that his body is not ballast – something that weights him to the world and gives him the protection of solidity like a moat or a castle wall – but something that holds him back from where he wants to go. And he's started to realise where it is he wants to go and it's in pursuit of money and a decent job because he thinks that it's money helps you to run fast, takes you anywhere you want to go in the world. That it's money is the wall that keeps you safe. What he wants to do is earn money, more money than anyone else and when in the future he sees Chapman, Rollo, Leechy and all the others like them standing on the same street corner, he'll be smiling out at them from the wheel of his black car with its tinted glass and when he lowers his electric window, he'll give them the finger before leaving them forever in his dust and never have to see them again.

Something else has started to happen to him. The thought of it is still edged with a flush of shame because it doesn't seem right. His relationship with Lara is changing. Now as she runs, he has the type of thoughts he's never had before and he's started to look at her in different ways, sometimes slipping into a fantasy where she's almost overpowered by the dogs and he bursts in and saves her and she turns her tiger eyes to him and smiles her thanks. Sometimes as he plays, he finds himself stirring and stiffening to the encouragement of her sighs and sometimes when he's sleeping it's his name she calls over and over, and even in the dampness and embarrassment of the morning light he senses for a fleeting second what it must be like to be loved.

But it's not just Lara. He's started to look at girls, just like he's looking at this girl beside him playing the machine where she's won the money and he was wrong – there are things which distinguish her from others. There's the shiny fall and curve of her hair, the creamy pale spots the size of coins on her temples where her hair is clipped back, the slender shape of her body inside her clothes, the rounded perfection of her upturned heel as she stands with one foot on tiptoe. He'd like to go up behind her and envelop her in the tightness of his arms, make her love him, but instead he says, 'How did you manage to win?' Without looking up and without breaking her concentration, she answers, 'Pure luck, just pure luck.' He wants some of that pure luck, thinks he can find it if he tries hard enough but then as her game ends she looks up at him for the first time and he sees how he looks in her eyes. He turns away and takes the first door he can find which leads out to a deck. Though the wind slaps his face with its coldness and stings his eyes, he walks along its deserted length until he finds a tight little space where he wedges himself for shelter.

He thinks of Rachel and for the first time realises that in all the time they were brother and sister they never spoke to each other, not about anything that was important so she never knew what he felt and he has no idea about what went on inside her head. It makes him sad, conscious of the terrible waste, and he tries to think of some way that he can make up for it, make amends, but there is only the slice and whip of the wind as it shreds the skin off the sea. Then as he huddles in his narrow metal crevice, his hand touches the mobile phone and he thinks that maybe there is a way and he doesn't know if it's a real way or a stupid, childish, pretend way but he's driven by a need that he's never felt before and which scares him a little bit. So taking the phone he holds it to his ear and after a few moments he speaks in it. Speaks to her. And he tells her he's sorry he wasn't a better brother, that he wasn't able to look out for her. He tells her, too, that sometimes she was a snobby bitch who looked down her nose at him because he wasn't as smart as her and as the wind whines and frets the waves he tells her with shame and sadness that there were times he hated her because he thought that she had taken all the luck in their family and that there wasn't any left for him. And because she had all the luck she got almost all their parents' love so he only got the little bit that was left and that wasn't fair. It wasn't friggin' fair. He feels the first tears start, tells himself that it's the spray of the sea. He tells her that everything's going to be different for him now though, because he's going to work hard, learn all the things he needs and shape himself into something better. Tells her it's really sad for him that she won't be there to help him when he doesn't know how to do things, because he needs lots of help. And one of the thing he needs help with, because he doesn't know what he's supposed to do, is Mum and Dad. He tells her he's scared and that if they go on like this something terrible's going to happen but he doesn't know what he can do to stop it, so if she knows will she please tell him. He listens for some answer, some voice on the end of the phone, but all he hears is the restless moan of the rising wind. His tears taste of salt. He catches them on the tip of his tongue, tells himself that it's the spray of the sea.

*

He's driven through the estate but there's no sign of the black four-wheel drive and then something Rob said comes back into his mind and he drives back out the short distance to the private leisure complex. As he approaches it he can see the floodlit tennis courts and the outdoor pool behind the high fencing. He follows a car into the car park, drives slowly round. It's full of BMWs, expensive cars and scores of four-wheel drives and it takes him a few minutes before he finds the one he's looking for, with its tinted glass and personalised number plate. It's parked up near the doors. He stops behind it and checks again that it's the right one. He's sure.

Two women in crisp ice-blue tracksuits are going through the entrance doors, their sports bags slung snugly on their shoulders. Even their hair is the same blonde colour. He sits in his parked car and watches a family come out, the mother and father holding the arms of their son so he can swing between them, then stopping to give the other boy his turn. It feels like a different world through the doors, a world that is far from his own and one in which he doesn't belong. It stirs a new sense of his anger because he knows there are people out there whose lives never cross the rigid boundary lines which separate them from what is dirty or unpleasant, people who never get closer than television pictures. But then if someone had offered him the chance to join them, to be a member of their club, he would have taken it. But no one's going to ask him, no one's ever going to want him or his family as members and that's all right because he knows now that he's on his own, more on his own than he's ever been. With this knowledge comes no sense of loneliness, instead only a feeling of lightness and the freedom to do what has to be done. Before he had told himself that it was for Rachel, but it was always a lie and he knows that it's for him, for his pain, for the future that's been ripped from him. The truth can never hurt. So it's finally time for him to bring to book, to pay back. Time for him to take his stance like the man he's almost forgotten how to be.

He gets out of the car, and walks towards the doors. He walks quickly, both hands plunged into the pockets of his coat, locking himself into his own space. Someone coming out holds the door for him but he doesn't say thanks or look at him and then he's in the foyer and striding past the reception desk where a young woman smiles at him and says, 'Good evening,' before she takes a second look and asks him if she can help him. He shakes his head and keeps on walking.

'Excuse me sir, are you a member?' she calls but he keeps on walking. 'Excuse me sir, you can't go in unless you're a member.' Her voice is a shout now as he vaults the turnstile and he knows without looking that she's lifting a phone. He's in the changing rooms, amidst the smell of talc and shampoo, heads turning to look at him and then he's walking through the weights area, striding quickly past people on rowing and cycling machines, past people pounding on running machines. Sweat-beaded faces turn to look at him for a few seconds of curiosity before returning to their strain. Some faces are turned away from him and he has to move closer to satisfy himself that they're not the one, stepping over weights and bits of exercise machinery. Then he's in the corridor again and into the swimming area. The sudden heat flannels against his face and now there's two attendants on the other side of the pool pointing at him but they're too late because he's seen him.

He's one of four men in the jacuzzi, their heads lolling backwards to rest on the rim, their arms stretched round its circumference. There is the glint of a gold identity bracelet and at his neck hangs a golden chain. They're too bound up with their own laughter, the pleasure of their bodies to see him until he's standing over them.

'Well, look what the cat dragged in,' Jaunty says. 'Didn't think you had the money for this sort of place, Marty. Most people take their clothes off when they go for a swim.' The other three men smile at the joke as they stare up at him.

'I have something belonging to you,' he says.

'And what's that, Marty?'

'This,' he says, taking the plastic bag of drugs out of his pocket and sprinkling the contents into the water with a shake of his hand as if he's sowing seed. 'For fuck's sake, Marty, are you off your head?' Jaunty asks. 'Yes that's right, I am. Off my head.'

'You need to take care, Marty,' he says, the narrowest of smiles slinking across his face.

'You'll be telling me next that I'm a dead man walking.'

'Maybe not so far from the truth,' Jaunty says, massaging his throat with his hand.

The two attendants are starting to make their way round the pool. There is the sound of a phone ringing.

'This is the truth, Jaunty,' he says, taking the gun out of his pocket. As he points it, he worries that his hand will shake but it's perfectly still even when the screaming starts and people are clambering out of the pool, bumping into each other, shoving past those deemed too slow, everyone running with their heads craned to look. The two attendants are frozen to the spot, their arms suddenly touching, their heads looking back towards the changing rooms, not wanting to draw attention by sudden movement. It is the power of fear. He tells himself that it's the sweetest thing. It's what his father felt that night when he opened his door to a stranger. In the jacuzzi the only movement is the flurry and bubble of the water.

'Jesus, Marty, you can't be serious,' Jaunty says, his two hands pulled from below the water and laid flat on its surface.

He doesn't answer but looking at the other three men moves his head slightly and at the signal they slip sideways, pressing their backs against the tiles, trying to move away without causing any more disturbance in the water.

'Jesus, Marty, let's talk about this. Everybody knows you're angry about what happened to your daughter and you've every right. Everybody feels bad about it, swear to God. But let's talk about it.'

'I've nothin' to say. I was never any good at talkin',' he answers.

'We go back a long way, Marty – we were soldiers together. We fought in the war,' Jaunty says, holding his hands palm upwards in a begging gesture.

'We were never soldiers,' he answers, releasing the safety catch. 'We were just kids with our heads full of crap. And if we believed anything, it was that we were protecting our people. Now all you and the rest do, is live off the back of them, pump this shit into it.' The water goes still and flat.

'Okay, Marty, you shoot me but you can't stop there because I'm just small fry so you're gonna need to shoot an awful lot of people.' Jaunty's voice is high-pitched, starting to break; he wipes his eyes with the back of his hands, looks round for help that isn't coming.

He lowers the gun for a second, then raises it again. His head is spinning, the heat mixed with the smell of chlorine is making him feel sick. He straightens his arm but the gun feels suddenly heavy in his hand. Take your stand. Show him, Martin. Make his eyes water. Make him step back. He drops the gun to his side and turns away and in his ears he hears a voice calling him 'a bastard', 'a useless little cunt'. But then it's Jaunty shouting, and his voice is suddenly buoyant, inflated with relief.

'Respect, Marty, you need to learn some fuckin' re-spect!'

'Respect' the word rattles and buzzes round his brain and he can't still it. He stops. Jaunty is standing in the middle of the water, his hands arched on his hips, his head held high. He walks slowly back and in each step he sees a vision of him toppling back in the water, his head banging on the tiles and a spume of red foaming to the surface. He raises the gun again and Jaunty suddenly cowers down in the water.

'Respect?' he says, looking at the new flush of fear in his eyes. 'Respect?' Then he steps on to the rim and sprays his piss into the water. They squirm and shudder away from its gush, their eyes blinking and hands pawing at the water.

'That much respect,' he says, then walking round to where Jaunty huddles, he kneels down and without speaking lets the barrel of the gun rest across his cheek. Then he walks quickly away, and back out through the foyer but no one comes near him or attempts to stop him as he walks through the building and out to the car.

He's down on the carriageway when the police car passes him, its lights blazing, its screaming siren torturing the stillness of the night. He drives quickly, mindless of other cars and his wake is littered with the angry blare of their horns but nothing registers with him beyond one thing. Everything else is falling away, borne away in the tightening noose of neon that constricts his thinking and hurts his eyes. He can hardly focus on the road – the lights straddling the road, the heat and speed of the car, the unrelenting pounding inside his head, all bleed into each other, and rub raw-edged. If he doesn't stop he'll lose control and crash the car, so as he cuts back along side roads, he stops in the entrance to a field and crouching down on one knee is sick, his stomach heaving even in its emptiness.

*

There's so little time, so much to do – he must work quickly if he's to get it done. He lifts the books from the book-rack followed by the ones which sit between the dressing table and the wardrobe, places them in one of the boxes piled up on the landing, making sure they're in the exact order she had them and remembering which title follows which. Next he empties the wardrobe, forcing himself not to linger or dwell on what he touches, driving himself on by a constant reminder of the need for urgency. All the clothes are folded over on themselves, kept on their hangers and placed in the boxes. At the very back he finds her school uniform, hanging complete on one hanger – blazer, blouse, skirt. There are pens in the inside pocket of the blazer, a hymn book and a homework diary. Then he folds it and places it in a box with all the rest.

At the bottom of the wardrobe he finds a blue swimming float, hockey equipment and a small case he doesn't recognise. Kneeling on the floor he opens it to find a dozen pairs of shoes, lifts out the ones he remembers as the first pair she ever had, lets them rest a second in the palm of his hand. He wonders at their smallness then places them back with all the others and closes the lid again. Standing on a chair, he lifts down a tennis racquet, two box files full of school stuff, rolled-up posters and empty shoe boxes from the top of the wardrobe. He groups it all together in one half of a box.

He hesitates a little at the dresser – it seems the most personal – but tells himself that it has to be done, that he's doing it for her. He uses a plastic bag for what's on top of it, carefully storing the combs – one has a long hair, almost too light to be seen, trapped in the teeth that trails in the air as he lifts it – the cosmetics, the jewellery, the little ornaments. Then he opens the drawers and transfers the contents to the boxes. He carries the full boxes down the stairs and out to the transit van he's driven from the museum, piles them on top of each other to leave as much space for all that has to be brought. There's so much to do, so little time – he has to hurry. Then it's her desk, the place where so often he stopped to watch her work, and delicately and with reverence even in his haste he gathers and stores the pink pebble, the fossil fish, the ball of plasticine, the personal stereo, the tiny elephant, the spangled wooden box that contains a tangle of rings and earrings, the picture in a shell frame. There is a hand-held black lacquered mirror and he lifts it with the glass face down so that he doesn't see himself. He clears the rest of the desktop including the essay she was working on and finds a safe place for everything, pausing only to remind himself where everything belongs, rehearsing the sequence and order.

He doesn't rest because there is much work to do and he knows that on his own it's not going to be easy but he's doing it for her and that tells him he can make it, that he can see it done. The wardrobe isn't heavy and he's able to slide it on its back down the stairs, then walk it corner by corner to the van and pull it into the back before securing it with one of the straps. He does the dresser the same way but first removes the drawers to make it lighter and easier to manoeuvre. It bangs against his shins and is more awkward to get down the stairs, but eventually he has it stored beside the wardrobe and ties it with a length of rope to prevent it sliding about. When he goes back into the almost empty room he sees the hidden spot where he couldn't get the wallpaper to join, remembers the struggle of the job and how pleased she was when everything was finished, how important it was to her that everything matched.

He takes the posters off the wall and rolls them inside each other, slips an elastic band round them, then turns to the bed, unscrewing the white quilted headboard that just above the pillows bears the faint tarnish of her hair. Folding the quilt and sheets he takes them down and places them inside the wardrobe. He finds the mattress difficult as it buckles and slips in his grip and it's too big to fold or tuck under his arm so he struggles with it and stumbles before it's finally in the back of the van. When everything from the room's stored, he takes one last look to make sure he has it all. The emptiness of the room presses against his senses and as he stands in the doorway, he leans against the frame for support. But it has to be done – he understands that now and knows that it is the right thing, as right as anything can be. He's just about to go when he sees the snow-shaker on the window ledge, partly hidden by the curtain. As he lifts it, the glass feels cold against his skin as if somehow the snow inside it is real. And then when he tries to stop the fall by turning it upside down it only makes it worse. He hides it from his sight by dropping it into his pocket and as he goes round the house turning off all the lights, in each room he imagines the silent swirl that he's powerless to stop.

There aren't many cars on the roads at this time of night and he makes good time, so it only takes him twenty minutes and he's there in front of the gates. He's got little threads of different colour on the heavy bunch of keys for everything he needs to open, so he finds the right one quickly and it's turning in the padlock and he's able to open the double gates, drive through and close them again in a matter of minutes. He drives round the rear of the building and parks at the back doors beside the lift and loading bay. Another key, a lengthy punched security code and he's inside, lighting his way with his torch. Already he's aware that it's not silent in the way he imagined it would be in the middle of the night, that the empty building hums and stirs with little sparks and currents of sound that emanate from pipes and distant corridors. Sometimes the whole building seems to shiver and stretch itself in the bed of its broken sleep before settling again. He stands and listens as the sounds filter their way towards him in hollow criss-crossed echoes and for a moment he feels afraid but he uses the light from his torch to illuminate the familiar fabric of the walls and floor, then turns back to what he has to do.

He unloads the lightest boxes first, piling them gently on top of each other in the open service lift, then brings the furniture out piece by piece and packs everything into the lift, using all the available space, so there's barely room for him to squeeze in and press the button to close the door and travel to Level Four. When the doors open there is a green, seeping half-light from the night lights and exit signs and he starts the process of unloading, carrying everything to the middle of the gallery which is about to be cleared of the students' work. Some of it has been taken already and there are bare spaces on the walls where paintings have been removed.

In the middle of the gallery there is a clear, raised wooden area and it's here he begins his work. This time he starts with the furniture and it's the bed he puts together first, screwing the headboard back in place, then adding the clothes and quilt, straightening and smoothing everything. He's placed the torch on the floor and once as he moves about the bed he kicks it, sending a Catherine wheel of light spinning round the gallery and an echo that skims onwards like a stone through water before sinking into silence in some distant corner of the building. He freezes, listening to its journey, then returns with determination to what he has to do, pacing out the spot where the wardrobe has to go, only filling it with its contents when he's absolutely sure that he's got it in the correct position. He puts the same objects back on top and in the bottom, but keeping back the case of shoes. Her desk takes a long time, as he gets a little confused about the order of the objects which sit on it, can't remember at first whether the alabaster elephant should be in the box or not. Finally he decides that it should and when he opens the lid a sweet scent puffs up and it makes him feel that everything so far has been right, that everything he has done already is staking its claim.

When he's finished the desk he moves the torch over it, checking that everything's where it should be, sometimes stopping to straighten or alter the spacing. The light catches the ball of plasticine and he pauses, wondering why she had it, shines the torch more closely on it, and for the first time sees the whorled print of her thumb. It's there, the press of her thumb and more than anything else it makes him stumble, threatens to halt him in his tracks. He feels it all welling up inside again, a carbon copy of everything that has already been felt and he knows if he allows it admittance, that he'll be overwhelmed, borne away on the flood, so he struggles as he's never struggled before, shaking his head and walking fierce, stubborn circles of himself. He goes over to the windows which look out on the roof garden and presses his cheek against the glass, holds his hands above his head, their palms also pushed against the glass, and feels the damp coldness freeze his skin. In his head he counts sixteen beautiful stone axes, smoothes them polished and perfect in his memory, traces with his eye the great waterwheels and steam engines, imagines the turn of the wheels and the shuddering throb of the pistons. It's not enough; he presses his palms more tightly against the glass, recites the words, 'Man goeth forth unto his work and to his labour until the evening.' Over and over. 'Man goeth forth unto his work and to his labour until the evening.' Over and over and sometimes he mixes in whatever words come into his head, words that make no sense to him but which slowly dissipate what's rising inside him and then he drops coins into the water, one after the other until he can see their shimmer below the surface. But his only wish is that he will have the strength to finish what he has started.

Slowly he lets his hands squeak down the glass and feels his breathing returning to normal. He squats on the floor for a few final moments and then returns to his work, completing what's left methodically and meticulously, never flinching again from what his hand touches. On the wall behind, he pins her posters and the postcard of Mount Fuji, the pictures of Etna and Everest. His eye catches the sequence of white ceramic masks which are still on the wall and not wanting them there, roughly pulls each free from its fittings and stuffs them out of sight in a corner.

Finally it's almost finished – there's only one last thing he wants to do, something he hadn't planned but which now seems right, so kneeling down beside the case he unpacks the pairs of shoes, matches them, and at the edge of the wooden area, in front of her completed room, places them side by side in their chronological sequence. None is polished or shiny, all bear the scuffs and scores of use. In some, the ends of the laces are frayed, or eyelets are buckled out of shape, in others the heels worn down on one side. On one the toe is a lattice of scratches and he realises it's one of the pair she had when she got her first bike – the bike that was slightly too big for her – and this is the foot she used as a brake. There's a pair of red summer sandals which look light as air and a heavy black formal pair she got for starting secondary school. He sets them all in line and then he's finished.

It's done, it's truly done and she's here in this place where the past is cared for and preserved, where nothing is allowed to decay or be destroyed. He tells himself she's safe now, held in the arms of a place that won't let her be discarded on the pages of a tattered paper, or brushed aside into the faded yesterdays of people's memories. She's here for ever and the knowledge lifts a burden from his shoulders but as it lifts he feels a rush of weariness take its place – he feels more tired than he's ever felt, every part of his body weighted like branches layered with the heaviness of snow. He has to rest or he won't be able to go on, won't be able to do the other things that need to be done, so he goes to the bed and sits on the end. The weariness is inside his head, straining against his temples. He suddenly sees her as his child again and she's run too far ahead. He hears himself calling out: Stay where we can see you. Don't go too fast or you'll fall. If you run too fast you'll fall and skin your knees. Wait there until I catch up. I'm coming. Hold on, I'm coming.

He has other things to do, other things to finish, but if he's to do them he has to be rid of this weariness, so he lies on the top of the bed and curls into a ball. He'll only take a few minutes, just rest his eyes until he gets his strength back. The pillow is soft under his head and he lies and listens to the currents of sound that travel along the conduits and through the pipes, the sudden shards of noise that pierce the soft skin of the building. Then there is only the slow drift into sleep and with it a sense of release, of rest at the end of work, of things falling inexorably away and free-falling into a deep and distant valley.

And at first his sleep is borne along on this sense of untrammelled release and he's in the tepee with a flickering, flitting transfer of light projected on the screen of his naked body and he's wearing a wind-stirred screen of leaves, or a white-ridged climb of waves and the world is turning and turning endlessly in the perfection of its orbit. Shoals of orange fish glide over beds of gold coins and then at some wordless command, the great water-wheels which stand fixed in the building below begin to turn after their century of stillness, and droplets of silver water glisten against the brass and shoot off the metal in whispering sprays. And each turn is accompanied by the rising voices of women who sing in the mills and their voices and the fall and sluice of water echo each other. Hands are claiming their stone axes and they slice the milky sap-filled branches of the trees and flints spark kindling into fire, at first a tiny puff of grey and then the crackle and shoot of flame that warms and stirs everything into life.

A spark ignites the sleeping looms and the shuttles begin to fly, joining the rising chorus of voices. And in the glass cases all the pinned insects and the butterflies waken and flutter and ping against the glass. Polished pistons pound with the hiss and spurt of released energy. Everywhere there is the rising tide of light, running through the shadowy corridors and everything which is burnished by its touch throws off the shackles of sleep and quickens into the newness of its former life.

Clack, clack, clack – the tiny, running feet in their best Sunday shoes shoot through the corridors as if a shot of electricity and these too are part of the awakening. So let her run through the galleries and the floors where everything is hers for the touch and let her pause only where her desire takes her. Let her ask her child's questions, as many questions as she wants because here there'll always be answers.

'Where does the sun go at night?'

'What are clouds made of?'

'What would happen if two stars bumped into each other?'

Questions that spin and spiral, each one as serious as her voice. Let her run, the clack of her heels, a pulse of this new life, a world that he, too, is part of, his very skin a screen for the turning world to show its once hidden self. So let her run, let her run ahead – he'll follow the drum-beat of her heels wherever they lead. But now there's something wrong – she's got too far ahead, the sound of her feet are growing fainter, fading into the echoing shadows of distant corners. He tries to run faster but his feet are weighted and he's slowing down, and the singing voices of the women are fading like the mist of the morning as the sun rises and strengthens. Everything is falling asleep again, everything is quenched and staunched. He tries to run faster, to catch her up as the quickening flames collapse and tumble into ash but he's powerless to force his limbs into speed, so he calls out to her, calls again and again. Hold on, I'm coming. Wait there until I come. Please wait there for me. And when there is only the answer of silence his cries become more frantic, screeching like gulls against the engulfing darkness, their voices borne away on the rising fury of the storm.

He's reached the second floor and he thinks he hears her, searches around the glass cases but she's not there and he stumbles on, calling and calling in a voice which is collapsing in on itself. He knows now where his steps are taking him but there's nothing he can do to stop himself and in his dream he's standing at the foot of the glass case where the young woman Takabuti sleeps, wrapped tightly in her linen dress, one hand and one foot exposed, her black wizened face with its walnut eyes looking at him as if awaiting his arrival. But when he looks again, it's the face of his daughter and the lighting above his head is a relentless glare that washes her skin blue and cold. Then the light blinks and stutters out and when his eyes are able to see, he's looking at the painted breast of the coffin where a beautiful young woman is kneeling with out-stretched wings. It's the goddess of the skies who wears the bright ball of the sun in her hair, who swallows it whole every night and then pours it out each dawn. It's where the sun goes, he tells Rachel. It's where the sun goes and she tells him she understands but then she's fading from his sight and as hard as he tries to hold her image in his head, it's drifting into the darkest spaces of the night where the stars are frozen and fixed in silence.

The silence is inside his head. He has no voice to call her, to tell her all the things he wants to and she, too, has no voice as she travels ever further, out to the very edge of his memory. It is the terrible silence that shakes him with its shiver into the grey light of dawn which has started to snake through the gallery. He's cold to the bone, and his whole body aches. He clambers slowly off the bed trying to stretch the pain and the coldness out of his body, blowing his breath into the frozen knobs of his hands. His throat feels sore and raw as if he's been shouting and he needs something to drink but he pauses first to smooth the cover of the bed, brushing out the imprint of his body with the palm of his hand. The first edges of a hardening light slant through the windows and define the roof garden outside and as he goes to the glass he wants to go out, breathe in the air, try to warm himself with whatever heat the new day is able to muster.

THE BIG SNOW David Park
£6.99 0 7475 6141 9

'Bewitching ... triumphant ... if you like Ian McEwan's *Atonement*,
you will adore this' *Daily Mail*

Northern Ireland, 1963. In a house with windows flung defiantly wide, a wife dies before
her husband can make his confession. Elsewhere, an old woman searched desperately for a
wedding dress in her dream of love. And in the very heart of the city, the purity of snow is
tainted by the murder of a young woman, leaving one man in a race against time – to find
the murderer before the snow melts.

'A very good murder mystery ... Park is a writer if startling grace and integrity ...
darkness seeps in to meet the relentless snow in this new world of black and white, and
Park's characters burn like the candles they light against it, shivering but bright'
Daily Telegraph

'Luminously written ... intense and extraordinarily compelling' *The Times*

'Ingenious' *Sunday Times*

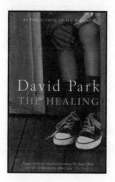

THE HEALING David Park
£6.99 0 7475 7163 5

Winner of the Authors' Club First Novel Award

'Deserves to be numbered among the finest first novels of this or any other year'
The Times

In rural Northern Ireland, a boy sees his father shot dead before his eyes: another helpless victim of sectarian violence. The traumatised boy loses the ability to speak, so to escape the past his mother moves them both to Belfast. Here, in the city, an elderly man is grieving for his own loss and the shattered world around him. When the boy's life becomes entwined with his own, the old man believes he has found at last in the silent child the instrument of healing.

'A beautifully written story ... sheer magically descriptive writing ... the beauty of Park's work lies in the simplicity of the telling, the exquisiteness of his language and a blazing tension ... He is, one feels, interested in the truth' *Irish Independent*

'Park beings to the interior life of the child the eloquent sympathy that distinguished his collection, *Oranges From Spain***'** *Independent*

To order from Bookpost PO Box 29 Douglas Isle of Man IM99 1BQ www.bookpost.co.uk
email: bookshop@enterprise.net fax: 01624 837033 tel: 01624 836000

bloomsburypbks

www.bloomsbury.com/davidpark

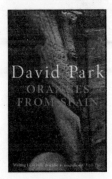

ORANGES FROM SPAIN David Park
£6.99 0 7475 7162 7

'Writing I can only describe as magnificent' *Irish Times*

Oranges From Spain is a collection of stories about of the trials of growing up in a community where tension, confusion and violence hold sway. Here, among other tales, a youthful seaside romance crosses the religious divide, a gang take turns at the wheel of a stolen car, and an exceptional student stirs the resentment of her troubled teacher. Set in Northern Ireland against the background of the troubles, these vignettes capture the spirit of adolescence in difficult times.

'If there has been a better first collection than David Park's *Oranges From Spain* in the last year then I fear I have not read it ... he is capable of amazing tenderness and sympathy ... one could recommend these stories for their author's formal dexterity alone: what raises them above the common ruck, however, is his ear for the murmurs of the heart' *Telegraph*

'David Park writes beautifully about growing up in Belfast – of childhoods under God and the gun. Somehow, against all the odds, his stories are gentle, vivid, life-affirming'
Christopher Hope, author of *Serenity House*

bloomsburypbks

www.bloomsbury.com/davidark